Finding Bess

FINDING BESS

Victoria Gordon

Five Star • Waterville, Maine

First Edition
First Printing: April 2004

Set in 11 pt. Plantin by Liana M. Walker.

Printed in the United States on permanent paper.

Library of Congress Cataloging-in-Publication Data

Gordon, Victoria, 1942–
    Finding Bess / Victoria Gordon.—1st ed.
        p. cm.
    "Five Star first edition titles"—T.p. verso.
    ISBN 1-59414-101-0 (hc : alk. paper)
    1. Fiction—Authorship—Fiction. 2. Americans—
Australia—Fiction. 3. Arranged marriage—Fiction.
    4. Women novelists—Fiction. 5. Kidnapping—Fiction.
    6. Tasmania—Fiction. I. Title.
    PS3557.O7155F56 2004
    823'.92—dc22   2003065568

This book must, of course, be first and foremost for Deni.
But there is an "Ida" who played a part in it all.

CHAPTER ONE

"For Bess," it said. Then:

I fear that I'm headed for trouble, and I don't know what to do
For something in life is changing, and I know it's to do with you
All of which makes it difficult, as we've never really met
   And yet . . . there are things about you
   So many things about you
Things I must know about you, and they're starting to make me fret
It is more that I need to know, not less, but so far I can do nought
Unless you reply in words that I know, then I'll stay overwrought
So let's get with it, lady; I'm waiting on you now
   If you don't know how to do it
   Aren't brave enough to do it
Then we'll just have to get together, and I'll try to show you how.

No title; no signature. And none needed; there it was on Geoffrey Barrett's website, after all. Bess Carson Bradley felt her cheeks bake. Underneath the poem was one of her book covers. ELIZABETH CARSON, it said in gold foil. Then, in red foil, SWEET PRIMITIVE PASSION. Depicted above the title, a cowboy was about to ravage a beautiful woman. True, Bess had written the "ravage scene." True, the artist had vividly transformed her words into flesh—lots of flesh— and blood. True, *Passion* had been her best-selling book, her readers titillated by the cover art.

But despite the ooohs and ahhhs the cover had prompted,

Bess hated it. Always had. And now . . . well . . .

The cowboy's bare chest rivaled Conan the Barbarian's, and his rugged features were shadowed by a Stetson. Swooning in his arms, the heroine's white riding shirt molded her breasts. Anyone with the imagination of a pre-pubescent teenager could see the heroine's nipples, even though the artist hadn't depicted nipples. On the book's cover, the heroine's face had conveyed one-third apprehension, one-third terror, one-third anticipation. Now, on the website, it conveyed . . . herself!

Geoffrey Barrett—well who else? It was his website, after all—had somehow substituted a head-shot of Bess, her neck melding into the vee of the heroine's shirt, her forehead merging into the lush russet hair that fanned out and, eventually, spilled over the heroine's shoulders.

It would have been clever, even funny, if it hadn't been so . . . No! Bess wouldn't go there; had sworn never to go there.

"Oh, Geoffrey," she said with a sigh. "What in the name of all that's holy are you trying to do? Why that awful 'bodice-ripper' book cover, and what do you mean by 'headed for trouble'?"

Of course, he couldn't know how insensitive he'd been. No one knew about the opera-inspired climax to her marriage; tragic and deadly. No one knew what had gone down, and wasn't that a horrible pun?

Her eyes were drawn once more to the poem, scanning the lines yet again before she turned to stare blankly out her window at the bright Colorado autumn day, at the cacophony of dying leaf colors. Seeing them, but not seeing them, half her mind in the small Australian island of Tasmania where Geoffrey—her friend Geoffrey—seemed to have lost his marbles.

Or had he? Maybe he'd meant the poem for someone else. Although . . . was it logical to think that Geoffrey Barrett had an entire harem of girls named Bess, all of whom he'd met via the Internet?

And why include her book cover? Why substitute the author-photo that had once graced an article in *Romantic Times* magazine?

Geoffrey's verse maintained the cadence of *The Highwayman*, and Bess was the only one with whom he shared a straight-from-childhood fascination with the famous Alfred Noyes poem. His mother had read it to him in the cradle, as hers had done for her, and each of them had always found the rather morbid poem comforting, perhaps because of its evocative inner music. Bess had, in fact, written a romance novel based on the poem, but Geoffrey was the only other person she'd ever run across who'd actually memorized every stanza.

Her gaze returned to the computer screen. She stared hard, as if she could mentally move his Highwayman parody—and the damn book cover—from this all-too-public website to her own private E-mail address. Where, if anywhere, it surely belonged. Then she keystroked back to his home page, graced by a color photo of a seemingly tall, dark-haired man with pale green eyes and the look of a pirate or brigand on a lean, tanned face.

The first time she'd seen the picture it had been difficult to imagine that face on the man who'd sent her an E-mail some two years back when her marriage was destroyed, her unborn baby lost, and her life blasted apart in a million tiny, tortuous shreds. She had, impulsively, made mention of her problems on Novelists Inc., an authors' E-mail loop she used, filled mostly with romance authors whose compassion had helped others through a host of personal problems. Her NincLink friends had responded, and their help had assisted her through the post-miscarriage depression and the trauma of seeing madness take the man who had turned out to be anything but the person she thought she had married.

But Geoffrey Barrett went one step further, given that neither had ever so much as spoken to the other, even by E-mail. His message had been so gentle, so warm, filled with genuine compassion and yet a determined attitude that she should take steps now, immediately, if she was to deal with it all successfully.

She had sent him a brief, polite reply and thank you, and only then had begun to notice—really notice—his contributions to the link. His descriptions of his "child bride" and the problems she caused him were so filled with love that Bess envied the girl, and through comments from friends knew she wasn't alone. Yet his posts were also alive with a risqué humor that suggested Geoffrey was really using the list to rid himself of annoying angst, on occasion. He adored the child bride, but she was slowly driving him crazy, Bess had thought. And knew she was right when the loving, gentle, humorous contributions gradually and slowly dried up.

Then he came back with a comment that really didn't say much at all, yet somehow told her that his wonderful marriage was over. How she knew, she never quite figured out. But she did know. So after a suitable interval, she'd sent him an E-mail of her own, trying to emulate the favor he'd done for her, something to ease the pain.

It was two months before he responded, but his reply held the same warm friendliness his first E-mail had contained. Which—almost a year ago, now—had been when it all really began. Gradually their communication became more regular, if a tad . . . formal. Polite. When she finally got her own website set up, he wrote to congratulate her but made no comment about the carefully-selected photo she had used, one that complimented her wild mane of auburn hair and as much of her figure as it was allowed to reveal. Which wasn't much. Of course, she had never so much as mentioned his own photo, much less the fact that she now realized she'd been about half in love with him from the time of his very first E-mail.

What sense to that? Her home, her life, was here in Colorado Springs, while his was half the world away and in, she knew full well, a place he loved at least as much as she did her own. Of course, they had a lot in common. She wrote steamy western romances that gave no hint of her own personal barrenness. Her romances were filled with heroes that often— she had realized one day—strongly resembled Geoffrey. And, when he wasn't busy playing with his business interests and training his gundogs, he wrote rawboned Australian historical novels filled with rich, vivid description in words that often were to be found in no American dictionary, but always managed to convey their meaning clearly enough.

Yet neither had ever so much as hinted at any sort of relationship, or the need for one, beyond what they had. Never! Not in any way! She was quite certain of that, because she had found they could almost read each other's minds. Or so it seemed. She had frequently drawn nuances from his E-mails and replied with answers to what he'd meant, rather what he'd actually written. And he—all too frequently—did the same. Only never about anything truly personal.

"And never, damn it, on your website," she muttered, scowling again out the window into the fading light of evening.

Other website visitors might consider Geoffrey's poem and doctored book cover a harmless prank, or even worse, "cute." But to Bess, his glib innuendoes seemed as explicit and well-marked as the hot crimson patches that undoubtedly stained her cheekbones. And how long had she been sitting here, she wondered, realizing she'd used up about two hours of net time and accomplished absolutely nothing.

A sudden chill permeated the room, and she shivered as she keyed back to what had already become in her mind "that damned poem and book cover." The cover's half-naked, swooning heroine seemed to mock her, and the poem hadn't changed by a single word. It still mimicked the structure and cadence of *The Highwayman,* but it was aimed at Bess herself, not the landlord's black-eyed daughter of the poem. That much was all too obvious.

What to do about it, however, was not. Nor did it become any more obvious after a nervous, restless night's sleep in which she kept hearing the *tlot-tlot* of horses' hooves on some ancient pavement.

Staring into the mirror the next morning, she saw raccoon-eyes beneath a haystack of auburn hair that looked as if it had been combed with a pitchfork.

Cranky, as much with herself as with Geoffrey, she thumbed on her computer and was about to call for her E-mail messages when her finger halted as if striking an invisible wall.

What if he'd put some similar nonsense on NincLink? She couldn't fathom why he would, unless he assumed she hadn't seen his Web page yet. Yesterday he'd written an enigmatic message, directing people there. She'd gone like some lemming, but she hadn't reacted yesterday, at least not to him. So maybe . . .

"No," she said. And then said it again, more firmly this time. Surely he wouldn't dare. It was simply ludicrous. None of which explained why after she finally clicked on her E-mails, she slowly and carefully read through each and every message, then sat and stared at the NincLink icon. Usually it was her first check-in of the day, a splendid collection of comments, questions and replies from authors spanning the globe with their interests and shared concerns for their chosen profession.

The icon stared back, a ghostly galleon tossed upon cloudy seas, and Bess reared back as the *Highwayman* refrain bounced through her brain. Her half-filled coffee cup lifted as her knee struck the keyboard shelf and only a frantic swipe of her right hand saved her by flicking the cup, contents spraying everywhere, off the corner of her desk.

Stumbling to the kitchen for paper towels and cleaning spray, she was only too aware of the way her knees were shaking below the oversized Goofy tee-shirt she wore for sleep.

"You're a romance writer; you should sleep in a negligee," someone had once commented. Had that been Geoffrey? she wondered, then scowled at even having thought it. And yet, her Goofy tee was just the sort of thing she might have joked about after a day of spectacular creative energy.

She remembered her exact reply, if not the questioner. "A negligee is for sleeping with someone, or getting ready to. I sleep alone," she had written. And imagined she had exhibited a smug expression like Kipling's cat that walked by itself.

The thought turned her generous lips into a half-smile that revealed a slightly crooked front tooth. Straightening her entire five-foot-two frame, she faced the computer once more.

"If you've posted an innuendo on NincLink," she mumbled at the distant Geoffrey, "I'll kill you off in my next book. I will . . . I swear I will . . ."

Drawing a deep breath, she scanned through her digest, only to find her apprehensions unwarranted.

Maybe, lacking an immediate response, he'd deleted the

cover and poem from his Web page. Hope flickering, her fingers flashed, the computer hummed and whistled at her like a demented teapot, and up came Geoffrey's website.

The cover was still there, as well as the damned poem. Only now he'd added another verse! Even as she admired his skill, angry tears filled her eyes and the parody blurred. Yet she managed to brand her brain with the last four lines. "No good to hide in distance," he'd typed. "You can't hide behind your words. So plait your dark red love knot. Know my interest you have caught. And give me a sign, Bess darling, to let me know you've heard." The two stanzas practically screamed at her. Bess shook her head in silent fury. How could a poem scream?

Maybe she was overreacting. The book cover could be nothing more than a practical joke, and Geoffrey's poem didn't shout cyber-sex, so what had made her nerves so raw?

"If you don't know how to do it, aren't brave enough to do it," she whispered, "you're the lousiest wife in the world."

She was busy pouring her second coffee when the computer, still on line, burbled to announce an incoming E-mail. And it was only by the grace of some fate or another that she left the cup on the kitchen counter when she strolled back into the office to confront the screen.

The first message on her authors' digest was only one word: WAITING!

Waiting for what? Leaning down closer, she read the E-mail address. Geoffrey!

A surge of temper flared her turquoise eyes into fire. It was a temper she sometimes hated, but its one saving grace was its impermanence. Usually.

"I'll give you waiting," she snapped, and reached out to punch the off-button, almost doing so without bothering to go through the brief but oh-so-important procedure that allowed the computer to be safely shut down without risking damage.

The sigh that followed was part anger, part relief. Half her current book was in there, she had realized at the last instant. In there, unsaved, vulnerable. But not as vulnerable as Bess felt. Nor were the tortures about to be unleashed upon her heroine by ravening Apaches—an Elizabeth Carson trademark—anything compared to what her fertile mind was imagining for Geoffrey.

Trembling fingers picked up the new coffee when she returned to the kitchen, and she found herself turning to look back toward the computer as if it were suddenly animate, suddenly alien to her modest home in Colorado Springs.

The image of the altered book cover filled her mind. She tried to blot it out. Might as well try and stop an avalanche by thinking: STOP, SNOW!

And then it was all too familiar, that empty, gasping feeling in her tummy, the same feeling she'd experienced the first time Paul had suddenly, without warning or reason, punched her in the stomach, then driven her to the floor with a smashing, open-handed slap across the face.

"I control things here, bitch," he'd cursed in a voice she had never before heard, hadn't recognized, couldn't comprehend. It had sliced through the ringing in her ears like a razor, only to be followed by the slam of the front door as her husband—surely that wasn't her loving husband Paul Bradley!—surged through the open doorway and into the night.

She had lain there, half-fainting, for what seemed hours before daring to clamber to her feet, to make her way to the bathroom where a livid cheek proved the assault, even if the pain in her middle had dared to deny it. Paul's assault made no sense, had no logic, but it was real.

Something's happened to him, had been her first thought.

He's been drugged or suddenly developed a brain tumor. Some . . . something!

Why else would a formerly loving and caring man punch his pregnant wife in the stomach just for informing him with pride that their first-born would be a girl?

Paul had never struck her; never so much as raised his pleasant, exceedingly light voice to her. He had, in fact, treated her like royalty, which considering he was an employee of her father's huge international conglomerate, she was, in a way. But a very small way, in her own mind.

Even her position as her father's confidential secretary had been, in her view, small. It wasn't as if she'd been his personal assistant or anything, not that she had the drive or the passion for power such a job required.

Still, she had at first wondered about Paul's attentiveness, his almost shy demeanor whenever they crossed paths in the multi-story New York complex where the conglomerate was based. The attentiveness had been easy enough to accept, but the shyness from someone of Paul's status had seemed unusual.

It was as she stared at her reddened cheek in the mirror, still clenching her tummy against the pain, that Bess suddenly found herself realizing she hadn't actually seen that vulnerable shyness for quite some time. Not since their highly-publicized wedding, in fact. And with that realization, the turquoise eyes in the mirror narrowed as repressed synapses began to click into synchronization.

Perceptions blurred by the sheer delight of the courtship, once Paul had shrugged off sufficient shyness to actually court her, and then the majesty of the wedding, sharpened in that instant to a reality that smacked Bess at least as hard as her husband just had. Paul's promotion, announced with their engagement, stood out as it never had before. As did his

reaction to it, which now seemed a totally different color.

"Just enough to keep him hungry," her father had said in the privacy of his huge penthouse office. "Enough to warrant his commitment to you, and to us. But not too much; let's keep him a bit lean and mean."

Dover Warren Cornwall, known throughout the multi-faceted industrial kingdom he controlled as "War" Cornwall, had seemed only a tiny bit discomfited by finding one of his employees pursuing Bess. Certainly he hadn't opposed it, but even then Bess had realized he must have been disappointed. Cornwall had often theorized about the splendid potential his daughter offered as part of what he liked to term a "merger marriage," but had stopped doing so out loud when he noticed the disgust on her face at hearing the term once too often.

Now, as she stared at the stranger in the mirror, she found herself linking Paul's face to the statement. And wondering if he, too, had seen his marriage in such disreputable terms. Could this be the reason for the sudden shift of temperament? Did he see her as the foundation, the brood bitch, for a new dynasty within the Cornwall empire? Certainly his faintly disapproving, almost condescending acceptance of the promotion suggested . . . something.

And as his I-control-things-here-bitch flashed through her mind, to join that part of her earlier thought in a picture of sudden, vivid obscenity, she bent over the sink and released the roiling contents of her pained, convulsing tummy.

Had Paul been cracking up right from the start? But how could she not have noticed? No, she thought, scrubbing her face and teeth. It must be pressures of work, something to do with his new responsibilities. She would speak to her father; he could intervene. Dover Warren Cornwall could fix anything.

Which was why her first words to her returning husband had been, "Paul, darling, don't let this upset you so much. I'll speak to Father. Surely he can fix things . . . make some changes."

"Changes?"

And the light voice she had so often thought soft screeched in her ears, the cadence that of a spoiled child having a tantrum. Then she could hardly hear at all as open-handed slaps drove her head from side to side and back again. Much less could she focus on the letter he wrenched from an inner suit jacket pocket and thrust in her face.

"Do you think he's going to change this?" the voice raged in a tinny whine, and through the tears she caught words like "accounting review" and "audit".

"Well, bitch?"

But she couldn't answer, only stare through tear-smudged, puffy eyes at the madman who faced her, his eyes ablaze with anger and rage. No, worse than that, with blatant hatred and contempt. Evil . . . evil and more. Obscene.

"And he can't fix this, either," the deathwind voice screeched as one clenched fist followed the other into the rounded softness of her already painful stomach.

His blows bent her double, stole her breath, then smashed her upright again so the process could begin again. And with the progress of the beating, Paul's language became stronger, more hostile, more filled with hatred.

When his rage could no longer keep her upright, Bess collapsed to the carpet, her face branded with slap marks on both sides, her eyes blinded by tears, her stomach a well of roiling, heaving pain. Then the final degradation had begun. She felt herself being hauled to her hands and knees, was only vaguely aware of her long, loose skirt being thrown above her back, her panties being torn from her body as if made of

paper. But she was too, too aware of the violation that followed, a violation punctuated, as her beating had been, by curses, by hatred.

And by her own self-loathing, a deep sensation of having been treated as filth, of having been turned to filth, of being filth. And it went on until she thought he, and it, would never, ever, stop.

Even when he finally left her, kicking out in a final gesture of his contempt for her, screaming for the millionth time his disgust that she had dared to spawn a female child instead of the son he demanded, Bess couldn't have moved if she'd tried. She remained crouched there on the home-office carpet, a spent, discarded brood-bitch in her own mind as well as his, barely noticing that Paul had marched to the desk and yanked a gun from a drawer.

It was only when he raged, "I should use this on you," that she peered upward to catch a blurred image of him standing before her, the weapon aimed at the air between them.

"But at least I've had some satisfaction out of you," he continued, his shoe crushing her panties. "Even if you always were the lousiest wife in the world."

He didn't mean wife, he meant something much more graphic, and the words washed over her, adding another layer of filth. Her eyes widened, or tried to, at what he said next.

"But your old man won't get his satisfaction," Paul snarled, pressing the gun's muzzle against his forehead. "He'll have to live with your brat in my name, but he won't have me to take the rap for the rest. I'll see him in . . ."

The muzzle blast drowned his final words even as it drove Bess that decisive step toward merciful oblivion, one from which she emerged in the sterility of a private hospital room—no longer a mother-to-be, no longer a wife, no longer a woman, and barely still a person.

19

Two years, two months and seventeen days ago; a thousand lifetimes ago. Shaking her uncombed hair, she stared at the blank computer screen as the pain and nausea magically left her middle.

The pain gone, but a vestige of the other remaining, a vestige she had never managed to erase from her feeling of self. Six months of serious counseling, regular visits to a skilled therapist . . . but always that vestige remained with her, a part of her. Filth. Sometimes the feeling was so strong she could taste it, smell it . . . Enough! If the therapy had done nothing else, it had taught her that dwelling on the past only led into an increasingly rapid downhill spiral of mood that could put her back in the hospital.

Far better to expend the energy on something positive. She had half a book to write and a deadline to meet for a short story. She had a shower and a warm computer waiting, a maiden pleading to be rescued from certain ravishment. And she really ought to shave her legs, she thought, smiling at the absurdity of that last thought.

But when she emerged from the shower, her mane of auburn hair now a sleek stream of color that would all too soon begin springing back to its natural unruliness, the only thing she could think of was that damn book cover and poem and what, if anything, she might do about it.

To do nothing was unthinkable. To fall into Geoffrey's trap was far, far worse. It was only too obvious that he had decided the time had come for them to have some serious changes in their relationship. He couldn't realize, of course, how totally impossible that was. And he mustn't!

Bess sat staring at the computer screen, which stared back accusingly, mocking her, almost daring her to reach out and hit the start switch.

Suddenly infuriated by her computer's smartass stance,

she punched the on button, stabbing at it fiercely with one unvarnished nail. And when the start-up nonsense was over, she thumbed the trackball until she could, yet again, click on Geoffrey's website.

Ignoring the book cover, she read the poem. Then read it again, all the while feeling the surge of adrenaline building inside her, feeling the anger and now consciously feeding it. How dare he invade her privacy like this? There would be dozens, perhaps hundreds of people—other authors, her peers, damn it!—who could read between the lines and know without question which Bess Geoffrey had aimed his poisoned cursor at. The inclusion of her "bodice-ripper" cover was a punctuation mark, an exclamation point. Overkill!

The majority of her colleagues knew her as Bess. She even used Bess in her E-mail address, a get-back aimed at her father. While her mother had named her for a favorite aunt (and the Noyes poem), her father told everyone she was named for the Queen of England, and he'd never called her anything other than Elizabeth. The pen name had been her editor's suggestion; Carson for her mother's maiden name, Elizabeth because it was more syllabic.

Then there was Geoffrey and Bess's mutual fascination with *The Highwayman*, well known because they'd discussed it on a couple of authors' links, hoping to find kindred spirits.

She felt the galloping refrain of the poem's cadence begin to fill her skull and pulse through her consciousness like some voodoo drum. Her nervous fingers spread lines of "a"s and "s"s and "z"s across the screen, causing her to vent curses at the damned machine as she then had to remove them before she could begin. And all the while, the refrain from his poem—no, her poem—throbbed with the intensity of a migraine behind her eyes.

Until . . .

Bess, the landlord's daughter
The landlord's . . .

And she stalled, her mind suddenly blank. What was turquoise . . . blue or green? It could have been purple, for all the good the question did her, and the next thing she knew she was running to the bathroom and staring myopically into the mirror, her confused mind trying to find the proper color for what she saw.

Her eyes, she decided, were the eyes of a deranged stranger, a stranger with shimmering auburn hair that streamed like a fiery curtain down past her shoulders. A stranger whose flushed cheeks were those of one of her heroines, about to reach the ecstasy of climax in the arms of a hero that looked too much like Geoffrey Barrett.

Bess shook her head. Blue, green . . . what difference did it make? She turned away from herself, from the vision of herself, now dressed in scruffy, faded jeans and a worse T-shirt, then strode back into the office with fire in her eyes.

Bess, the landlord's daughter
The landlord's green-eyed daughter
Stood straight and still at the window;
*   the musket by her side*
Geoffrey Barrett's a bit dim
Hopelessly lost in his own whim
Bess has nothing for such as him;
*   slink back to your cave and hide.*

All of which took her what seemed like the entire day to work her way through, changing words, searching for the right cadence, the proper mix of scorn and contempt that would make him end this nonsense once and for all. She didn't want a new, or different relationship with him; what they had was just fine, thank you very much. Ten thousand miles between them and never the need to meet as physical beings was about all she could handle just now.

Just now. She found herself repeating those final two words like some foreign mantra, some alien sound combination that had driven the lyrics of *The Highwayman*—and her own attempt with it—out of her mind entirely.

Just now . . .

Bess shook her head violently, curls going everywhere. What on earth was she thinking? There was no "just now" about it. She had nothing to offer any relationship, any man. Except sorrow for them both, perhaps.

"No!" She spat out the word like something that tasted bad.

And manipulated the trackball to where her heroine waited so patiently for rescue. This, at least, she could handle. For some reason—one analyst had described it as unconscious therapy—Bess had no problem dealing with suicide, murder, rape, torture and degradation in her novels, which were actually infamous for the strength of her heroines in recovering from the trauma they suffered.

Easy stuff, that. Easy enough to let a fictional character be captured by outlaws or savages, stripped, humiliated, forced to endure sexual torments that no woman should have to think about, much less endure. And then let that same woman find a brave, honest, handsome hero who could take her away from the inner demons, banish them, slay them, and then ride off into the sunset, heroine on his saddle, to a life happy ever after . . .

But not herself! The violation, the shame of what she had endured at Paul's hands was like a stigmata on her soul, and no amount of cleansing could ever make her fit for any man. The lousiest "wife" in the world, he'd called her. And meant it. Forget that he must have been quite insane at the time, perhaps even forget—although she knew she never, ever, could—the bestial way in which he'd used her at the end. The fact remained that Paul had been a man of some considerable expertise in sexual matters. He had to have been. He was thirty-five to her twenty-three when they married; he'd been all over the world in his work, would have had many women. Even if his remark had been meant only to hurt—and she was certain of that—it had held a ring of truth she couldn't deny. Even though for her he was the first, it wasn't as if she had gone into the marriage knowing nothing. She had known plenty, and the proof was, if nowhere else, in her novels.

In one, she had even managed to contrive her heroine being forced into sexual congress while on the saddle of an outlaw's horse. It hadn't been rape, exactly. Surely difficult in such a position, but it could be done. Bess was positive in her own mind—and comments from readers had confirmed it—that both parties enjoyed themselves immensely.

Writing brought her a good living, it was perhaps as therapeutic as the analyst had suggested, and despite all the blood and guts and rapine, it was inestimably, thoroughly, unarguably safe.

When she'd fled to Colorado after her own ordeal and hospital treatment, her father had done his best to persuade her against it. New York, he had said, was the only place in the country worth living in. "Nothing in Colorado but horses and cows and mountains," he'd said. And finally, faced with her determination and unable to budge her, he had relented with the prophetic, "You'll be back before you know it; mark my words."

Well, she'd marked them all right. And now knew she would never go back to New York. Or, given a choice, to any other mega-city where everyone was a stranger at best and at the very least a potential threat.

To be fair—and Bess had always considered herself a reasonably fair person—her father knew only about Paul's suicide. The awful prelude to it was something only she knew. Shame had prevented her from revealing it, even to the high-powered bloc of analysts her father had brought in to help in her recovery.

Damn! Enough of this wallowing in self-pity. She knew it didn't work, seldom indulged because of that. Better to let something positive drive her emotions, and Geoffrey Barrett, bless his rotten sense of timing, had done just that.

Once her own poetic contribution was finished, not exactly to her total satisfaction but there had to be limits to these things, she was on the phone to the delightfully gay young man who was her computer expert, website designer, and dear, safe friend.

"This is Bess," she said upon reaching his voice mail. Mouse—and if he had a proper name, Bess had never heard it—had a total disregard for conventional ways of doing things; if you wanted him, it was the voice mail or nothing, and it was impossible to tell if he was even there, because he used technology so well that he could be anywhere at all, despite calling back within ninety seconds.

They exchanged the usual pleasantries, asked each other how their love lives were going. Bess lied, and, she thought, did it very well too; whether Mouse lied, she was never quite sure. Eventually, they got to the point.

"Mouse, how difficult would it be for you to hack into somebody's website and deposit something there? Without it being realized until it was too late, and without getting caught, of course."

"Hacking in is easy as pie, darling. Getting out is only marginally more difficult. Why? One of your many lovers hassling you? Turn him over to me, and when the mouse that roars gets through with him, he will bother you nevermore."

"Something like that. If I send you a little poem and the website address, would you be willing to try? I'd pay, of course."

"Not me, you wouldn't. Not ever in matters *d'amour*. After all, darling, if the great lovers of the world don't stand up for each other, then who's going to? You just send over what I'll need and leave it all in my furry little paws, although I will expect a detailed explanation sooner or later about what's going on. Fair?"

"Fair," Bess agreed. But it wasn't, and she knew it.

So she fired up the computer, called up Geoffrey's website, stared at the book cover, read the seemingly innocent poem, then allowed her indignation to build again, let it feed her emotions, fuel her fear and her anger.

And, within a few minutes, felt much, much better.

CHAPTER TWO

Maybe he'd overdone it with the book cover, Geoffrey Barrett thought. He had pictured Bess laughing at his crafty modification. But, in retrospect, it had been a stupid idea. "A guy-thing," his friend Ida would say, and she'd be spot-on.

The dulcet tones of Loreena McKennitt floated like bubbles through the air of Geoffrey's office. Her Celtic music usually provided a delightful background, especially when he worked at his computer, but on this late Tasmanian evening he was only marginally aware of it.

He was sitting, staring at his own website on the screen before him, long fingers stroking his strong chin, his pale eyes alight with a mixture of excitement and annoyance. Shaking his head to try and clear it after an eighteen-hour day, he looked absently out the window beside him, gazing into the darkness as if it could tell him something.

But when he looked back again, the poem was still there, a contemptuous reply to the one he'd sweated blood to create only days before. So engrossed was he that for once McKennitt's version of *The Highwayman* played all the way through without drawing his usual grunt of annoyance whenever her emphasis on some words didn't match his own. He even missed the part where a section of the poem had been deleted from the otherwise poignant song.

It wasn't until his CD player stopped of its own accord that he twisted his mobile mouth in a tight grin, then shot a glare at the computer screen, a glare that would have had a living miscreant shaking in terror.

And when he finally spoke, talking as much to himself as to the invisible, distant creator of the second poem, it was in a voice reminiscent of gravel inside a tin can.

"Gotcha!" he said vehemently. But the laugh that followed was at total variance with the fierceness of the face from which it came. It was a rich, vibrant laugh, a laugh so filled with good humor, so genuinely happy, that any onlooker would have been hard put not to join in.

Tipping his chair back as far it would go, he folded his arms across his chest, then reached out and idly clicked up the picture of Bess. Months ago he had downloaded the picture from her website so he could bring it up from his own computer menu. Folding his arms again, he just sat and stared . . . and stared.

His eyes hardly moved, but his mind, by comparison, seemed impossible to stop. It was, he decided for about the thousandth time, ridiculous in the extreme to find himself falling in love with a woman he knew only from electronic communications and a single picture.

"And that's putting it mildly," he muttered. "Ridiculous is the tamest of words. Let's try idiotic, insane. I haven't only got wallabies loose in the top paddock; they're full grown 'roos and there are thousands of the buggers, all hopping in different directions."

None of which did anything to dispel the truth. He already had fallen in love with Bess. The question now was what to do about it. He was so intrinsically involved in business problems at the moment, he didn't dare leave the state, much less the country. Which prohibited a flying visit to Colorado.

How in hell he could convince her to come to him, he didn't know. But there had to be a way, and he'd find it.

And then he did . . . or rather it was done for him.

Idly shifting back and forth between the link messages he had received during the day, he came across a brief announcement that seemed to leap off the screen at him and yell: *Hey, look at me!*

A mystery writer in The States and a romance writer here in, of all places, Tasmania, were announcing their intention to collaborate on a book. That's all that was said, but it was enough. Geoffrey's brain went into overdrive.

So much for sleep after his eighteen-hour day! He was still awake when dawn cast a pink blanket over the city of Launceston. Tired, to be sure, but not exhausted. Weary, to be sure, but so exhilarated he couldn't be bothered noticing.

He had his bait. Now all he had to figure out was which pond to throw it in. His own website, where patience would be the key to success? Or a private E-mail to Bess, which would force an answer more quickly, but might force it too quickly, and therefore make it the wrong answer?

"Bugger . . . bugger . . . bugger," he muttered, tossing the choices around like a handful of peanuts. It was, Geoffrey realized, a decision of vital importance. He knew without exactly knowing why that Bess was a woman of extreme complexity. A vulnerability had surfaced at the time of her earliest link messages. Ever since, she'd displayed a coolness that was sometimes daunting. And yet, despite her ice-maiden's masquerade, she was a caring, thoughtful, warm person.

Geoffrey's broad shoulders gave the semblance of a shrug. In the passionate, often chilling, passages of her books, where murder and rapine surged to life, there was . . . something else. And although he sensed he might be alone in seeing it, he also wondered if he wasn't sometimes making it up.

"No," he said, his fingers still suspended above his keyboard. "Nobody could be that obsessed with those elements, and she is bloody obsessed. I'd bet the farm on it. She has to have a dark side, too damned dark for words, or she's been there herself. So think carefully on what you're about to do, young Geoffrey. Because whatever else, it isn't going to be bloody easy."

Impatience got to him in the end, and although he identified it, Geoffrey was incapable of dealing with it. So he chose private E-mail.

"My dear Ms. Carson," he wrote, using her pen name because he knew of no other for her. It was probably her mother's maiden name, he thought, assuming she had followed that quaint American custom.

"Loved your responsive poem, although it was perhaps a bit over-reactive.

"But now that I have your attention, as the man with the four-by-two said to the mule, may I ask you to open your mind and read the attachment, which is an outline of a book proposal for which I desperately need your help."

He paused several times during even that short introduction, then sighed and got stuck into it again. In for a penny; in for a pound.

"The concept seems to me to fall squarely between my area of expertise and your own. Given that it involves both our countries during the frontier times we both favor writing about, and given that it involves more romance than I am used to dealing with, and given that I think it will go into territory with which I am totally unfamiliar, I propose that we collaborate."

He rubbed at his suddenly tired eyes and stared blearily at the word "propose," wondering if he shouldn't change it, wondering if it would prove the provocative, proverbial last straw, then wondering if he wasn't making far too much of this in his own mind.

"Bloody cheek calling her obsessive," he muttered. "If it wasn't impossible business-wise, I'd just fly there, toss her over my shoulder, and bring her home. We could sort out all the rest later."

"What I suggest—and honestly, Bess, I am deadly serious here," he continued, "is that you think about flying to Tasmania for a few weeks. At my expense, of course. So that we can thrash this concept out and have a bash at seeing if we can work together. Because I can't do this one alone, and I am bound and convinced it's worth doing. It would shove both of our careers in a somewhat new direction, perhaps, but surely there is nothing wrong in having more than one iron in the fire.

"So please, give it serious thought and an honest evaluation and let me know. Being aware that while I will take 'no' for an answer, I will nonetheless do my best to change your mind."

Enough? Too much? Geoffrey decided he was too damned tired to worry about it. Adding the attachment, which outlined the book proposal he had just spent all night creating from nothing at all, he sighed with a mixture of despair and excitement.

And sent the damned thing.

"You're not going to seriously consider this, are you darling?"

Mouse raised one eyebrow and peered at Bess with a scowl that was fiercely, comfortingly protective. Then he shook his so-ugly-it-was-beautiful, gnome like head in a gesture both sad and provocative.

"Of course you are," he said. "What a dreadfully silly question. But why, darling? I mean, Australia? Worse than Australia, Tasmania!"

"Mouse, please."

His eyes widened in mock shock. "Isn't Tasmania that little bit that hangs off the bottom of an Australian map . . . like an afterthought?"

"Yes, Mouse," she replied, then quickly added, "and no, Mouse. Tasmania is not on my agenda. There, does that answer your question?"

"Answers mine, but I guarantee it doesn't answer yours," he snapped, then softened the remark with a grin. "Don't ever play cat-and-mouse with me, darling, because it's a game you can't win, so let's not go there."

"I won't, believe me. But why should I want to go all the way to Australia to collaborate on a book with a man I don't even know? I have a book here that's half-finished and really should get finished soon, even if I haven't a strict deadline for this one. And I have a dozen ideas for others. And I don't even have a passport. I've never been out of the continental United States in my life. And—"

"Okay, you can stop now. You've convinced me," Mouse growled with a shake of his head. Then he whooped with almost childish laughter. "Now listen, I have some absolutely fabulous ideas for positively decimating this guy's website. We could have him so busy running around chasing his tail, he wouldn't have time to bother you."

"No, Mouse. Please. I appreciate the thought and I know you'd love the challenge, but it wouldn't be right. He is, whatever else, a professional colleague. So thanks, but no thanks. And I mean it," she added, doing her best to look formidable.

"All right, dear, I'll leave him alone . . . for now. But if he keeps bothering you, I'll roar."

"I doubt it will come to that, honest." She glanced at her watch. "I've got to get back, Mouse. My story is finally submitted. However, my book isn't going all that well and I have to whip it into shape before I lose it entirely."

She was about to leave and travel through the labyrinth of passages that led to the street when Mouse muttered something she couldn't quite hear, so Bess turned back to see him positively beaming at her. She raised one eyebrow, which only caused the beam to turn into a veritable beacon.

"What did you say, Mouse? And don't you dare say you didn't say anything, or I'll cut off your tail with a carving knife."

Standing, Mouse was six feet, four inches tall. He shrugged his massive ex-football-player shoulders, not one whit dismayed by her show of strength.

"I didn't actually say anything, Bess darling. I just asked if you've applied for your passport yet."

He grinned, then laughed as she turned and fled.

Because, of course, she had applied for the passport. Her Mouse visit was in the nature of seeking validation, after suffering through many vivid second thoughts.

The passport was nothing in itself. She had occasionally been invited to address groups where a passport would have been needed, and had at the time graciously declined. Now she could, if she desired, go to England, where she had been invited three times. Or New Zealand (once). Or Australia.

"This," she said with a sigh some few weeks later, "is totally insane. I think I must be losing it." And she stared at the still half-finished novel, no longer sure whether she liked the heroine, the story, the work she'd done so far, or even the idea of facing her recalcitrant computer again tomorrow.

She had replied to Geoffrey, politely but firmly declining his kind offer. Only to find the next time she accessed his website that he had made the offer public.

"Quit doing that," she had replied on his personal E-mail address. Only to be ignored. And Mouse, with care, managed to do his best to make things worse.

"I told you to stop messing with Geoffrey's website!" she shouted at his answering machine a few days later, after Geoffrey's picture had somehow been replaced by one of a cartoon Taz, whirling like a dervish, wearing a bright pink tutu. "Damn it, Mouse, pick up your phone. This minute!"

"He started it." Mouse hardly sounded contrite, displaying a belligerent tone in his usually silky voice that Bess had never heard before.

"I can fight my own battles, Mouse. Will you please just lay off? Please, please, please! I am begging you, here, you rotten rat."

"Oooh. Aren't you the one? Sticks and stones, darling, sticks and stones. Or should I be talking about getting more bees with honey than with vinegar?"

"You should be talking about stopping this inane vendetta," Bess snapped. "Damn it, Mouse, I want it stopped. Now do it, or I'll find another computer guru and never speak to you again as long as I live."

Obviously, Mouse didn't believe her. The next E-mail from Geoffrey was so sarcastic, she thought her computer might melt.

"Call off your tame wolf—or else," it ended, and that statement was the most gentle comment in it.

"He's not a wolf, he's a Mouse," she replied without bothering to stop and think. "And he's out of control, having decided to make this into some sort of vendetta, for reasons I cannot imagine. I'm truly sorry, Geoffrey, but I think it's beyond me. I don't even know why he's doing it."

"He's probably in love with you," was the next morning's reply, a remark that had her sputtering coffee all over her desk.

Which did nothing to ease her mood, much less ease her growing anger with Mouse.

"I rather doubt that," she finally typed, thankful that, by this time, they seemed to have confined the issue to private E-mails. "Mouse is gay. So I think there's some other agenda here, although I can't for the life of me figure out what it is."

"Maybe he's in love with me, then," came the reply. "Poor little bugger's on a hiding to nothing if that's the case, but there you go. Anyway, just to change the subject, have you got your passport yet?"

How to answer that one, she wondered, looking down at the pristine document that stared accusing up at her from the desktop. Then, rising to her feet, she walked to the bathroom and stared into the mirror at a face flushed with emotions that had somehow sneaked under her usually rigid guard. Her turquoise eyes were more like opals, filled with fiery colors that seemed to flash in conjunction with the fire of her hair as she shook her head.

She could not go to Australia, could not go to Geoffrey's home and become professionally intimate with him. The intimacy that was required to collaborate on his book might lead to another kind of intimacy. She wasn't ready for that, and this time there was no "just now" about it!

So why was it that his book idea filled her mind, having driven out her own like an unwanted stray cat?

"Of course I have a passport," she eventually replied, deftly skirting the issue. "But that isn't the point. I simply do not feel we should be even thinking of such a project. I have a book half done and several others waiting their turn. I don't need this 'new challenge' as you put it. Besides, I hate to fly."

"You've done book signings and conferences all over the bloody country," Geoffrey wrote. "How did you get there . . . by Greyhound bus? Come-on, Bess, you're prevaricating here. You're just hunting up excuses, and your stock is getting pretty thin.

"Oh, by the way, there's an open-ended ticket waiting for you at the L.A. airport. All the way—L.A. to Melbourne to Launceston. I'll leave it to you to figure out how to get to L.A., but if you expect to be met at this end, you'd best let me know when you'll be arriving."

Her *huuumph* of annoyance echoed through the room. The nerve! The absolute bloody nerve! Wincing at her use of the undeniably Aussie word "bloody," she punched her way through the process of shutting down the computer. Then she flung herself into an indignant march around the apartment, heedless of the fact that she must look as ridiculous as she felt. She had to do something to wear off the frustration and confusion Geoffrey Barrett insisted upon stirring in her.

And she was still marching, still not the least bit mollified, when the telephone rang. Given the hour, Bess knew it could be only one person, and she absently picked up the receiver and said, "Yes, Father. What can I do for you?"

"Come home." Dover Warren Cornwall's staccato voice came through loud and clear. "I need you here, Elizabeth. Surely you can spare your father a portion of your life."

"I have no interest in returning to New York," she said firmly, not even bothering to keep the simmering anger from her voice.

"Your interests are not the only things to be considered," was the stern reply. "You might give a thought to the future of our holdings. After all, you'll inherit the whole kit and caboodle one day."

"By then I will be too old to care, Father. You're going to live forever and we both know it."

They had been here before, often, Bess thought. She had absolutely no desire to inherit the Cornwall interests. She was

36

making a perfectly satisfactory living doing work she enjoyed and—

"What happens when you get too old for your writing," he snapped, somehow managing to put the same connotation on the word writing as if he'd said garbage. "Or if your markets dry up? My sources in the publishing industry tell me the entire future is nothing but a round of merger after merger after merger. There are editors being replaced or displaced every day of the week. They'll be starting on authors, next."

"Then I'll do something else. It isn't as if I'm helpless. I could . . . I could wait tables if it came to that."

This, too, was old ground. She only tread upon it because she could be certain of stirring him up so much he might forget the reason for his call, if she was lucky.

She wasn't.

"There's someone here in New York that I want you to meet," her father said, sliding into his super-salesman's persona as if conveniently forgetting Bess had seen that one often enough to recognize it. However, tonight she was in no mood.

"Are you trying to marry me off again? How many times do we have to go through this, Father? I am not, repeat not, a company chattel. I am not interested in some corporate mating just to satisfy your shareholders."

"Our shareholders," he snapped back, obviously unable to help himself from acting like a corporate mogul, even in a discussion with his own daughter. "And I'm not trying to involve you in some corporate marriage. It's just that there's a man here from England whom I think would suit you very well. He has seen your picture and expressed an interest, so I said I would call you and try to arrange a get-together. Is that so wrong, Elizabeth? Does that make me out to be an ogre?"

Bess sighed. If she didn't give at least some ground, this

would go on for hours. Angry as she felt, she could hardly hang up on her own father for appearing to want to look after her. "No, it doesn't make you an ogre. It makes you a concerned father. But there's nothing to be concerned about. I'm an adult, running my own life my own way, and I intend to continue doing so. If this Englishman is so wonderful, introduce him to your hair stylist, your astrologer, your dietician, your personal train—"

"He says he prefers you. Apparently he's fond of natural redheads." A chuckle that was supposed to soften the chauvinism of the remark followed.

Bess, losing patience, didn't bother to hide the contempt in her voice. "Then keep him on ice for a week," she snapped. "By then it'll doubtless be natural blondes he fancies. Listen closely, Father. I . . . am . . . not . . . interested."

His pause gave her hope that he might, for a change, give up.

"Listen closely," he mimicked softly, too softly, warning Bess that he planned to drop a bombshell. "The man from England has to be in Denver next week on business. I gave him your address and phone number, so you can expect a call about Friday. This is supposed to be a secret, Elizabeth, but he asked me if you liked diamonds."

"Diamonds? I don't like di—"

"Or emeralds. I said emeralds. He went straight to Tiffany's. His name is . . ."

Her father got no further. Bess thumbed the disconnect button and ran out onto the balcony, tears of frustration pouring down her cheeks. When the phone rang again, she rushed back into the apartment, turned off the ringer and her answering machine, then fled back to the balcony. She needed—craved—fresh air.

Deciding sleep was the only immediate relief, she found

herself tossing on a sweat-soaked pillow, dreaming nightmares that brought her awake every five minutes, or so it seemed. In them, Paul lived again, the Highwayman's horse pranced and galloped, and the characters in Geoffrey Barrett's proposed book came to life and began to speak to her.

Morning brought the first frost of the season, and with it a sense of hopeless desperation tinged with the anger of frustration. Her anger with Geoffrey had long ago mellowed to a mild annoyance and Bess realized it was nothing compared to the anger she now felt for her father. Her own father! Giving out her address and telephone number, treating her as if she were some corporate whore!

To hell with him! He could send his Englishman next week at his leisure, because she wasn't going to be home to worry about it. Once the sun had melted the frost from her battered VW Cabriolet, she drove into downtown Colorado Springs and parked as close as she could get to her favorite travel agency, a firm she often used because she found them reliable, the staff friendly and helpful. Her meanderings across the country for book signings often presented unusual travel difficulties, and so far they hadn't let her down.

Nor did they this time. It was a matter of moments to confirm that yes, there was an open-ended ticket to Tasmania and return awaiting her in Los Angeles. The only problem would be the Australian tourist visa, but even that, it seemed, was easily solved.

"Your visa can be secured electronically," Sandi Pontius, the owner, assured Bess.

"If I left Wednesday, when would I arrive in Australia . . . Tasmania, Sandi? I'd have to be picked up at the airport, collected I guess he . . . they'd say."

"Depends, Bess. Do you want to lay over in Hawaii for a

couple of days? I'd advise it. Australia is a long, long journey, although I guess whoever wants you there must want you pretty bad. You've got a first-class ticket to get you from L.A. to Melbourne. And back again, of course." Wearing an impish grin, Sandi glanced up from beneath thick lashes as if to will Bess into admitting she had a rich lover footing the bill for all this.

First class! Bess might never have left the continental United States, but she knew about first class air travel. And how much it cost.

Her opinion of Geoffrey Barrett altered perceptibly as she drove home, her mind already occupied with what to pack, what not to pack, and the arrangements she would have to make before departing the following Wednesday morning.

The entire thing was daunting. But not even in the same league as waiting for her father's hedonistic business associate, who would wine her and dine her and give her expensive jewelry and expect compensation, which, of course, she was not willing to give, not even if her father threatened her with . . .

With what? It didn't matter. Her one and only rebellion, moving to Colorado, had brought a certain amount of relief. But she knew her father lurked, biding his time, hoping to permanently snare her in his sticky spider's web. And she feared his power—especially over her—more than she feared flying. Or Geoffrey Barrett.

Sometimes Father reminded Bess of Howard Hughes. Hughes wouldn't take no for an answer, either.

CHAPTER THREE

Tempted to bark into the speaker phone, Warren Cornwall bit down hard on his lower lip. Just in time and just as well, he thought, sliding easily into a more amenable tone of voice. He needed Reginald Bingham—not the other way around—and it wouldn't do to put the Brit off with an unseemly show of temper.

"Well really, Reg, I can't imagine what might have happened," Cornwall said in a voice that, even to his own ears, sounded false. "You say there's no sign of Elizabeth anywhere and she hasn't answered your telephone calls?"

As the conversation continued, Cornwall was forced to grasp more strongly at his temper. While his words to the rich British industrialist were honey-sweet, another part of his mind was cursing.

Once the phone call was over, he dropped the facade like a hot potato, punched the intercom as if it were some live opponent, and shouted, "Get Rossiter in here! Immediately, if not sooner!"

When Tom Rossiter, a huge, hulking ex-cop with a brain that belied his rumpled appearance, entered the opulent office, Cornwall's instructions were specific and to the point.

"Get out to Colorado Springs. Now. Take the Lear. Find my daughter and get her back here. I don't care if you have to kidnap her, but get her back before that damned Bingham returns from his tour of the Rockies."

The word "but" sprang to Tom's lips, and never got past them. He'd spent years with Cornwall, and knew when to speak and when not to. After darting a quick glance at Cornwall's framed photos of a young Howard Hughes in aviator garb and an older Hughes with actress Jane Russell, Tom turned and left the office.

But while his mouth had stayed silent, his mind raised a clamor. What the hell was the boss up to? Tom had always liked Elizabeth, although the feelings were confined only to her; he had actively disliked Paul Bradley and never bothered to hide it. He had positively rejoiced at Bradley's suicide, and quite enjoyed his own part in helping to orchestrate it. The only drawback was that Elizabeth had been there to witness Bradley's "execution." Tom had always thought she deserved better, and was dead certain she deserved better when it came to fathers.

A feeling of raw trepidation burned in his guts when he phoned from Colorado Springs. It had taken little time to ascertain what facts were immediately apparent.

"She's gone," he said without preamble. "Mail's canceled, paper's canceled. Her car's here, which tells me nothing, and the neighbors aren't talking. Seems they took a dislike to Bingham, if that means anything, and now any stranger is suspect."

"Find her. I don't care what it takes, but find her. And drag her back here by the hair if you have to. Check the bus lines, airlines . . . hell, Rossiter, you know the drill. She can't have gone very far."

"I think I could get into her apartment, maybe check her computer and see if it tells me anything. And her answering machine." Tom was cautious in raising this. Despite Cornwall's insistence, the old man might not like having his daughter's privacy invaded. And Tom had been at the sharp end of Cornwall's legendary wrath often enough; he didn't relish a repeat performance.

"Whatever it takes, do it," Cornwall barked. And the phone at the other end crashed down.

Once back in New York, Tom was even more apprehensive about facing his boss. The news was not good.

"Australia?" Cornwall's huge fist slammed down upon the surface of his custom-built executive desk with sufficient force to rock the enormous structure. "You can't be serious. Elizabeth doesn't even have a passport. What the hell would she be doing in Australia? Writing about kangaroos?"

"I don't—"

"Then find out! That's what I pay you for!"

"I got into her apartment, but it was a waste of time," Tom said patiently. "She's been using a laptop hooked up to a monitor, and she must have taken it with her. I did think it was worthwhile trying the local travel agents, and sure enough she left for Australia last Wednesday, mostly on someone else's money."

"What the hell is that supposed to mean?"

Tom shrugged. "Someone organized an open ticket for her in L.A., according to the travel agent. Then the woman started getting spooked and wouldn't tell me any more. I've got people checking out there now, but it's still the middle of the night. No one in L.A. gets up before noon, it seems."

"Get somebody up! Get somebody up and working on this, damn it, or tell them to start looking for another job!"

Tom again chose silence as the best course, and left the huge penthouse office without speaking further. This was going to be a bastard of a job, and although he wasn't, and never had been, a superstitious man, he felt tremors of black dread running along his spine.

Inside his penthouse office, Dover Warren Cornwall was

over his tantrum. Now he was merely fuming, staring at the wall and wondering how he could have made such a hash of this whole business with Elizabeth. Ever since her mother's untimely death, he seemed to have had increased problems with the girl. In retrospect, letting her marry Paul Bradley had been a huge mistake, but at the time he'd been thinking more of an heir to his empire. He had determined that a child raised at least partly by Bradley—with his own influence, of course—could emerge a winner.

Well, that hadn't worked out. They'd gotten rid of Bradley, but Elizabeth was still too damned independent for her own—and his!—ultimate good.

Australia? That simply made no sense. What the hell was she up to now?

Bess leaned forward in her seat to see the landscape of Tasmania sprawling below her in a welter of greens and browns.

Her mind raced as her meeting with Geoffrey loomed like a specter before her. What in God's name was she doing here? What had ever possessed her to believe this choice was a better one than having it out with her father, once and for all?

"Because with Father there is no once and for all," she muttered, as the plane touched down and taxied toward the terminal. "He never stops trying, never stops pushing and shoving and manipulating. He's like a dog with a bone, a big, mean, powerful dog. One that always wins in the end."

Luckily there was no one in the seat beside her, and the flight attendant merely gave Bess a puzzled smile.

Damn it, now she was talking to herself! What next?

Come to think of it, E-mails were like talking to yourself, Bess thought. She had often read introspective posts, followed by an apology saying the poster had hit the send button

44

too quickly. If Miss Bess-make-a-mountain-out-of-a-mole-hill had simply ignored Geoffrey's Web page book cover and poem, would she be halfway around the world, visiting a man she'd never met? Well, technically—and technologically—she'd met him. But what if the picture on Geoffrey's website wasn't his picture? How many times had she heard stories about men luring women to one place or another via the internet? Sometimes they even faked their photos, altering the features of a Sean Connery or a Brad Pitt . . . or a Mel Gibson.

Geoffrey could have done that! After all, he'd altered her *Sweet Primitive Passion* book cover easily enough. Come to think of it, no author photo had ever graced his books. And his website photo looked like the kind of picture found at a discount mart; a handsome 5×7 executive, athlete or cowboy, smiling from hundreds and thousands of marked-down-for-quick-sale frames.

"Nonsense," Bess said, giving the flight attendant a dark look, daring her to produce another puzzled smile. "A stalker wouldn't pay for first class tickets to Australia, would he? That's a tad extravagant, even for Jack-the-Rich-Ripper."

Still, Bess wished she could just huddle in her seat. Perhaps she would be overlooked and allowed to return to Melbourne and, eventually, home. Indeed, she did let everyone else off the plane before she managed to summon up the nerve to follow. Grabbing her laptop case and purse, she stumbled her way to the exit door, mumbling thanks to the staff as she emerged into sunlight so bright it almost blinded her. Then, straggling along at the tail of the line of passengers moving toward the terminal, she finally stepped inside to meet another form of blindness, and realized that her pupils had shrunk.

As passengers ahead of her dispersed like so many pigeons, Bess found herself waiting for her eyes to adjust so she could search the recesses of the terminal for some recognizable sign of Geoffrey.

Logically, he should also be looking for her . . .

And there he was, leaning against a pillar about twenty feet away, a lean, trim figure in checked shirt and moleskin trousers. He sported shiny, low-heeled boots, quite different from American riding boots, and his arms were folded across his chest as he scanned the crowd . . . above her head!

Bess would have laughed if it hadn't been such a common phenomenon. She was so short it happened every time she was met by a stranger at a railway station, airport or bus station. Or restaurant or theatre . . . just about anywhere.

Ducking her head so she wouldn't meet his eyes, she tried to alter her gait, to shift into the shuffling, nondescript movements of a teenager at that worst stage of development, where neither child nor adult is fully in charge. Her mane of auburn hair obscured her face, and was such a riotous rats-nest of curls after her long flight that she was certain it—and she—looked nothing like her photo.

She moved at an angle, ending up beside Geoffrey, but sufficiently out of his line of vision. Her sense of fear and apprehension had disappeared, replaced by a wave of puckish humor she had never in her life been able to control.

"Hello, sugah, are you lookin' for me?" she said in a Scarlett O'Hara drawl, batting her eyelashes shamelessly as Geoffrey turned to stare down at her. A long way down; he was all of six feet tall. Green eyes met turquoise, widened in recognition in a movement so fleeting she wasn't totally sure of having seen it, then narrowed in deliberation as his gaze swiftly flickered up and down her body, touching her breasts in a tangible caress, lingering between her thighs, flashing along the inch or so of leg between her culottes and her leather boots. It occurred to her that he'd never seen her below the waist, as his gaze rose to meet her eyes again while his mobile mouth twisted into a wry half-grin.

"Frankly, my dear, you'll do very nicely," he said, sounding exactly like Clark Gable. "Tell you what, darlin'. If you come along with me, I'll . . ." He paused, as if to let her fill in the blanks. Then he simple said, "I'll carry your bags for you."

He laughed, a totally masculine laugh so filled with fun, with delight, with genuine pleasure that Bess couldn't help but join him. Whereupon, he stepped back a pace and bowed . . . actually bowed! And reached out with long, graceful fingers to take her hand and raise it to his lips as his eyes searched her face, searching for a reaction . . . demanding a reaction. And getting one. Bess blushed, but couldn't tear her gaze away as his lips brushed her knuckles ever-so-slightly. A butterfly kiss, barely felt but impossible not to remember.

"Welcome to Tasmania, Ms. Carson," he then said very formally. "Shall we collect your bags now, or wait until the scrum dies down a bit?"

"Let's wait," she found herself saying, wondering why he hadn't released her fingers, yet glad he hadn't. If only he would stop undressing her with his eyes.

"Forgive me," he said, as if he had read her mind. And something in his eyes changed, the predator sign going off to be replaced by one of warm welcome. "It's just that . . . well, you're much more attractive than your picture reveals."

"A lot shorter, too." Bess grinned, and would have laughed aloud at the expression on his face, except that he seemed genuinely contrite. "I wouldn't worry about it, Geoffrey. Happens all the time."

His second burst of laughter was even more contagious. "You snuck up on me, didn't you? I suppose I should have expected it, but I didn't, even though I obviously deserved it. Guess that'll teach me not to underestimate you, Bess."

Somehow the way he said her name was a sigh, a soft wind against her cheek that flowed in an eddy down the hollow of her throat to lodge in the hollow of her breasts, and Bess sighed in response. She couldn't check it, didn't try, didn't care. At least not for that single, never-to-be-forgotten instant. Then all her panic mechanisms came alive, and without realizing it she was stumbling backwards, away from him, almost falling. Would have, had he not reached out quickly to grasp her arm and hold her upright.

"You okay?" And the concern in his eyes—those damned brigand's eyes—was genuine enough, as was his voice.

"Fine," she managed. "Just . . . just stiff from sitting too long, I guess."

As good a lie as any, and not all that far from the truth. Bess saw his eyes narrow in speculation, and realized she must be very, very careful with Mr. Geoffrey Barrett. He was far too astute for comfort.

Too considerate for her comfort as well, she decided. He maintained his grip on her arm as they moved to the baggage trolleys, now mostly empty, then was forced to release her so he could pick up her suitcases.

Moving side-by-side out and across to the airport parking lot, he seemed to be totally aware of her movements, ready to drop her bags and grab her again if she should stumble or—as perhaps he feared—faint. She did neither, and within minutes they were at the rear of a large four-wheel-drive Land Cruiser in which a bouncing, demented small dog danced as if heralding their arrival.

"Wait," Geoffrey said absently, as he pressed a button on his key ring to unlock the vehicle's doors, then reached out to open the rear door. He raised one finger silently, and the brown-and-white spaniel backed halfway along the rear compartment and obediently sat down, eyes flickering wildly from Bess to Geoffrey and back again.

"This is Lady," Geoffrey said, and at the sound of her name the spaniel flopped over and began to wriggle with excitement.

"Bloody fool of a dog. Who'd have a Springer spaniel, eh? Who could love a dog like you?" Geoffrey reached out to tickle those few parts of the dog that would hold still long enough. "And if you piddle in the car, my girl, we're going to have words. Now settle down. Bess came to see me, not watch you make a fool of yourself."

Then, to Bess, "I'd rather you didn't pet her right now, although I can see you're dying to, because if you do, she will piddle, I guarantee it. It's the one thing about her I can always be sure of. Time enough when we get home, okay?"

"Okay," Bess replied, somewhat disappointed. She backed out of the way so Geoffrey could load her baggage in beside the still-wriggling spaniel, then clambered up into the passenger seat, after having first attempted to get in on the driver's side, which would have been the passenger side at home.

She'd have blushed at that faux pas, had not Geoffrey chuckled softly. "I did that almost daily for a week, last time I was in New York," he said with a slow smile that diffused her embarrassment without adding to it. Of course, the fact that he took her arm to help her into the passenger seat after holding the door for her didn't hurt.

Too smooth, too polite, too . . . everything, Bess thought, and spent the fifteen minute trip to town rebuilding her defenses. Which, she realized, badly needed rebuilding. Geoffrey Barrett was—and why, after exchanging E-mails with him all this time, hadn't she expected it?—apparently on a wave length so close to her own that it was almost impossible not to be relaxed in his presence. Almost impossible not to laugh with him, because the humor they shared had taught her to know when he was spoofing and when he was serious.

She wondered what Mouse would say. "You're in trouble now, dear," he'd say. "Such terrible trouble." And Bess resolved to raise the drawbridge at the first opportunity and keep it raised. Surely she could work with this man professionally and not succumb to the potential for personal involvement. She couldn't get involved, couldn't allow such a thing to happen. It would only result in disappointment for Geoffrey. And, worse, for herself.

During the trip into town, Geoffrey pointed out this and that, but Bess could only oooh and aaah and then immediately forget. She was so busy putting a check rein on her emotions, she barely registered the fact that they had pulled into the driveway of a large, oldish-style house, and that Lady clearly knew where they were. The little spaniel was doing cartwheels at the end of her tether.

"Home again, home again," Geoffrey said with a grin. Then added, as he opened the rear of the vehicle and reached in for the tether clasp, "Now don't say I didn't warn you about this, Ms. Carson. Just stand still, and if you're lucky . . . well . . . we shall see."

"Wait!" he said to the spaniel. And then, "Okay!"

A whirling dervish of brown and white and speckles sailed to the ground and spun around Bess's feet. The flying tail also managing to whip droplets of piddle everywhere as the dog did her amazing dance.

Bess whooped with surprise, but that only added to the astonishing performance. Geoffrey just stood there and laughed, making no attempt to control the mad animal.

Okay, Bess thought, *I guess it's up to me.*

"Lady," she said softly but firmly. When the dog paused long enough to meet her eyes, she raised one finger as she had seen Geoffrey do, and commanded, "Sit!" And to her astonishment—and perhaps the dog's as well—it worked. "Wait," Bess added, putting her hand down toward the dog like a traffic cop halting traffic. And that worked too!

"Bloody hell," Geoffrey said. "You didn't tell me you were a dog person."

"You never asked," Bess said with a grin, not about to admit that she had only become a dog person in the past fifteen minutes. Or, to be honest, one minute. Her father had never allowed what he called "scruffy canines" inside his Long Island mansion. He had dabbled in horse racing, but when his million-dollar auction choice, Queen Elizabeth, lost her first race, Father—in a fit of rage—sold the mare. Her mother had possessed a regal, squashy-faced cat, but Bess had only been seven years old. After the death of her mother's cat, Noyes, not so much as a goldfish had invaded the Cornwall estates, and Bess, craving some semblance of petting, longing to pet, had satisfied herself with a menagerie of stuffed animals.

"You've made a conquest," Geoffrey said, staring at Lady. "Not that it takes much with this one. She's the biggest tart I've ever seen, aren't you my little sausage?" Which put paid to Bess and her dog handling. The dervish began again, only this time it was around Geoffrey's legs.

"Enough," he griped, picking up the suitcases and starting toward the back door of the house. "Go and kennel."

Lady dutifully scooted toward a purpose-built kennel adjacent to the back door, giving her owner a positively filthy look as he shut the gate on her.

"Now, Ms. Carson, let's see what we're going to do with you." Geoffrey led the way down a hall, then elbowed open the door to a spacious guest room with its own en-suite bath-room and a balcony that overlooked portions of the city below.

"I would expect you'll want to freshen up or maybe even have a nap," he said to Bess, as he dropped her suitcases. "Just do whatever satisfies your needs, come find me when you're ready, and we'll go out for some tucker. Okay?"

"Sure," she replied, somewhat taken aback by the casual-ness of his approach. "But . . . uhm . . . where do I look for you?"

"Oh, I'll be somewhere round the house." His grin was truly wicked. "And it'll give you a chance to snoop with a proper excuse."

Whereupon her host bowed politely, just before he shut the door. But he left Bess the image of that wicked, fanciful grin, and the eternal wisdom behind it.

Definitely a man to be very careful of, she decided, cranking up the chains on her emotional drawbridge by an-other notch. She took his advice and flopped face down on the bed. Asleep within seconds, she stayed that way for sev-eral hours as her body clock made an attempt to sort out the loss of a day and the transposition of too many hours.

She awoke feeling grubby, stiff, and—after a lengthy shower followed by a vain attempt to tame her auburn curls—decidedly hungry. So she dressed quickly and casually in jeans and an over-large Denver Broncos sweatshirt, then began her investigation of Geoffrey Barrett's home.

Bess had a vague memory of him describing it in one of his E-mails as "Federation Style," whatever that meant. How-ever, it was spacious, nicely planned, and delightfully deco-rated. He obviously had an eye for art; there were several paintings that caught her eye and imagination, plus a variety of wood carvings that sat or stood, each one gleaming polished in the late afternoon sun, each begging to be touched, fondled, admired in a tactile sense.

One, she especially loved. It was a chunk of what had obviously been driftwood of some sort, but now from its depths peered the bearded face of an almost mystic personage. Her mind shouted: *Druid*.

She found his office, empty and yet not empty. His presence was palpable. She could almost see him sitting at the computer, whittling away in his mind at the poem he had used to lure her to Tasmania. There was an indentation in the aging leather couch that told her he often napped there.

His bedroom, into which she only peeped, was austere. A large bed, dressing table, a single chair. The only touch of whimsy was a huge piggy-bank, almost child-like in its simplicity. There was one painting on plain, off-white walls that surely cried out for more. The painting showed a surrealistic figure, a nude without blatant nudity, decidedly feminine but without blatant sexuality. It was beautiful, ethereal, almost haunting. Bess felt something reach out from the painting and touch her, even as she closed her eyes and the bedroom door at the same moment.

She eventually found the kitchen, and Geoffrey with it, sprawled in a chair with a coffee cup close to his hand and a faraway look in his ice-green eyes. He was staring out the window, seeing something in the garden that was invisible to Bess. Then, aware of her presence, he rose to his feet.

"Feeling better?" His voice was gentle, its rough texture tamed by softness. But his eyes had suddenly become lasers, scanning her from crown to insole, missing no detail, then returning to rest on her face like a distant caress.

"Much. Although I'd kill for a cup of that coffee, Geoffrey, and some food. I'm famished. May I raid your fridge, or is that something not done by guests in this country?"

"Any guest in my house is free to do whatever takes their fancy, up to a point," he replied. "The coffee's just freeze-dried instant. I'll show you how to boil the jug. And I had been hoping to take you out for a meal. I'm a reasonable cook, but it's been a sort of hectic day and I've nothing planned."

"Good thing you plan to do the cooking," Bess said with a slow smile. "Because, although I can cook if I have to, it isn't something I enjoy very much, and I do it primitively at best."

"Not a problem here. Living in the town like this, there are heaps of choices, all within walking distance, at least for me. Do you enjoy walking, Bess?"

"Yes."

If only he could manage to say her name without that sensual caress in his voice, she thought. No, not a caress. The suggestion of a caress, the hint of something more than she heard, something coming.

She found herself hearing the Ray Bradbury title: *Something Wicked This Way Comes*. And she shivered inside, hoping it didn't show. However, as Geoffrey switched on the electric kettle, she was unable to ignore the economy of his movements, the lithe, almost feline grace as he moved across the kitchen.

"Will I have to get dressed? For dinner, I mean," she added, then looked away to try and hide the fanciful thoughts that accompanied her question. Although Geoffrey considered her words carefully, she expected him to grin and say something about eating in the nude. What on earth was going on in her head? Every time she came into this man's presence her entire system seemed to conspire against her.

"No, we're pretty casual mostly," he finally replied. "Unless you've a fancy to visit the Casino, or some really posh restaurant, we can go as we are." He looked pointedly down at her bare feet and raised one dark eyebrow. "Although I suppose you'll have to put some shoes on."

"Yes, well . . . the thought did occur to me, too. First, coffee. Okay?"

Shortly thereafter they were strolling down the city streets of Launceston. But Geoffrey didn't bother with much touristy talk, merely answered her occasional question, then suggested they drop in at O'Keefe's for a counter meal.

"Which is . . . ?"

"A pub meal. You have them in The States, but I can't remember what they're called, I'm afraid. Just good, wholesome tucker, not awfully expensive, not great shakes for atmosphere, but quick and satisfying. Suit you?"

"Lead on," Bess said, her stomach telling her she was looking forward to food, and at this stage it didn't matter where it came from.

They had barely entered the place when a barmaid called out, "Hey Geoff . . . ow ya goin'?" The woman smiled as he replied sadly, "Without, as usual." She then shot Bess a look that could only mean: *why-was-Geoff-going-without?*

For his part, Geoffrey could only nod to Bess and mutter, "Sorry . . . old joke."

And an old friend too, she surmised, but said nothing, merely nodded back. The food was plentiful and more than satisfying, and the only real difference Bess noticed in service was the business of paying at the bar when the meal was ordered, rather than waiting for the bill at the end.

"I'll get the tip, if that's okay," she said when they had finished eating and were dawdling over the remains of some splendid local beer.

"No need," was the reply. "Tipping isn't very common in

Australia, and even less so in Tasmania."

Bess was astonished. "How do these people make a living? I waited tables in Colorado, and believe me, when you only make about two dollars an hour, tipping is what it's all about."

"You? A waitress? Well bugger me dead," he said, surprise evident on his face. "Sorry . . . very much an Australianism, that. I just wouldn't have thought—"

"I was good enough to average eighty dollars or more a night in tips, but it's hard work, very stressful. And please don't apologize for your language. I've heard it all before. It doesn't bother me in the slightest." And then, coming from nowhere, certainly not from her logical mind, she added, "Just don't pinch my butt. That really pisses me off." And she could have crawled under the table.

"I wouldn't dream of it," he said, face set in what had to be fake seriousness. "But while we're on the subject, or near it, would you please see if you can manage to call me just Geoff? My mother called me Geoffrey and one . . . close friend . . . does too, but it sounds very strange in my ears hearing it from anyone else."

"Okay, Just Geoff, so long as you continue to lay off the Ms. stuff and call me Bess. Deal?"

"Done."

"And now I think it's time you took me home to bed because I can feel an attack of jet lag coming on. Ohmigosh! Did I say take me home to bed? I can't believe I said that. I mean—"

"I know exactly what you mean, Bess. Loosen up a bit, please. We'll never be able to work together if you throw a . . . what do you Yanks call it? . . . hissy fit . . . every time one of us makes a Freudian slip."

"It wasn't a Freudian slip. It was a figure of speech."

"And a very nice figure at that," he replied, appraising her jeans and tee. "Now, let's get you home to your own bed, alone, before you stop making sense entirely."

Which was what they did. Walking in silence all the way. Bess would have thought he was annoyed with her, except that somewhere along the journey she tripped, and having taken her hand to steady her, he kept holding it . . .

And she never even thought to try and free herself.

CHAPTER FOUR

They started on The Book two days later. Geoff wanted to call it Our Book, but Bess insisted it would be The Book until it had a genuine title.

Actually it was a case of Bess making her start, since Geoff had already roughed out the first chapter as he saw it. Now it was up to her, he suggested, to determine if she could make the transition from his work to a second chapter that was her work.

Great in theory. Impossible to implement. Their writing styles were too different.

"We can't do it this way," Bess announced at lunch time, when he said they should walk downtown to have a beer and sandwich somewhere. "And I'd rather discuss this in private, Geoff. Surely I can make us a sandwich while we thrash this out here."

"No bread," was the almost-brusque reply. "And more importantly, no beer."

"And no one, I suppose, who'd be prepared to just go and get such things. Are you angling for a public discussion to keep me from making a scene or screaming at you?"

"Precisely. We're still sorting ourselves out, Bess. Tempers could flare, and don't deny it. You're not wearing all that red hair for nothing, I suspect."

"I'm one third Irish and one third Jewish," she said, fighting for calm. Damn it but he could be annoying when he chose to be. "Which, my mother used to say, means I have an

Irish temper and Jewish guilt. It does not, however, make me a person who stages scenes or loses my cool at the drop of a hat."

"Of course not," he said. "But you don't know about me. Indeed, for all you know, I like to throw the occasional hissy fit where the world can see and appreciate it."

Bess broke up. She couldn't help it. The thought of Geoffrey Barrett throwing a hissy fit in public was so ludicrous, her sense of humor couldn't deal with it. She started with a giggle, but within seconds had tears running down her cheeks and could hardly sit upright.

Geoff just stood there, shaking his head sadly, until she finally regained some shred of composure. "I'm sorry," she said. "It's just that . . ." And she lost it again, dissolving into giggles once more.

All of which was far, far too much for Lady, who had gamely sat through the first session with only a token wriggle. Now she went into her dervish mode, spinning round Bess's feet, sprinkling as she spun.

"Oh, Lady. See what you've done. You didn't name her properly at all, Geoff. She ought to have been named Cyclone."

He handed over a roll of paper towels. "Here. You started it, you get to clean it up. Then, I'm leaving for a beer and sandwich, whether you choose to come with me or not. Lady! Go and kennel."

Geoff headed for the door with the spaniel at his heels. Lady looked back as if asking Bess if it was all right to follow him. Smiling at the dog, she knelt to wipe up the piddle, thankful it had happened on the polished kitchen floorboards instead of the living room—no, here it was lounge room—carpet.

"Right, I'm off," Geoff said, having locked up his recalcitrant Lady. "You coming or not?"

"Not," she replied, hardly bothering to think about it. "I'll just raid the fridge and try to make some sense out of this collaboration thing. If we don't get it sorted out, you've spent a lot of money for me to play tourist and—"

"Your principles won't allow it. Damn it, Bess, even you have to eat. Especially you. There's hardly anything of you in the first place."

To which she merely snorted. There was more than enough of her for the size of her frame. A fellow author had once said: "It's not that I'm overweight, it's just that I'm under tall." Then there was the old cliché: "You can never be too rich or too thin." Well, she'd been too rich, thank you very much, and too thin wasn't her style.

"Besides, the walk will do you good," Geoff persisted. "Clear away the cobwebs so we can look at our problems from a different perspective."

"Is this your way of telling me you have some new and exciting ideas about how to approach it, or are you angling for company?"

"Both. Now put your shoes on and let's go. I'm getting decidedly peckish."

As they meandered down the streets, Bess did her best to explain to Geoff why she thought they would have to try something different if their collaboration was to succeed.

"Look, you've got this American heroine, Kate, who is caught up in a press-gang raid in San Francisco, protected by a pirate all the way to Australia. Then she winds up on the Ballarat gold fields, which is the setting for Chapter One. I'm sorry, Geoff, but I think that's a poor choice from the get-go. Especially when you want the reader to believe she's still a virgin."

"Innocent. I said innocent, not virginal. There is a difference, you know."

"Probably better than you do!" Bess, who felt neither innocent nor virginal, wished Geoff would stop looking at her that way every time so much as a word was mentioned that had the slightest sexual connotation. It was as if those brigand's eyes were able to slice through her defenses like a cutlass, and it was damned disconcerting.

"Okay, I suppose so," he said, "but your point is?"

"I think you should start where she starts, in San Francisco. Otherwise, there's too much flashback, which is no place to try and explain how she manages to maintain her . . . innocence . . . for so long under such difficult circumstances. And we have to explain how she got into those circumstances in the first place. After all, she's a decent girl, isn't she? What was she doing getting involved in a press-gang raid?"

"I explained all that in my outline. Didn't you read the outline?"

"Don't be so defensive. Of course I read it. Unfortunately, it isn't detailed enough for my puny female mind to follow." Bess felt her Irish temper flare, then simmer. His outline had been filled with promise. However, her emotions had been tangled at the time, and it now seemed to be all smoke and mirrors. "The problem is," she continued, "and I don't want to hurt your feelings, but the problem is . . ." She took a deep breath. "It's all puff and little substance."

Bess was right, of course, thought Geoff. His outline wasn't detailed enough. But he didn't dare admit to her at this stage that he'd made the thing up from the whole cloth the very night he'd sent it. She'd have his guts for garters if he did that. So he would just have to brazen it out and hope that somehow he could trick her into creating some of that substance. But how?

"If we started the book in your country," he said, thinking out loud, "you would have to take charge of the beginning.

You will have to 'become' Kate anyway, one would suspect, given that it's the American speaking patterns and attitudes and, admittedly, some of the history and geography that I have the most problem with."

"So now you want me to start the book? And do you expect me to write the whole thing too? Because I couldn't. You must do that!" Her simmering temper boiled over. "Damn it, Geoff, half the book is set here in Australia, about which I know less than nothing."

"Ah, but you know Kate," he replied enigmatically, then switched tack as they reached the Royal Oak on the corner by City Park. "There's a local brew on tap here that I'm rather fond of, and the tucker's quite good too, of course."

"Of course," Bess said, for the first time consciously realizing that Geoff's Kate was, in fact, herself, or herself as he perceived her. Red-headed heroines were hardly uncommon in historical romances, but his enigmatic comment had dropped the penny. An Aussie expression, dropped the penny, one which Geoff often used while dealing with his fractious dog. Bess liked the expression, and was determined to use it more in The Book.

She also liked lunch and the local beer, Hazard, but going straight home to write was suddenly removed from her agenda. No, Geoff insisted, they would wander through City Park for a bit, enjoy the sunshine, visit the monkeys.

So they did, but if Bess had expected this to be an opportunity to discuss their collaboration, she was quickly disappointed. In fact, Geoff seemed to be avoiding the subject rather than embracing it.

Geoff stifled a sigh. His lovely American wench was still fretting over the bloody book, he thought, observing her half-clenched fists and the subtle pout of her generous mouth. Unfortunately, he had no more idea where their book was

going than she did. Perhaps less. He'd exhausted all his ener-
gies creating a believable outline and hadn't thought beyond
its effectiveness in baiting his trap. As they paused to watch
the City Park monkeys in their walled enclosure, he concentrated on his original lunch mission: evading any in-depth
book discussion.

Bess fumed silently. Not only didn't Geoff want to discuss
the book, but as they strolled through the park he took her
hand in his and matched his stride to her shorter one. He
didn't do it seductively, but simply as if it was the most natural thing in the world. And while all her instincts cried out
for her to put a stop to this right now, she didn't. Because it
seemed natural to her, too.

It wasn't as if they were lovers, she reasoned. Just two
people who happened to be extremely comfortable in each
other's company. At least most of the time. Why not enjoy
this gracious park on a gorgeous day, after a wonderful lunch,
with the skies blue and bright and the sun warm upon them?
Why not . . . what were Geoff's words . . . loosen up a bit?

"What's the other third?" he asked.

"Excuse me?"

"You said you were one third Jewish and one third Irish."

She considered saying one third Dover Warren Cornwall,
but Geoff wouldn't understand, and she really didn't want to
talk about her father right now. It was her mother who'd been
half Jewish, half Irish, which made Bess fifty percent . . .
what?

"Iconoclast," she blurted without thinking any further.
Then felt her cheeks bake.

Geoff remained silent for six or seven heartbeats. "Interesting," he finally said. "I'm a bit of a pagan myself. Or by
iconoclast, did you mean 'devil's advocate'?"

"If you mean faultfinder or bubble-burster, I certainly

hope not." She tried to grin, and failed. "Actually, it was my father who liked to burst bubbles."

"Was? Is he dead?"

"Yes." With sudden clarity, Bess realized how . . . iconoclastic . . . her father had always behaved toward her. Bubbleburster? An understatement if she ever heard one. Father was dead, at least to her, because she would never let him manipulate her again. Never!

Misinterpreting the anguished expression that flitted across her face, Geoff squeezed her hand. "I'm sorry," he said. Then he led her back to the monkey enclosure and suggested he and Bess christen the monkeys with people-names.

I'd rather name our book characters, she thought, even as she played along. "Okay, Geoff, the one over there in the corner is Tommy Frontario, my first boyfriend. And the big one, the one who looks like he's wearing a rumpled suit, is Tom Rossiter."

Geoff laughed, then leaned over and stage-whispered, "I do believe your Tommy is a Tomasina, darling."

As always, his laughter was contagious, and Bess let loose with a series of unrestrained giggles, suddenly happy to be alive, happy to be with Geoff.

But when they returned home and he announced he would be gone for the rest of the afternoon on business, she was equally glad to be rid of him, to get some time to herself, to try and work out something on the book, not to mention working out more than a few somethings about the effect Geoff was having on her.

It was all very disconcerting. She was a guest, but also a sort of partner. She was collaborating, but on what? Every time she looked at what he had done thus far, the substance of the book grew more and more ephemeral.

Before leaving her alone, Geoff had been adamant . . . if

she was going to have Lady in the house, Bess must refrain from undue excitement. So she found herself moving slowly, thus thinking slowly. Because, as Geoff had predicted, the mad dog was alert to her every move. Often, it seemed, before Bess even knew she was planning to move.

"That damned dog piddles on my office carpet, and you, missy, are going to be in big trouble," Geoff had warned. But Bess, watching him try and hide his grin, had surmised that if Lady watered his office carpet, it wouldn't be the first time or the last. What had Geoff said over lunch? Something about how maturity, assuming it ever arrived in a dog as spinny as a working-bred English Springer Spaniel, removed at least the damp aspects of the demented frenzy that appeared at the slightest stimulus.

He could have been talking about Bess Carson, she thought wryly. Without a doubt, Mrs. Paul Bradley had been the most immature female on the face of the earth. Except Mrs. Paul Bradley hadn't been bred to work . . . just breed. Focusing on Geoff's computer, Bess was determined to forget her own past and solve Kate's dilemma. After all, Bess Carson's demons were nothing compared to the demons that haunted Kate No-last-name-yet.

When the telephone rang about an hour after Geoff's departure, Bess picked up the receiver without thinking and answered with a simple "Hello." After a few beats of silence, the man on the other end asked for Geoffrey Barrett. Bess politely told him Geoff was out, would perhaps be back by tea time, then asked if she could tell Mr. Barrett who'd called, and if there was a message.

"No," was the reply. "I expect I know where to find him, so I'll catch him there. If not, I can always phone back later."

Her mind was partly on the book and partly on the distinction between tea time as afternoon tea and tea time as dinner time, and it wasn't until after she'd hung up that she found herself thinking the caller's voice had sounded strangely familiar.

Definitely American, she thought, just before the mailman came by on his motorbike, Lady went ballistic, and she forgot all about the phone call.

She had reluctantly abandoned the book and was in the back yard playing with the demented dog when Geoff returned late in the afternoon. Standing near Lady's kennel, Bess looked on in some confusion as Geoff started unloading a huge sheet of plywood from the roof of his four-wheel-drive.

"Well don't just stand there, come give me a hand with this," he said, as the panel tipped and threatened to score the Land Cruiser's paintwork.

So she did, then helped him manipulate the plywood into the house and, by virtue of several back-and-fill maneuvers, into the hall outside his office.

Then Bess helped him move furniture so he could lay the plywood on the floor in front of his desk. She stood rooted in further confusion as he strode out to his vehicle and returned with a smallish, gas-lift secretary's chair, on castors. The chair was similar to his, except Geoff's had a bigger, more luxurious seat.

"What on earth are you doing?" she asked, realizing even as she spoke that there was only one logical explanation.

"Giving you a place to sit while we collaborate, of course. I think there'll be a lot of chopping and changing at the keyboard, and I hate to think of you having to leap up from the couch every time I need you."

"Do you expect me to just sit there while you're typing? What are you going to do when it's my turn? Twiddle your thumbs?"

66

"No. I'm going to sit on my chair and watch you. Very pleasant occupation, that."

The grin that followed was the brigand's grin she had come to fear most, the one that warned her there was a gangplank only inches away, and he was the one with the cutlass. Bess shook her head, auburn curls flying. Then she decided enough was enough, this conversation was heading into deep water, and she hadn't even tried out the chair yet.

"Oh, you had a phone call," she said, suddenly remembering. "An American. He didn't leave his name or any message; just said he'd find you."

Geoff's eyes grew bleak and the smile vanished. "I found him, and the only thing he and I could manage to agree on was that my new secretary, that's you, had a most professional telephone manner and a very pleasant voice to go with it."

"So it wasn't a very productive meeting, I'd guess."

"Not for him." And there was that pirate's grin again. Only with his eyes still bitter, the grin now held more than a hint of danger, and something in Geoff's expression was positively menacing. "If he calls back, tell him to go and get stuffed. In your most professional manner, of course."

"Yes, sir. Anything else, sir?"

"Nothing I'd like to hear coming out of your pretty mouth," was the laconic reply. "But I'm damned sick of buggering around with this mob, and I'm afraid it will get worse instead of better unless I start getting exceedingly hard-nosed about things."

"What things? I suppose I shouldn't ask, but . . ."

"You shouldn't. Especially since the corporation concerned is one of your mob. American, that is. They've been after a company I own for about a year now, and they don't seem inclined to take no for an answer despite the fact that it's the only answer they're going to get. I control the damned company and if I don't want to let it go, I bloody well won't."

It was the word, more than the tone of voice, but when Bess heard "control," an involuntary shiver flew along her spine. And it must have shown on her face, because Geoff immediately looked concerned and moved closer . . . the worst possible thing he could have done.

"Are you all right?" he asked, reaching out to catch her as she backed away and almost fell over the new chair.

"I . . . I'm fine," Bess stammered. "A touch of heartburn, I think."

Which gained her a quizzical look. "Oysters," he said.

"What?"

"You once told me you really like oysters. And do I know a place. Unless your heartburn is more than a touch."

"No," Bess assured him. "You just said the magic word. Oysters. Do I have to dress up?"

"Not really, but it isn't a bad idea. I haven't seen you wear legs since you landed at the airport. Tell you what. You wear legs and I'll wear a tie. You may not think it a fair trade, but you don't know how long it's been since I wore a tie, much less how I hate the damned things."

Bess couldn't help but smile, thinking it had probably been about as long since he'd worn a tie as it had been since she'd worn a mini-skirt. And she'd packed one!

In his suite at the Country Club Casino, the Asia-Pacific manager for the Cornwall group, Gerald Coolidge, couldn't stop thinking about the voice he'd heard on Geoffrey Barrett's phone. Why had the voice sounded so familiar? American, definitely, but why should he think he knew it?

The penny dropped about three minutes after Tom Rossiter walked through his door. Even then Coolidge wasn't sure. But he'd trained himself never to believe in coincidences, no matter how ridiculous they might seem on the surface, and so far that ability had paid off in spades.

"You're a long way from your turf, Tom," he said in greeting to his old friend. "What are you drinking and what are you doing in this god-forsaken hole?"

"Whiskey and water, and make it a double," Rossiter said. "God only knows I need it. The old man's going off the deep end, Gerry, and it's all I can do to keep from going with him."

Coolidge shrugged. "He's always doing that. What's the flap this time?"

"He's never gone this far before. I think he's losing it, I really do. Can you believe I've been sent here to track down his daughter and drag her home by the pigtails? I'm supposed to kidnap her. I mean, how the hell can I kidnap someone I can't even find, much less get them from here, if she really is here, back to New York? Hell, this isn't some little kid, Gerry. This is the old man's full-grown, adult daughter and heir!"

Whereupon the penny dropped from a wondrous height, and Gerald Coolidge could only stand there with his mouth open and his brain on fire as the coincidences came together. "How bad is the old man, Tom? It's been a year since I saw him in person, you know, but I have to agree he's been sounding more and more out of control whenever he phones."

Rossiter grunted, took a huge slurp from his drink, then lowered his hulking body into a chair. "I've noticed during the last six months that he's getting more and more erratic, and far more volatile, which is saying something for old War. And vindictive? Gerry, you wouldn't believe some of the crap he's been pulling. Remember the pictures in his office? I think he thinks he's Howard Hughes. You're lucky to be so far away from headquarters."

"What about his daughter?"

"He's concocted some weird scheme involving this Englishman who's fixated on Elizabeth. Never so much as met her, but he's seen her picture and he wants her. And if the old man has anything to do with it, he'll get her. Lucky bastard. She's probably the most drop-dead gorgeous woman I've ever seen. Nicely padded, not too skinny like . . . like one of those scrawny models. Elizabeth should have been a movie star, not buried somewhere in Colorado. The old man said she moved there because she loves football and she's a Denver Broncos fan."

"And the old man's going to . . . what . . . sell her? Marry her off like he did before to that idiot, Bradley? Wasn't he a piece of work? We've done a few things over the years I've at least half-regretted, Tom, but putting that jerk through the hoops almost bordered on fun."

"Personally, I think it's too bad he shot himself. Better he should have lived and suffered some more."

"Yeah, right." Coolidge paused, then reached out to snatch the almost-empty glass from Rossiter's hand. When he refilled it, it was more than a double.

"Listen, Tom," he said, after Rossiter had slugged back a mouthful. "How do you think the old man would feel if his daughter helped him with this stubborn son of a bitch down here? The one we're trying to dicker with? Before you kidnap her and drag her home, I mean."

"What?" Rossiter's surprise was total. He almost gagged on the next slug of whiskey, then sat there dumbfounded, the glass swamped by his enormous hand, his eyes glaring with suspicion. "Okay, Gerry. You obviously know something I don't. Of course! I forgot the old man sent instructions to everybody and his dog to keep an eye out for the girl. And you found her, didn't you?"

If they hadn't been old friends, hadn't gone through the Cornwall corporate wars together, and if their corporate interests weren't in totally different if complimentary directions, Gerald Coolidge would have lied. But he owed Tom Rossiter, and vice versa, and they went back a long way, with many bodies buried along the track.

"I didn't realize I'd found her until you walked in the door," he said. "What's worse, I never got any instructions from the old man about Elizabeth, which means I'll have somebody's balls for bookends when I get back to Singapore. But yeah, I'm almost sure I know where she is. Why, I can't imagine to save my life because it makes no sense at all, but it could be just the ticket for both of us, Tom. A ticket to fame, fortune and the American dream."

Whereupon he poured himself a drink, most unusual in the middle of the morning, and sat down to relate to Rossiter the curious tale of his phone call, as well as his last abortive meeting with Geoffrey Barrett.

"Now, friend Tom," he said, after refilling their glasses. "I think we have to have a plan, and I think I've got one that serves both our needs. Interested?"

"Cautious," was the brief reply. "But I'll listen."

"Good. First, we have to make sure it is the old man's daughter. Did you happen to bring a picture or two along? Of course you did; how handy. You and I can't go anywhere near the place since she knows both of us by sight. But I just happen to have an ambitious bootlicker called 'Rambo.' Rambo's as sleazy as they come and Elizabeth doesn't know him. So, first thing we do is send him around to confirm her identity. Easy enough to get Barrett out of the way. A phone call should do it."

Rossiter merely raised one eyebrow. "Okay, so assume we're sure it's the right girl. Then what?"

"We find out what the hell she's doing here. Rambo's an electronics wizard, one of the reasons I hired him, so I expect it won't be much of a job for him to tap the phones. I was going to do it anyway, because we've got bugger-all leverage on Barrett. But this is double the excuse and maybe ten times the payoff."

"I don't quite follow."

"She didn't come all the way down here to shake Crocodile Dundee's hand, did she? Barrett paid for her trip, right?"

"Someone did."

"If it was Barrett, he didn't pay all that money just for the hell of it. They're both writers. It's not hard to figure out what they're doing when they're not writing. Barrett's probably boffing her six ways from Sunday every day of the week."

"Well . . ."

"No well about it. I mean, she's a widow. She's used to getting her share, and it's been a while. I bet she hardly got off the plane before she tripped him and beat him to the floor."

"Okay, let's assume she's living in his house and they're sleeping together. What advantage does that give us?"

Coolidge grinned, but there was no humor in it. "Want to bet Barrett doesn't know who our girl really is? You'll get no takers here. He can't possibly know. He hates the old man even worse than I do, which is saying a lot. But Elizabeth has to know who Barrett is. She was the old man's personal secretary. Wonder what she'd do to keep him from finding out about her?"

"And what if you're off on some tangent somewhere? It sounds damned sketchy to me."

"Trust me, Tom. It's been a long, long time since I was wrong. If the girl I heard is Elizabeth, and I'm certain it is, we kidnap her. Then we ransom her back to Barrett for his agreement on the old man's deal."

"Then we kidnap her again and tote her back to her father?"

"Why not? It's only what you were going to do anyway. Hell, Tom, what's it going to cost us but a bit of extra time?"

"A lot of time, and most of it spent behind bars, although I suppose it couldn't hurt to let your guy check out the situation. I'll go along that far, for now."

"Good. I like a man who makes decisions."

Coolidge filled their glasses again. After all, a toast was in order. A toast to the old man, his daughter Elizabeth, and the bloody American dream.

CHAPTER FIVE

Geoff's idea of collaboration went much more smoothly than Bess would ever have imagined. With the office carpet protected from the castors by the sheet of plywood, they skittered back and forth, editing each other's contributions, entering their own, squabbling like children over some passages and issues, laughing like idiots at others.

"I think we should have a steamy bit," Geoff said, sitting back in his chair.

"Isn't it too soon?"

"Bloody hell, my little possum, it's almost too late!"

Bess wondered why he'd called her a possum, then decided she liked it.

"We've spent pages and pages on the earthquake," Geoff continued. "We've explained how Kate got separated from her family, her fiancé, and everybody else she knew intimately, even her bloody cat."

"I didn't say intimately."

"Yes, you did." He scrolled back a few pages.

"Oh. But I meant familiar, chummy, not intimate in an amorous sense."

"So did I." He flashed Bess a grin. "She was chummy with her fiancé, eh?"

"Wipe that smirk off your face, Geoffrey Barrett. Back in the eighteen-sixties, Kate and Leonardo would have been chums, not lovers, and frankly I see nothing wrong with that. If more people today were friends first, lovers later—"

"Okay, okay, but it means we'll have to deflower Kate carefully." He gave a small shrug. "For the record, Bess, my women protagonists have never been deprived of their virginity, at least not on the pages of my novels."

"Mine have," she said, and her tone of voice must have conveyed something because she saw his eyebrow slant upward. "It's no big deal, Geoff. One burst of incredible pain and then it's over."

He wanted to refute her statement because in her books—and he'd read them all—she seemed to dwell on that pain. He had never "deflowered" a virgin, had never even asked his various partners how they'd felt at the moment of deflowerization . . . if that was a word. Suddenly, he wanted to ask Bess how she'd felt, but it was too personal, so he merely said, "We'll give Kate an 'intimate' moment with Leonardo, and bugger all Victorian morals. Is that okay with you?"

"Sure. She can blush furiously every time she thinks about it."

"And while we're on the subject, Victorian morals I mean, do we really need one whole page devoted to *Little Women*?"

It took Bess a moment. "Oh, you mean the book."

"Yes, the book. The bloody book Kate sneaks onto the ship by hiding it . . . the book, not the ship . . . under her wrap."

"Most cloaks had pockets."

"I have to admit it was poignant. I mean, Kate trying to read through the small slice of sunshine that leaks into her cell of a room. She really should have tried to hide a reading lamp beneath her cloak. Or, at the very least, candles and matches."

Bess giggled. "Not to mention fish and chips. If we don't let her eat her moldy bread soon, she'll waste away to nothing. Look, Geoff, I only mentioned the book so that readers can date the scene. *Little Women* was published in 1868."

"And no one will notice that Kate survived the 1868 earthquake, eh?" Geoff quirked his eyebrow again.

"You have a point, dar . . ." Bess paused to issue forth a fake cough. She'd almost said darling, and she knew the word would have sounded intimate rather than chummy. "You have a point," she repeated. "Darkness would have kept Kate from reading, so we'll delete *Little Women*."

"Good. Then we'll have more space for our spicy scene."

"No problem." Bess instinctively flexed her fingers. At the same time, she pushed against the plywood with her sneakers.

"Just a minute." Geoff stopped her chair with one large, arrogant foot. "This is my area of expertise."

"You're kidding. You're not kidding. I thought I was airfreighted to Tasmania because of my expertise. 'Given that it involves more romance than I am used to, I propose that we collaborate.' That's what you said, or close."

"Close," he replied with a grin. "But what I have in mind isn't romance, Bess. What I have in mind is sex."

"What's the difference?"

Was *she* kidding? No, she wasn't. With an effort, Geoff kept his face impassive. "The difference," he began, fumbling in his mind for words. "Okay, suppose we take one of your book heroines? If she's being ravaged by outlaws or revolutionaries, that's sex. When she . . . what's an American expression?"

"Gets it on?"

"When she gets it on with the hero, that's romance."

"I beg to differ, Geoff. It's all sex. The romance is in the courting, the sex is in the consummation."

"Well then," he challenged, "let me prove you wrong."

"Okay. And just to be fair, I'll go to the bathroom . . . I mean, the loo."

Geoff's fingers attacked the keyboard. When she returned, he had completed two full pages. She sank into her chair, then maneuvered it toward the computer. She had always prided herself on her ability to construe a sex scene, be it ravishment by an evil Apache or "getting it on" with a handsome cowboy. She truly doubted Geoff could match her expertise, but she was willing to give him the benefit of the doubt.

Then, reading what he'd written, she had to stifle a giggle. It was all so very, very Victorian, even prudish. And because they'd been having such fun, when she spoke it was without the caution a saner Bess might have shown.

"For goodness sake, Geoff," she jibed, not bothering to look at him, her entire attention on the computer screen. "What do you think this book is going to be? A Victorian melodrama? I'd hate to be the girl you marry if this is what you consider steamy."

She was already reaching for the keyboard when a long arm shot out to spin her chair around so that they faced each other like two people on an old-fashioned love seat.

"You would, would you?" he said in a voice that somehow managed to shout and whisper at the same time. Eyes like green sea ice flashed lightning into her own as his strong fingers reached out to gather the front of her ragged, ancient Denver Broncos football sweatshirt and yank her up and over into his lap, somehow without tearing the shirt into shreds.

Bess started to squeal, but no sound emerged because his mouth was already there to stop it, lips swooping to plunder her mouth as his left arm gathered round her to keep her in position. She was overwhelmed by the suddenness of it all, then by the taste of him, the sensation of his tongue as it leapt to dance with her own.

She shuddered, but it was not the shudder of fear that her mind tried vainly to demand of her. Her breasts were being crushed against his chest, her breath seemed to have deserted her entirely. And still his tongue danced with her own in a primitive, savage and yet somehow teasing, languid tempo that sent fluttering, pulsating messages to her tummy, then lower still.

Then he paused, gave back her mouth, and she thought she heard him whisper something . . . a single word that could have been a curse or a prayer. And his free hand lifted to touch her cheek, her throat, moving like moth wings as it explored and caressed, guided and directed. And when his mouth returned to claim her, it was in a kiss that was almost tentative, his mobile lips touching and retreating; another dance, but this one to a totally different melody.

His fingers spread so that he could caress her jaw line and the soft hollow behind her ear at the same time, stroking her neck and rousing, with no logic she could determine, her nipples. She felt them straining against her bra, against him. And so did he; she knew it, although he made no move to touch her there. Had no need to . . . he knew!

And he reacted. Against her bottom she could feel him throbbing, growing, expanding, his erection threatening to lift her from his lap entirely. And she knew, and knew that he knew, of the flood of desire that flowed from her in reply. Bess wriggled, couldn't help it and didn't want to, betrayed by a part of her body that craved only to get closer to his swollen groin, that wanted to use this sudden and unexpected flood of desire to engulf him, too.

"Nnnnoooo." The sound emerged from her in a combined wail of agony and sigh of desire, and she flung her arm out wildly, defying fingers that wanted only to weave through his hair, thrill to the touch of his neck.

"Nnnnoooo!" And this time he listened. In a single gesture, he was on his feet, strong arms depositing her back into her own chair with an urgency that equaled that of his kisses. Eyes hot with passion and yet somehow tinged with sadness bored into her own, fighting their way through her tears, and she saw, rather than heard, his mouth saying "Sorry" before he turned away and stumbled from the room.

Bess slumped, elbows on her knees, her eyes, first closed, then open and staring at the floor, her fingers trembling. Her entire body shook with the aftermath of a physical reaction more intense than anything she had ever experienced, ever even dreamed of experiencing.

Her gaze strayed to her crotch, her mind certain that her jeans must be soaked to the knees. Not a sign. It didn't seem possible, but then, was any of this possible? Could she really have climaxed just from the feel of his erection through their clothing and the intensity of her own response to him? How else, she wondered, could she be left with a tummy throbbing as if filled with dying butterflies? Why else did she still feel her sex muscles clenching and unclenching as if still reaching for him?

Was what she had experienced even a climax? Difficult to judge when you've never had one, and she never had. Even when her marriage was at its best, she had thrilled to Paul's spurting releases, but faked her ultimate responses.

Hardly any wonder he'd called her the worst "wife" in the world, she found herself thinking. And then wondering what Geoff would have thought had she followed her instincts and allowed him to continue . . . helped him to continue.

Because that was what she had wanted, and Bess wasn't fool enough to lie to herself about something so basic. As she had felt herself rise on the passionate lift of his erection, her every instinct had been to reach down and assist it, to dissolve into his embrace and allow him do whatever he wished.

And why not, she was thinking; at least there would be physical pleasure for both of them, even if their relationship couldn't go anywhere, wouldn't go anywhere beyond their book collaboration and perhaps Geoff's bedroom. Why shouldn't she take what pleasure she could? That concept was surging through her head and starting to re-heat her body when Geoff stuck his head through the office door.

"I think we both need some fresh air," he said without bothering to further apologize. "Do you want to come and help me train my idiot of a dog? There's a trial soon and she could use the work."

Bess didn't trust herself to speak. Just looking at Geoff right now was like staring into the sun; it made her light-headed and giddy and totally unsure of herself. And perhaps a little bit peeved, as well. Here she was, not sure if she dared get out of the chair, half-afraid her legs would collapse from under her, and here he was, all prepared to go dog training as if nothing had happened.

Still, she nodded her acceptance and forced herself to walk straight, without revealing the turmoil inside her.

They stopped first at a local store, where Geoff insisted upon buying her some rubber boots . . . gumboots they called them here. Bess found herself still reacting to him sexually as he knelt to help her try on the boots. Just the touch of his fingers on her ankle sent spasms straight to the core of her being.

"You'll need gumboots," he explained. "The place where I train is tidal. And if the tide happens to be in, there are parts of the track that get more than just a little damp."

Then he drove to Hobler's Bridge, where he parked and let the dog run free. They walked side by side along a well-constructed track that led for what seemed like miles along the North Esk River at almost the limit of tidal influence. As he had predicted, she was glad of the rubber boots, especially when she saw her first Australian snake slithering away into the waist-high undergrowth.

Fortunately, Lady never saw it. Geoff said that snakebite was a risk for dogs throughout Australia. "In February and March, when the tiger snakes get to mating, they can be fairly aggressive," he said, "but mostly we trial in the winter, when there's less risk."

Lady, whose pedigreed name was Wrangham Ladybird, was what Geoff termed a working-bred English Springer Spaniel. She'd been bred by Rachel Greaves, considered the country's leading breeder of working spaniels, and was significantly different from those English springers one might encounter in the show ring.

"If you tried to put her in a dog show you'd get laughed out the place," he said with a grin. "But bring one of those poofter show spaniels into the field, and Lady would run him into the ground in no time. They've bred most of the working ability out of the show strain, although I do know a bloke who trialed Welshies . . . that's Welsh springers . . . with a degree of success."

They walked on several yards before Bess's curiosity got the better of her, and she had to demand an explanation of his word "poofter." Which made Geoff laugh the huge, friendly laugh she had come to associate with him.

"It's what you Yanks would call 'sissy,' " he said. "Often as not, it's sort of an affectionate jibe used between friends. Like calling someone a bastard, which sounds horrible, but as often as not is a term of genuine endearment."

Bess wanted to talk more; it was comforting to her, helping her past the surprising physical and emotional reaction she had experienced in his arms. But Geoff, it seemed, was through talking for now. Instead, he gave her a bag full of

81

dummies, which looked like small canvas-covered boat bumpers, and sent her off about a hundred fifty yards down the paddock.

"When you see me point, you throw one as high in the air as you can, so it lands just on the edge of the heavy cover over there," he said. "That's the biggest problem with bloody spaniels. They're bred to work at gun range, and getting them to go beyond it even to retrieve is the devil's own job, sometimes."

Bess did as she was told, and was pleased to see that Lady flowed across the space between them, moving so lightly and so quickly it was if the dog could fly. Then it all fell apart. Lady picked up the dummy, looked back at Geoff, then trotted over and sat facing Bess, lifting her face as if demanding that Bess accept some valuable present.

"Bloody dog! You want shooting, my little sausage," Geoff grumbled as he stomped the entire distance between them, took the dummy from the dog's mouth, and handed it to Bess before returning to his starting place. "You . . . heel!" he said to Lady, and to Bess, "When she gets down here, don't look at her. Keep your eyes averted, pretend she isn't there."

Which, to Bess's surprise, somehow worked. Lady did her job, apparently, to Geoff's satisfaction, then they all wandered along the track for some distance as he put her through a series of other retrieving exercises. But it was when the dog was free to just run and enjoy herself that Bess could see what Geoff had meant about what Lady had been bred to do. She charged around, quartering back and forth in front of them, never getting more than about thirty yards away before turning and working slightly closer, or waiting impatiently for them to catch up. And her nose never stopped. She had to sniff everything, investigate every patch of cover.

Gradually, they covered the entire track, all the way to the Henry Street bridge, then worked their way back again to where Geoff had parked the Land Cruiser. In places, the track was covered by water, in which Lady gamboled with delight. Where the backwaters allowed for it, Geoff put her through a series of water retrieves that resulted in all three of them getting soaked. Lady brought back the dummy, delivered it, then shook herself, creating an instant shower.

"Well, my little sausage, haven't you had a wonderful day?" Geoff said to the dog, who wriggled in response and tried to shake some more dampness from her coat. "And what about you, Bess? Interesting, at least?"

"I had a wonderful day too," she replied.

Then she shivered delightfully inside. Because it had been wonderful. She only hoped he'd interpret her remark as applying to this part of the day.

If honest, Bess had to admit that Geoff's brief foray into love-making had been the true highlight. No, damn it, she reminded herself, not lovemaking. Sex. Yet, as they drove homeward, it was all she could do to keep from staring at Geoff, drinking in his features, memorizing them . . . not that she needed to.

His buccaneering good looks disguised a sensitivity and a gentleness that showed him to be well-balanced, mature, caring. But still a man, and his mouth and touch had imprinted that fact on her far more than any words could do.

She had told him—was it only this morning?—that romance was in the courting and everything else was sex. She had to believe that, couldn't let it slip away, otherwise it would mean she'd had no romance in her life. None at all.

Admittedly, Paul's wooing had been non-aggressive, which she had attributed to an inherent shyness. But now, thinking about him objectively—could she think about him objectively?—she realized that his hugs had been respectful, his kisses diplomatic. Never, not once during their courtship, had his tongue danced inside her mouth. Never had she felt even the semblance of an erection.

She hadn't been untouched when Paul began pressing his suit. Other men had openly expressed their lust, if not love, for her. And, in the back of her mind she'd always thought: "They want something from me. They want something from my father." But Paul already worked for her father, so he must have loved her for herself alone . . . at least, that's what she had believed.

Warren Cornwall, even then, had been molding Bess into his corporate whore, although she hadn't thought of it in those terms, preferring the word "merger." How could her own father sell his daughter's body to the highest bidder? She had appreciated Paul's restraint and adored him for it. She had idolized his . . . formality. Love, she reasoned, would come later. And actually believed it had when Paul's passivity turned to passion. If she didn't respond, she told herself, the fault was hers, not his. In other words, sex had raised its ugly head and romance had gone down the drain. Which was natural in a marriage, she justified over and over again. Hadn't Mother been totally malleable, her one and only rebellion the squashy-faced cat?

Geoff didn't want anything from her father, Bess thought, admiring the ripple of his thigh muscles as his foot found the clutch pedal. So, what did he want from her? The book? He'd already secured her cooperation. Her body? If he wanted a body, there were barmaids, and unless she was terribly mistaken, Geoffrey Barrett wasn't the kind of man who enjoyed conquest for its own sake.

Had she goaded him into his seduction with her thoughtless jibes? Of course she had. But after his icy-eyed glower, after his angry transference of her body to his chair, after the urgent plunder of her mouth, he'd turned surprisingly tender. Not passive. Tender. Every time she conjured up the scene in his office, which she'd done on and off all afternoon, she could feel him gently sculpting her jaw line, caressing her cheek, stroking the arch of her neck. Even now, as the twilight vista blurred past her open window, she could feel her nipples strain against her bra.

They finished the day with a slapped-together meal of cold meats and cheese and bikkies—biscuits—then Geoff, thankfully, excused himself to "go hide in the office and attend to some work that can't wait."

Which left Bess free to call it an early night, although it was one in which the sleeping time available to her was disrupted by too many thoughts and a body that suddenly held too many disruptive memories.

And the dreams! If she hadn't climaxed in Geoff's arms, on his lap, she surely did so within the sanctuary of sleep. When she looked in the mirror next morning her face was flushed, her eyes radiant, her body tingling. And her mind not one whit more settled than it had been the day before.

CHAPTER SIX

Rambo was, at heart, a braggart. Right now he wanted to crow, considering how easy it had been for him. And yet he knew it was better to be valued for having completed a tough assignment.

"Piece of cake," he finally said, unable to swallow one small boast. "I mean, the identification part. She's definitely the girl you want. The girl anybody would want," he added with a sly grin. "Talk about drop-dead bloody gorgeous!"

"We know that," Coolidge snapped. He was pleased the kid had accomplished his mission, but they could do without gratuitous comments. "What about getting into the house? No problems there?"

"Well, it wasn't the easiest job I've ever done. Had to take some pretty fancy risks," lied Rambo, who had simply slipped a patio door lock, done what he'd come to do, and walked out without the slightest hitch. "But yeah, I managed to bug the phones and arrange things so I can hack into his computer. I really wanted to bug the whole house, but didn't have time. One thing for sure. I've got the perfect spot to lift the girl, if you decide that's what you want to do. Before I tapped the phones, I followed them. They took this dog down along the river below Newstead, and you couldn't ask for a better situation. Not a blessed soul around, plenty of places to set up an ambush. I don't know if she'd walk the dog down there by herself, which would be perfect, but—"

"It's a bit early to worry about that," Rossiter cut in, then

86

stared at Coolidge. "Besides, there's no way we'll do it. She knows us."

"I'll bring in some people from Sydney, Tom. There's really no great hurry. The old man isn't expecting miracles. Even the great War Cornwall understands that Barrett won't give in without a fight." Coolidge smirked at his own pun. "But at least now we've got something to work with, and if the bugged phones show a relationship between Barrett and Elizabeth, it will make it all that much easier."

Turning to Rambo, Coolidge issued his instructions. "I want you to put together a team to monitor everything. Every phone call, every E-mail. You'll have to bring people in from Sydney for that, too, so get on it damn quick."

"Yes, sir." Rambo's fingernails, which had been picking at one of the many scabs that adorned his face, joined the rest of his hand to offer Gerald Coolidge a brief salute. On his way out, Rambo tried to avoid the suite's mirror. The acne he'd endured since age thirteen didn't exactly make him a candidate for beer commercials. Still, his expertise at electronics had turned him into a minor pub celebrity. Hooray for home computers. Girls needed him, and were willing to pay dearly to get him, even when he said money wasn't his toll. Problem was, none of those girls even came close to Elizabeth Carson Bradley.

"How much time are we going to give this before we decide on the next step?" Rossiter asked, after Rambo had shut the door.

"As long as it takes. I want to be sure about the relationship issue, although you wouldn't find me with something that choice underfoot and not be making use of it. Barrett's doing her . . . you can bet on it. But just to be safe, we'll wait for proof of some kind. Pity that fool kid couldn't have bugged the bedrooms."

"I don't think it's going to be that simple," Rossiter said with a shake of his head. "I got to know Elizabeth fairly well when she worked with the old man, and she never struck me as being the type for a casual fling."

Coolidge looked his companion up and down, eyeing with distaste the rumpled suit and tie, the un-shined shoes, the shambling, unkempt look which had always been a part of the man's persona. Tom Rossiter was immensely clever, but obviously not clever enough to realize that appearance counted, and that he was his own worst enemy on that score. Coolidge couldn't imagine Rossiter getting close enough to Elizabeth to recognize what her character might be like.

"It doesn't matter what Barrett values her for," he finally said. "All that matters is that he does value her, enough to come to the party when we put the screws on him."

Bess paused to rub her eyes. She felt more exhilarated than tired, but sometimes her eyes seemed glued to the computer screen. Not that one could glue eyes, she thought, having just deleted "Kate dropped her eyes" and changed it to "Kate looked down."

Working side-by-side with Geoff, playing this absurd game of musical chairs, actually seemed to work. He did most of the writing, and it was powerful stuff. But her job of Americanizing the language of the heroine and ensuring the accuracy of the book's American beginning kept her own mind active, and was clearly going to be an important element in the finished product. Which, to her dismay, still didn't have a title and hardly any plot line.

"I do wish we could put a name to our book," she said, not for the first time. "I always like to have a title before I start. It helps me keep it together."

"And I always find a title leaping out at me when the time

is right," Geoff replied, not even bothering to look up. "The title is in here someplace, and it will come to us, so stop fretting about it."

"Fine," she said. Only to suggest, not ten minutes later, "But couldn't we at least give it a working title?"

"Be my guest."

"You're not very helpful."

"It isn't my problem. Call it 'The Catharsis of Kate.' How does that grab you?"

"Ah, so her name really is Kate. I was beginning to wonder. Half the time you call her Kate, but I hesitate to mention how often you've called her Bess. I'm constantly changing it."

"Continuity is part of your job," he said in a low voice that was almost too calm, too controlled. "But maybe we should call her Bess temporarily, and use the search-and-replace mechanism to change it later. Ultimately, we can't use Bess."

"Why can't we?" Bess knew she was being deliberately argumentative, but seemed unable to stop baiting him.

"Because you are Bess, ignorant American wench. We can't have a heroine named Bess in a book co-written by an author named Bess, can we? First off, it's not an autobiography. Second, it would drive the readers crazy."

"Co-authored by Elizabeth Carson, not Bess Carson, and I was only kidding."

"Good," he said, his gaze still focused on the screen.

"Because I can't think of any Bess I know who would get stirred up by your incredibly pedestrian sex scenes. Honestly, Geoff, I thought this was supposed to be a collaborative romance, not a how-to manual for would-be Victorians."

Now she had his attention! He turned and fixed his gaze on her, lifting his hands from the keyboard and flexing his long, sensitive fingers as if preparing them for the task of throttling her . . . or worse.

"Have you got sex on the brain or something, dear Bess? What I am writing here, in case you hadn't noticed, is a descriptive scene of the San Francisco waterfront, from which, in the not-too-distant future, our chum Leonardo will follow his beloved fiancée to Australia. His beloved not-so-innocent Kate."

"She was never innocent. You forget, he . . . we deflowered her."

"Well then, call our book 'The Deflowerization of Kate.' "

"That's not a bad idea," she said, and watched his damn eyebrow slant upward for the umpteenth time. "I mean, how about calling it 'The Flower of Ballarat'?"

"Sure. For now. You're right, Bess," he added, as if thinking out loud.

"I am? About what?"

"Pedestrian sex scenes. I'm hopeless at writing spicy stuff, at least in this book. So there's another part of your input."

Geoff wasn't about to admit that Bess herself was the reason why he couldn't get into the sexy scenes the book required. She inhibited him, even though he knew she wasn't trying to. It was just that he felt embarrassed, writing such things with her sitting there beside him. Close enough to reach out and touch, which he dearly wanted to do. Had done, with almost disastrous results. And would do again, given half a chance and the slightest encouragement. He had wondered if her Victorian-sex-scene comment had been some sort of hint, then banished the thought. No. Bess was a professional. She was merely making a point.

"Another part of my input," Bess repeated. Although she had never been a hand-wringer in her whole life, today she wanted to wring her hands like a wet sponge. Her proximity to Geoff was becoming progressively more difficult to endure, if endure was the appropriate word. Where she had once been worried that their working so closely would result in him watching her too much, she now found that she did all the watching.

He was just so pleasant to watch. Even from a quarter-side angle, which was how she saw him most often while working. He had a habit of chewing on his lower lip when he concentrated, and the sight of those white, even teeth reminded her too often of his predatory potential. When he was satisfied with some sought-for word or phrase, his nostrils flared like those of a fine Arabian stallion, and there was an almost tangible aura of arrogant pride in the gesture.

Macho, in its finest definition, was a word that might have been coined for this man, she thought. He was totally, wholly, engrossingly masculine, but so completely confident in that element of himself that he didn't need to overplay the role to impress anyone. He clearly thought it no sin for a man to be sensitive, gentle, caring. And yet she couldn't help but remember his kisses, and her own still-vivid physical response to them.

Sitting hunched in her chair, she clenched her fists together and clamped them between her knees, fearing her knees were about to start trembling. Certainly there was that familiar stirring in her tummy, a slow, spreading warmth that seemed to flow lower and warmer the more she willed it to stop.

All she had to do was look at Geoff's broad shoulders, the flex of muscle as he occasionally stretched to ease his back, and Bess found her breath quickening. He needed a haircut, but she wanted to sift her fingers through the shock of hair at his nape before he trimmed it. Whereas she sometimes thought her own curly hair was as coarse as a horse's mane, his was unusually soft and fine, the waves that flowed above his ears like dove's wings, at least in her imagination.

Just as well, she thought, that Geoff usually spent the afternoons away on business, because a full day of this intensely intimate sharing of words and ideas might be more than she could handle. With him out of the way, she could edit the manuscript as it built on the computer, cutting and honing and polishing as she went along. And she knew she was doing it well. Geoff reviewed their work each day before starting anew, and hadn't so much as commented on the changes.

Unless he hadn't even noticed!

"You do good polishing," he said, as if reading her mind.

The remark brought her upright with a start, and she realized she'd been so lost in her own thoughts that she might as well have been asleep. "I try," was all she could think of to say. And it seemed to be enough because he returned to his typing without continuing the discussion, much less informing her about what had stirred his comment in the first place. Sometimes Geoffrey Barrett could be so . . . enigmatic.

As if I'm not, she thought. *We make a great pair!*

The night was uneventful, the next morning productive. Kate Still-no-last-name was now situated in the Captain's cabin, due to a fever that had her lingering between life and death. A bit of a cliché, Bess thought, except Geoff's expertise at narrative saved the scene. Bess honestly felt she was inside the cabin. She could feel the sway of the ship, suffer along with Kate, and suddenly her doubts about Geoff's sketchy outline were somewhat mollified.

When he left the office to make them more coffee, she took the opportunity to log on and check her E-mails, knowing there would be something from Mouse. Her friendly computer maven was faithful about keeping in touch, obviously still convinced that Bess had stuck her head in the lion's den and would need rescuing sooner or later.

She read today's message, then had to read it again, puzzled by the cryptic language. Mouse was almost always cryptic, when he wasn't rambling on effusively, but this . . .

"Do you remember the problem we had with Felix last year, Bess? I think we have to do it all over again, but in reverse this time. I should be around for the next 24 hours."

That was it! No hello, no goodbye, not even his usual sarcastic reference to "Lucifer"—his nickname for Geoff, inspired by the cat in Disney's *Cinderella*.

She was still staring at the message when Geoff returned with their coffee, and he glanced over her shoulder with casual interest.

"Your little mate always send such cryptic stuff?" he asked. "I tell you, Bess, if I didn't know better, I'd say he's a bit paranoid."

"That's it!" she cried, enlightenment dawning. "Thank you, Geoff. You're more clever than you realize. Have you got any change? I have to go into town and make a call."

He fished out what change there was in his pockets, then raided his bedside piggy-bank when Bess insisted she might need more than they had between them. "I've got a phone card here somewhere that I keep for emergencies," he said. "Why don't you use that? It'll be less of a hassle than standing in a phone box with twenty pounds of change."

"I'll take both, thank you," she replied. And did, skipping out the front door before Geoff could question her further. Mouse's message was crystal clear, now that Geoff had sparked her memory. It still didn't make total sense, but it would when she talked to him.

Perhaps a year earlier, she had indulged Mouse's intrinsic paranoia by letting him use her phone for an entire week, a week in which he insisted that a hacker named "Felix the

Cat" had somehow managed to bug his phone and E-mails. She never did learn all the details, but Mouse had declared himself eternally grateful when the week was over. He had either solved the problem, or taken his revenge, or both.

Now he was saying . . . what? The "in reverse" suggested a problem at her end, Bess thought, as she trudged down the hill toward town. Oh well, a call from the security of a pay phone would soon solve the riddle.

"Somebody's hacking into your E-mails, and probably bugging your entire phone system," Mouse explained. "They're good, but somebody got clumsy just once, and with the Mighty Mouse, once is all it takes."

"I don't understand, Mouse. Who? Why?"

"Beats me all to hell. Maybe your Aussie boyfriend's checking up on you."

"He's not my boyfriend. We're merely collaborating on a book. And why should he need to check up on me? I'm living in his house, using his computer for my E-mails."

"Maybe Lucifer has enemies. Didn't you tell me he had all sorts of business interests?"

"Yes, but—"

"What I'm saying is that Lucifer . . . Geoffrey Barrett's system is under surveillance. I can't find out more from here, and I certainly won't fly to Australia to help sort it out. I do not like that man! So just consider yourself warned, and don't say anything by E-mail, especially to me. And please don't say anything that could get either of us in trouble."

"I'll have to tell Geoff about this, Mouse. I mean, what if you're right? What if it is some business thing? He should be warned."

"That's up to you, darling Bess," Mouse said, as the money ran out and the call terminated, leaving her with more questions than answers.

"You say your little mate Mouse is a fair-dinkum expert?" Geoff asked, having listened to her story with a growing mix of skepticism and annoyance. But at least he hadn't made a fuss when she insisted they check on Lady, which got them outside the house to where, she hoped, it was safe to talk. If the phones were bugged, what else?

"Mouse is perhaps the best hacker in Colorado, if not the entire United States," she insisted. "If they ever caught him for a tenth of what he's done, he'd be in jail for life, although he assures me he's never done anything truly harmful. He's never stolen money, or ruined anybody's' system. He's just . . . curious."

"That kind of curiosity can propel a hacker right into the FBI witness protection program, Bess. You say your little rodent's not harmful? Have you checked your bank account lately?"

"Stop it, Geoff! You should be grateful he took the trouble to warn you."

"He didn't warn me. He warned you, which is quite a different kettle of fish. But yes, when you chat with him again, offer my heartfelt thanks. Just don't do it from here until we manage to sort out what's happening. Okay?"

"Well, obviously I'm not going to do it from here," she retorted. "And when you do get it figured out, I expect you to apologize for all the nasty things you've said about him. Mouse is one of my dearest friends."

"Any friend of yours, etcetera," Geoff replied, but his grin took the sting out of it. "Now, let's go back in the house and I'll make a phone call. Don't get your knickers in a knot at what I'm saying, just play along and stay cool."

Whereupon, Geoff walked straight into his office and punched out a phone number from memory. "Ida? Geoff here," he said. "How was Fiji? I'll bet you have a splendid tan, which I can hardly wait to investigate. Yes, of course all over, otherwise there'd be no fun to it, would there? However, I have something perhaps more interesting to suggest. There's this rather spiffy looking little redhead from America who's staying with me. She's very, very choice, and I wondered if you still got all hot and bothered over threesomes."

Bess was still gasping, open-mouthed, when he finished listening to whatever Ida had to say. "Terrific!" Geoff didn't quite shout, but his enthusiasm was unmistakable. "Yes, three o'clock would be spot on . . . give us time for a little fun and games, then we can all go on to dinner someplace . . . the casino, maybe."

Another pause. "Yes, darling, I'm sure she's brought something appropriate for the occasion. Bess is a very broadminded girl, for an American. What do you mean, how do I know? Darling, have I ever lied to you? Would I lie to you? But make sure you bring your gear, all of it. I wouldn't be surprised if we didn't need it all. Okay, I'll see you at three, and yes, the American and I will be prepared."

Geoff hung up the phone, turned to look directly at Bess, and signaled that she mustn't blow her stack. Confused and furious, she flung away his hand when he took her arm and tried to maneuver her outside. Still, she followed him, half prepared to deliver a swift kick to his rump.

"What the hell was that all about?" she said, once they'd reached the bottom of the garden and had somehow both accepted that it might be safe to talk there. "A threesome? What are you playing at, Geoffrey Barrett? It had better be a good explanation, because I am not one damned bit amused."

"Lighten up, Bess. Your little mate Mouse isn't the only person who can be cryptic, you know. I was arranging a bit of a diversion so we can find out if we're under surveillance, and if so, how so and how bad it is, that's all."

"With someone named Ida? Someone who is very clearly an old and familiar acquaintance, judging from the first part of your conversation?"

"That, dear lady, falls into the category of being none of your business."

Geoff's voice held sufficient steel to suggest it would not only be a waste of time to pursue the subject, but possibly dangerous as well. Bess took the hint, but she didn't feel very gracious.

She felt even less gracious when, at a quarter to three, Geoff instructed her to go and change into something sultry. "Did you happen to bring a peignoir, by any chance," he asked, and there was no tease in his tone. When she protested that of course she hadn't, he retreated to his own quarters. Soon he emerged with a heavy, silk brocade Chinese-style dressing gown, which he thrust at her with one hand as he gestured the need for discretion with his other. Then, as she emphatically shook her head, curls flying every which way, he pulled her into a quick embrace.

"Play along, damn it," he whispered into her ear. "We don't know yet if the whole damned house is bugged, and we have to assume that we may be watched as well. Change into the gown, and try not to act surprised when you come out and find me wearing something similar. Now go!"

A gentle pat on her buttocks sent Bess scrambling for her own room, all too aware of having opened a Pandora's Box she could have very well done without.

The gown fit her perfectly, which should have pleased her but somehow didn't. Worse was returning downstairs to find Geoff in a gown that was not only similar, but clearly part of a matched set. His fit perfectly, too, and served to enhance his masculinity, the pale jade color highlighting the color of his eyes.

Was this matched set left over from the "child bride" days he'd written about on their authors' loop? Or from some other liaison that Bess probably didn't want to know about? She considered asking, but the thought disappeared with the ringing of the door chimes. Whereupon, Geoff stopped closing various curtains and drapes and went off to answer the door.

Bess didn't know what she had expected Ida to look like, even though Geoff's phone conversation should have warned her. The vision who entered the room possessed pale, honey-blonde hair, and she was striking! Furthermore, Bess hadn't missed the way Geoff and Ida embraced in the entrance before strolling inside together, nor the tinge of jealousy that flickered through her own mind at the sight. No, not jealousy. Envy. Paul had never been demonstrative.

Ida was the same size as Bess—she could have worn this gown, Bess thought. Ida would never see forty again, but could have passed for thirty-five in most lights. Full-breasted, she had a figure most women of twenty-five would kill for. She wore clothing that conformed to her shape; a nicely-tailored suit that revealed beautiful legs, yet was business-like in the extreme, despite accentuating a wondrous tan. How a woman with her coloring could take such a tan, Bess—who burned if she sat too long near a light bulb—could not imagine. And to top it off, Ida had a smile that could melt male hearts.

"Ida, this is Bess," Geoff said by way of introduction. "She's visiting from Colorado, in America."

"Bess Carson." Reaching out to shake hands, Bess realized that Ida had one major asset that dwarfed all the others. She positively radiated sexuality.

There was nothing brazen about her, nothing cheap. She was clearly a lady, and a woman comfortable in herself and her world. But the sexuality hung about her like an aura, a perfume. She was a man's woman in every way, and Bess suddenly felt profoundly provincial, very much like Geoff's perception of Kate, the fictional "flower" of Victorian modesty. Too bad she didn't have a fever, Bess thought. Too bad she couldn't retreat to a Captain's cabin.

After giving Bess's hand a firm shake, Ida turned to Geoff. "Finish drawing the drapes, darling," she said, casually leading him over to where one set of drapes remained open.

Without so much as a glance at either the window or Bess, Ida flowed around Geoff, her arms gathering his head to bring it down to her mouth, then clenching at his shoulders as she met his lips with a kiss that Bess thought could have melted the ice in arctic wastes. In fact, Bess had never seen a kiss quite so arousing, and was staring in disbelief when she realized that the blonde had motioned to her.

"Maybe you ought to close the drapes, Colorado," Ida said. "I think perhaps we're a bit busy here." Her smile flashed in a gesture that could have meant laughter at Bess's discomfort or just delight at being alive and in a man's arms.

But the fun stopped the instant the final drape was drawn. "That was just to warm you up, Geoffrey darling," Ida said in a deliberately sultry voice. "Now let me see if your young lady here is as exquisitely sexy as she looks. You do make a lovely couple, you know, and she does have beautiful hair. I'd kill for that color. Try not to make too much noise or get too impatient, my darlings, at least not until the cameras are ready. Because the last time we did this, Geoffrey darling, the sound levels were quite horrid."

Bess stared. Geoff grinned wickedly and reached out to take her hand. As Ida delved into an enormous hat-box—the aforementioned gear, Bess assumed—Geoff motioned with an upraised finger for Bess to be silent, then led her over to the nearest sofa and sat her down beside him. "You ought to be able to fake this part; you've written about it often enough," he whispered in her ear. "Just moan a lot, but not too much or too loud, and pretend we're lost in passion."

It would have been easier to pretend, Bess thought, if Geoff hadn't been sitting two feet away, his gaze fixed on Ida as she moved around the room with some sort of instrument in her hands and a set of headphones clamped to her ears. And it would have been much easier if Geoff's moans hadn't sounded as phony as a three-dollar bill. But then her own couldn't have sounded much better, uttered as they were over the growing desire to giggle insanely at the whole scenario.

Ida, however, was not giggling, although she did occasionally add a sultry comment. Her lovely face was stern, no sign of a smile now. Whatever she was finding didn't please her at all.

"Keep on doing what you're doing, darlings," she finally said. "I have to make a little trip to the loo, then I'll come join you and we'll see if we can't really steam things up."

Her voice didn't match her expression, Bess thought, watching Ida stalk off, her instruments still in hand, her hips swinging, her gorgeous legs flexing with each stride. Geoff continued panting and sighing, and Bess tried to match the tempo he was creating. But giggles kept erupting in her throat like unladylike burps, and she didn't dare meet his eyes lest she lose it all together.

"It's all right to let yourself go," he suddenly said, and leaned over to gather her into his arms in a gesture so quick, so unexpected, she had no chance to defend herself. Then his lips were there, touching at her ear as he murmured delicious ideas in a stage whisper that should have carried across the room.

"Easy for you to say," she whispered back in a stage

whisper of her own, not having to fake the trembling in her voice as his fingers tucked back her hair and began to idly caress her neck and throat. "You don't have to compete with Ida."

"Compete? This isn't a competition, darling. This is just two wonderful ladies providing me with every man's secret dream. You and Ida . . . redhead and blonde . . . fire and ice. Both beautiful, both sensual, both . . ."

Whatever he was going to say next got lost in Ida's return. "Goodness, it's hot in here," she said, snatching up a camera. "Let us retire to the patio, darlings, so that I can get some happy-snaps of the two of you while there's still enough light outside."

Geoff scrambled to join Ida, and Bess felt an almost overwhelming sense of relief. She wanted nothing more than to get away from the effect Geoff's caresses were having on her, especially in front of Ida. That sort of thing, she found herself thinking, should be private, damn it, even if it was only a charade for . . . for what?

They moved to a bower at the rear of the patio. Ida smiled a great deal as she carefully posed Geoff and Bess for a series of pictures that, while perhaps suggestive, were nothing Bess couldn't have sent to her friends.

"The phones are bugged and I'd bet money they've hacked into your E-mail system," Ida whispered, while setting up a new pose. "I can't find anything else in the house, but I don't want to take a chance until I can do a better sweep with better equipment. Now, look radiant, Colorado. Think of Mel Gibson if it helps."

They returned to the house, where they hammed it up more and more until all three were howling with laughter. Ida had a genuine talent for such theatrics, and guided them expertly as she wandered through various rooms, using first one meter, then another, checking for any surveillance equipment she might have missed.

"Show's over," she finally announced. as all three walked outside again, away from the house. "And I'm sorry to inform you that unless this mob is better than I am, we've probably squandered our theatrical careers. Waste of good talent, that . . . we should all be on the stage. Anyway, Geoffrey darling, what do you want to do about your phones and computer?"

"You have a suggestion, I'm sure," he said with one of his wild, buccaneer grins. "I can see the light of battle in your baby blues. I know you too well, Ida."

"Ah yes, you do indeed."

Ida had the decency not to look at Bess as she spoke, but there was something in her sudden demureness that told Bess far more than she really wanted to know.

Then the moment passed, and Ida was all business again. "I think you should leave things as they are, Geoffrey darling. I'll put some of my people to work and see if we can't find out who's involved in this. Suit you?"

"Right down to the ground, but let's figure it out quickly, Ida. Because if I'm right, it has something to do with this damned take-over thing I've been fighting. And if they've reached the point where they want to play dirty pool, I might have to change my own tactics."

"Done. Now I suggest you both change clothes, and you, Geoffrey darling, can take us all to dinner at the Casino. I can get onto my mob by phone from there. I wouldn't even trust my cell phone here."

"Ida, you're a woman of stone," Geoff said with a shake of his head. "You're going to charge me an arm and a leg for this, and now you want dinner on top of it?"

"But of course, darling. After all, you didn't give me all the other wonderful things you promised. Which I know only too well you could," she added, a mischievous gleam in those wide blue eyes. "I'm sure Colorado just adores oysters. Don't you, love?"

"Yes I do, and, except for one measly dress-up dinner, all that cheapskate over there gives me is pub food," Bess found herself saying, falling in with Ida's mood.

She and Ida had a splendid time, uniting to harass poor Geoff until he threatened to leave them. Eventually, he joined in, helping to create an evening Bess thought she might never forget. The only slight note of discord was the way she felt when Ida waved goodbye, first bestowing her patented smile on Geoff.

"Now darlings, I leave you with two final thoughts," she said over her shoulder. "Be careful what you say inside that house until my people get through checking it tomorrow. And Geoffrey darling, I know how you adore oysters, just as Colorado here does, but remember that you've eaten four dozen between you, and if you go home and try to make all of them work you'll do yourselves an injury. Trust me!"

The remark set Bess's heart to thundering. And the champagne she'd consumed with dinner didn't exactly reduce her pulse rate.

CHAPTER SEVEN

"Your Ida is really something else." Bess said the words without thinking. She was still flying, the champagne having gone to her head.

"You've become a master of understatement," Geoff replied, not taking his eyes off the road. It was getting on for pub-closing time, and while he hadn't had enough champagne to worry about being breathalyzed, there were plenty out on the roads who drove with an uncaring recklessness.

"A mistress of understatement, Geoffrey darling. And do I detect a faint note of disapproval in your voice? That surprises me. I got the impression you and Ida knew each other very, very well."

"Just leave it there, Bess. It's not a subject we ought to be getting into."

"Why? I think she's really nice. And she's got your number, Geoffrey Barrett darling. It was quite sweet, really, to see the way she teased you."

Geoff said nothing, didn't so much as glance at her, but Bess saw the way his jaw muscles tightened, could see those sensitive nostrils flaring. Ida wasn't the only woman who could push his buttons, she thought, and without further consideration continued trying.

"Not that anyone could blame you, Geoffrey darling. She's very attractive, for her age. That figure, and those legs. I know women who'd kill to have legs like that." Bess didn't get into the fact that she'd seen Geoff, along with others at the casino, paying as much attention to her legs as they had to Ida's. "And she has the most beautiful smile I've ever seen. If she could patent it, she'd put the light-bulb people out of business . . ."

Bess let her voice drift away, but got no discernible reaction. Ah well, time to try harder, she thought, giggling inside. This was fun!

"And of course your Ida just oozes sex appeal, but I guess you know that. Hard not to, the way she was aiming it at you all evening. You two must have had some wonderful times together."

"One."

He said it so softly, Bess wasn't sure she'd even heard him. She cocked her head and looked at him, trying to decide if her ears were playing tricks on her. Then she went for broke. "You said one?"

"That's what it sounded like to me, not that it's any of your business, young lady. Now, will you please stop yammering and let me pay attention to the traffic."

"There isn't a car in sight!"

"All the more reason to concentrate. I dislike being taken by surprise."

"You dislike me asking personal questions, that's what you dislike. I'm a writer, sir, and people fascinate me. Ida fascinates me. So please unbend a little and tell me more. F'rinstance, where'd you meet?"

"At work. She used to be a contract cleaner, but after noticing how sloppy so many security firms are, she decided she could do it better. She went out on her own, and you've seen the result."

Bess was truly astonished. It was incredibly difficult to imagine the Ida she'd seen tonight washing floors and cleaning toilets in some office building.

"And before you ask," Geoff continued, "since I'm sure you noticed her Canadian accent, she's actually from Swift Current, Saskatchewan, which I guess makes you nearly neighbors. Any more silly questions?"

Only about a thousand, Bess thought, but held her peace. Until suddenly her mouth opened and the question popped out far ahead of her mental demand that it shouldn't. "Were you at your place then, for the once you mentioned? I did notice she seemed familiar with the layout, so I presume it was a fairly thorough once."

"It was an entire weekend, if you must know. I suppose 'once' isn't the most accurate word to describe it."

"I should certainly think not. Although I can't say I'm surprised. You two seemed awfully chummy for a one-night stand. In fact, you seemed awfully intimate for a two-night stand. I guess I shouldn't ask how many dozen oysters you ate that weekend."

"Stop fishing, woman! She's familiar with the layout because she's been there on a number of occasions. Ida and I are friends of long standing."

"The expression, I believe, is just good friends, although why people bother to say that I really don't know."

Geoff took his eyes off the road long enough to glance at her. Then he laughed, and it wasn't the friendliest laugh she'd ever heard from him.

"You shouldn't drink champagne in such quantities, young Bess," he said. "You're as pissed as forty cats, you are."

"If that means I'm drunk, I am not. I can hold my liquor as well as anyone," she retorted, only to belie the statement with an indiscreet hiccup that, try as she might, she couldn't disguise.

"Maybe fifty cats, actually. Good thing we're nearly

home. I cannot abide women who can't hold their grog."

That remark emerged as he turned into his driveway, making it, Bess thought, quite uncalled for and unnecessary. Spiteful, even.

"Ida drank more champagne than I did," she said, fumbling for the door handle that had mysteriously disappeared. "And I didn't notice you complaining about her."

"Ida's old enough to look after herself. And smart enough, too. You might not have noticed, love, but she had one of her people come to pick her up, just in case she might be over the limit."

"Well, bully for Ida." Bess's fumbling fingers found the door handle, tugged at it, and she came within an inch of falling out of the vehicle. As it was, her feet hit the ground with an almighty thud, and only her grip on the door handle saved her. "Are you saying she's old enough to look after herself, but I'm not?"

"So it would appear," Geoff said, suddenly there beside her, one arm around her waist as he kept her upright. "You'd best let me help you inside and up to your room, my tipsy possum. I'll take the chance you can find the bed by yourself, but the stairs might be a worry."

He was laughing at her! She struggled in his arms, but she might as well have tried to escape from a set of handcuffs. Even as she struggled, Geoff was gently easing her toward the front door, the keys in his free hand.

"Let me go," she said. "I'm fine, I tell you. It was just . . . just the fresh air after being in the stuffy warmth of the casino."

"It was two dozen oysters and too much champagne. Hasn't anyone ever told you that oysters may be good for some things . . ." He flashed her that devilish grin. "But for soaking up grog you need red meat, preferably raw. If you'd filled up on steak tartare, you'd be in better shape now."

Just the thought was enough . . . no, too much. Bess wrenched herself free of his grasp as soon as they entered the house, then stumbled her way toward the bathroom. When she returned some time later, she felt physically much better, but decidedly ashamed, although not enough to give in without a token rebuke.

"That was your fault," she said. "You deliberately had to bring up the subject of raw meat, didn't you?"

"I was merely attempting to educate you, you ignorant American wench. Now bugger off to bed before I turn you over my knee and educate you some more."

"You wouldn't dare!"

"Not only would I dare, I would positively enjoy it," Geoff said, rubbing his hands together like some silent movie villain. "Now are you going upstairs by yourself, or do I have to carry you up, which I warn you will have consequences you can't even imagine."

"Oh, I can imagine all right. Typical male chauvinist, using brute force instead of . . ." She paused, suddenly too close to sober, suddenly aware that whatever she said next might indeed lead to unknown consequences. The look in Geoff's eye told her that, practically guaranteed it.

Devils danced in those ice-green eyes. Worse than devils. Sirens, or whatever the male equivalent was. Dancing and laughing and challenging her, enticing her, luring her toward an indiscretion Bess knew she desired just as much as he did. She could only hope Geoff didn't realize that, and was terrified that he did, that indeed he was deliberately using her own nature against her.

"I want some coffee first," she found herself saying. Lying, knowing she was lying, and knowing he probably knew it too. What she really needed was three aspirins, some warm milk to hold them down with, and a good night's sleep to settle both her mind and her stomach.

"Don't be difficult, Bess. You'd be asleep on the floor before the jug was boiled. Which might be the safest thing after all, come to think of it. At least you'd be safe from me. I don't take advantage of girls when they're asleep."

"I wish I knew an Aussie word for . . . for horse feathers," she retorted, stepping past him en route to the kitchen. "Coffee I want and coffee I shall have, with a healthy slug of Bailey's Irish Cream in it, if you please."

"Are you always this damned stubborn?"

He was smiling properly now, that slow sweet smile she liked so much. Bess's tummy did a back flip. What would he do, she wondered, if she just flung herself into his arms, gave herself to him, gave in to herself, gave in to all the strange emotions that kept her entire body, her entire existence on edge, every time she found herself in Geoff's presence?

"Usually I'm worse," she said. "I would have thought you'd have figured that out by now. If you haven't, I'm being too subtle about the way our book is going."

"Subtle?" He snorted. "You change every second word, criticize my erotic bits, and tell me I can't talk American. Or that my characters can't, which is the same thing."

With the jug boiled, they sat across from each other at the kitchen table, and it was all Bess could do to keep from leaning on her elbows and staring into those incredible eyes. How could Ida let Geoff go after spending an entire weekend in bed with him?

And before Bess realized it, the question was flying off her tongue, and Geoff was rearing back in surprise at the directness of it.

"Bloody hell, woman! What do you want, a play-by-play description? Damn it, Bess, there's a limit to curiosity, you know, and you're way past it."

She just sat there, still staring at him, the Bailey's slowly warming her tummy into a gentle softness that seemed also to have gone to her brain. Even acknowledging the anger in his voice, she was unable to deflect her mind from its single track. "Was she good, Geoff? Utterly superb? The best there's ever been for you? Did she . . ." Bess had to search her slightly befuddled mind for the appropriate Australianism. "Did she root you absolutely stupid?"

And then Geoff was on his feet, his face flushed with either anger or embarrassment, she couldn't tell which.

"That's bloody well it," he said, reaching out to grab her by the shoulders and literally lift her from her chair as if she'd been a child of five.

Slinging her over his shoulder, he marched up the stairs. Into her room he charged, and for an instant she was positive he was going to throw her straight from the doorway to the bed . . . like a javelin. Instead, he carried her, and when he sat down on the bed, she suddenly found herself draped across his lap, bottom up, held so firmly she couldn't do a thing about it.

The first smack of his palm across her rump wasn't especially hard, nor did it hurt. Bess grunted, but didn't cry out. The second smack was more definite, and drew a gasp of surprise and a small squawk of alarm.

"Now," he said, "are you going to stop this bloody nonsense?"

Gritting her teeth, she refused to make a sound.

"Okay, Bess. But don't tell me later I didn't give you a chance."

To her astonishment, she felt her skirt being lifted. At which point, her mind and body disassociated entirely as hell reared up before her and she saw Paul's face, heard Paul's

whining, accusatory voice . . . lousiest wife in the world . . .
bitch . . . bitch . . .

She remained silent, trembling, terrified now by the pictures and voice in her head. Her jaw clenched. Her breasts flattened beneath her on one side of Geoff's lap. Her legs kicked to no avail.

And yet she was suddenly aware of the thrust of his erection against her tummy, and she found herself squirming against it, unable not to, not even wanting not to. Wanting anything, whatever it would take, just to end this, to get it over with. The movement of her hips caused his next light smack to miss her rump and land instead on her thigh, below her panties.

His gasp was a mixture of surprise and obvious dismay, but it emerged as a gasp and returned to his mouth as a soft, soughing sigh that she could feel all the way down to where his groin prodded at her. Bess sighed too, couldn't help it. He was Paul, sighing with contempt, and her own sigh was one of total submission, total subjugation.

The so-called spanking stopped, but Geoff's hand did not. It rubbed at the back of her thigh, moving in small, gentle circles, as if he was trying to erase the evidence of what he'd done. But all too soon it was moving further and further afield, his fingers tracing intricate, idle patterns down her thigh to the softness behind her knee, then returning along the back of her other leg, to halt at the edge of her panties.

Beneath her, she could feel his erection throbbing, twitching, attempting to lift her with a strength that seemed unreal, even when she squirmed against it, hating it, hating herself. Wishing she dared to reach down, somehow, and wrench it from him, break it like a dead stick. And then his hand was moving again, this time across the smoothness of her panties, seeking that soft, downy hollow at the base of her spine before advancing to snake between her legs, touching but not touching as it slid to her crotch.

She moaned, not aroused, but truly terrified. And despite her stubborn desire not to plead, the horror of memory took full control. "No . . . please," she whimpered. "No, Paul . . . please . . . not again . . . please. Please . . . please . . . please . . ."

Then it stopped. Everything stopped. The room seemed to spin, pulling her mind into a vortex that dizzied her, carried her in a frenzied whirlpool that spun her from the past to the present to the past to . . .

"My God, Bess, are you all right? What the hell have I done?"

She was upright now, although still in his lap, Geoff's lap, with Geoff's pale green eyes staring into her own, his eyes wide with anxiety. Bess shook her head, wild auburn curls flying everywhere, as she tried to assimilate, fought to understand.

"Bess?"

"Geoff? Oh, Geoff . . ." And she sagged in his grip, wallowing in the sudden safety his arms offered. Her own arms flung themselves around his neck, pulling him to her, letting her face nuzzle into the hollow of his throat as the tremors worsened, then subsided, then finally stilled.

Her nostrils drank in the scent of him, and it swept through her mind like a cleansing wind, driving out the memories, the pain, the humiliation. Replacing them, magically, with a surge of desire that plunged through her like a tidal wave.

"Geoff . . ." And now it was a whisper, teased from her throat as she lifted her head, blindly seeking his mouth with her own, unable to open her eyes, not wanting to open them, lest the dream be lost, lest it somehow vanish.

The lips she found claimed but didn't capture her mouth. They took her kisses tentatively, hesitantly, exploring as cautiously as her own lips tried to be bold, tried to dominate. Bess writhed in his arms, her lips burning, her tongue sliding past his teeth in a search for more response, seeking to conquer, demanding a response.

She let her tongue probe deeper, finding his, touching it, teasing it, seeking to initiate the dance, but frustrated because they were still out of step. She wriggled on his lap, felt the surge of reaction beneath her rump, wriggled some more as her tongue played against his teeth.

Both of them were sighing, and it was nothing like the charade they'd played earlier. Now there was only this tiny world of the bed, and them in it, and . . .

"This is crazy." Geoff's mouth managed the words, but she was pivoting in his hands, and whatever else he might have said was lost as their mouths searched for each other, found each other. She tangled fingers in his hair, dragging him down to her, holding him there as securely as he had held her across his lap.

Crazy, Geoff thought again, meeting her halfway, more than halfway, but not all the way. His body reacted, couldn't help but react. Yet his mind was stronger, alive with vibes that suddenly felt horribly, terribly wrong. He wanted Bess more than he had ever wanted a woman, but there were ghosts here. He and Bess were together, but not alone.

Paul . . . her ex-husband. No face to the name, yet he was somehow here, poisoning the air, giving the entire scenario an aura of . . . what? Geoff couldn't name it, could only sense it, fear it, despise it.

Bess's hand groped for one of his own, tugging at it, pulling it down to touch her breast, moaning as she felt his fingers sculpt. But even as part of Geoff reveled in the feel of

113

her, his sense of a wrongness grew and destroyed that pleasure.

"Crazy," he said again. Removing his hand, he began to use his greater strength against the almost manic tempo of Bess's seduction effort. The heat in their lovemaking dissipated, then died, until finally he was holding her and yet not holding her, looking down at her and seeing . . .

"Bess," he whispered. "No, please. Not here, not now. I just can't, won't. Can't," he finished, almost ashamed to meet her fevered, now confused eyes; those amazing, beautiful turquoise eyes; eyes that had haunted him for so long; eyes that would always haunt him.

Eyes that filled with pain as she felt his rejection. Filled with pain, then flared like shooting stars as the pain become anger, rage, a fury he'd never before seen in a woman's eyes.

"Bastard!"

She spat out the word as she recoiled from his arms, nearly falling to the floor when she scrambled off his lap. Then she scurried backwards until her spine was against the wall, her eyes wide and staring.

"Bess . . . I . . ." He got no further, couldn't find the words.

"Bastard! You . . . bloody bastard!"

Her eyes wavered, her mouth sagged into despair, and she turned and fled into the bathroom, the door slamming behind her.

Geoff sat for a moment on the edge of her bed, trying to work it out, failing, as confused by it all as Bess seemed to be, even though his primary emotion wasn't anger, but dismay. Then he shook himself like a wet dog and strode from the room, taking care to gently close the door as he left.

If he had learned one thing over the years, it was that there were times when nothing could be said, nothing could be done, nothing should even be attempted.

You're on a hiding to nothing here, boy. Just get out of it, and be glad you still can.

As he wandered down to the relative sanctity of his office—sleep impossible now, not even to be contemplated—he tried to fathom it all out, but found himself only getting more and more confused.

He padded to the kitchen and grabbed up the Bailey's from the fridge, then returned to the office and sat staring at the blank screen of his computer. He tilted the Bailey's bottle to his lips, taking small sips that gradually became larger ones, thinking small thoughts that also became larger, thoughts that began to take on nightmare proportions as the alcohol surged through his brain before it evolved into the depressant it was, and finally began to damp down his surging emotions and confusion. But when the last of the sweet liqueur was gone, he was still rattled, so he cracked open a bottle of scotch and sat sipping at that, his mind lost in a tempest that slowly succumbed to the grog, slowly began to fade into the obscurity of a bad, half-forgotten dream.

Eventually, he threw himself down on the sofa and lay staring at the ceiling until its spinning drew him into the vortex of sleep.

Bess tiptoed down the stairs, desperate for coffee, equally desperate to avoid the confrontation she knew had to come. Her memory of last night's incident was fragmented, blurry, tormenting her with visions of Paul, of humiliation, of rejection. And of Geoff's kisses, Geoff's touch, and even more rejection.

"Coffee," she muttered to herself as she filled the kettle, no, the jug. *Get it right, damn it,* she thought, spooning freeze-dried instant coffee into what had become "her" cup in this house.

Upon fleeing into the bathroom, so consumed with rage and humiliation she couldn't think, could hardly see, she had vomited once again, spewing out what remained of her dinner in a futile bid to purge herself of the torment inside. Futile, wasted, but it had at least allowed her to then peep out and, finding herself alone, to creep into the bed and let sleep relieve the pain . . . temporarily.

With morning comes a new day, she thought. And another after that. How many days before common sense took control and propelled her away from this house, away from this idiotic situation? Except that even in her despair, her professional pride was too strong to be lightly shaken off. She had come to do a job, she was doing a job, and she would somehow have to finish that job before she could depart Tasmania with a clear conscience.

That was uppermost in her mind as she picked up the coffee and went to confront Geoff's damned computer and Geoff's damned book.

No, their damned book!

But when she opened the office door to see Geoff sprawled, still fully clothed, on the sofa, her heart caught in her throat, threatening to strangle her, choke her. She turned, but it was too late. With the sense of a hunted animal, he had come awake and was staring at her through heavy-lidded eyes the color of winter sea ice.

Then he simply flowed upright and stood there, hair all tousled and the morning beard visible on his strong jaw. Looking at her with none of the contempt she might have imagined, none of the anger, just a warm, soft, gentleness. A gentleness tinged with a sadness so tangible she felt she could reach out and collect it in her hand.

"You're a glutton for punishment, you weird Yankee wench," he finally said, and a shadow of a smile played across his incredibly mobile mouth. "The last thing I could face this morning would be that bloody computer, and here you are itching to get to work."

She couldn't speak, couldn't force even a good-morning past lips that suddenly remembered the incredible taste of him.

"I'm glad you had the good sense to whip me into line last night," he continued. "Damned cheeky of me to accuse you of being into the grog, seeing it was me who fell apart at the finish. Try not to think too badly of me, Bess."

Then he was gone, slipping past without touching her, but also, having restored her dignity, without leaving her any response that would have made any sense at all.

CHAPTER EIGHT

They walked around each other like stray dogs for the next few days, saying little and choosing their words very carefully. Somehow, they managed to maneuver their way through the office, and the rest of the house, without physically touching.

Geoff spent a lot of time away on business, which suited Bess. But it slowed work on the book and gave her too much time to think, so she began editing in the mornings and strolling through the city every afternoon.

Sometimes she took Lady along for company. But all too soon she realized that having the demented dog only gave men an excuse to stop her and ask questions that quickly left the realm of dog interest and moved toward subjects she preferred to avoid. She did, however, make a mental note to pass this interesting bit of lore along to a few friends back home. Get a gundog and walk it where the men are; it's safer than wearing a mini-skirt and far more effective.

Bess visited the museum, checked out all the galleries and gift shops, even subscribed to Launceston's Theatre North, which offered dramas, opera, and musicals throughout the year. But mostly she just walked the streets, gradually extending her wanderings so that she covered all of the business district south of the River. Then she crossed over and meandered through Invermay, one of the city's older industrial and residential districts.

She spent a good deal of time in the library, trying to upgrade her knowledge of the period about which Geoff was writing. Australian history, so much like that of America on the surface, was almost totally different once the surface had been scratched. The language, the customs, the entire fabric was different. And, to Bess's mind, extremely difficult to comprehend. Still, it had to be done, and she enjoyed the learning experience.

One afternoon, having finished up at the library, she hurried through the Brisbane Street Mall, trying to get under cover before a looming shower decided to unload. Darting quick glances at a sky that had rapidly turned from dove-gray to steel-gray, she turned a corner and bounced off the burly form of Tom Rossiter.

"Elizabeth! What on earth are you doing here?" he said, astonishment obvious in his world-weary eyes.

"I could ask the same of you, Tom. Has father decided he wants to annex Tasmania or something? Whatever it is, it must be serious business, or have you given up being his number one fixer?"

"I guess I'm still doing the same old job, unless your father fired me and forgot to mention it."

To Bess's eyes, Tom Rossiter hadn't changed one bit since the last time she'd seen him . . . at Paul's funeral. Tom's suit was rumpled and looked slept in, his tie was askew, and his shoes were an absolute disgrace. But this large ungainly man had a strange aura of gentleness about him, so sometimes it wasn't all that difficult to ignore the kind of work he did for her father.

"Come on, let's find a place for coffee, or better yet, a drink," he said. Grasping her by the elbow, he led her to the Royal Hotel, chanced upon a reasonably private corner table, and ordered some cold beer.

Despite Rossiter's disheveled appearance, Bess felt self-conscious in her sturdy walking shoes, faded jeans, and oversized Denver Broncos tee-shirt. Maybe it was because her father had always insisted she maintain the "Cornwall image" by wearing tailored skirts and slacks. Fortunately, her Colorado friends didn't give a rat's spit if she wore cowboy boots with evening gowns, or air-conditioned-at-the-knees jeans, and Mouse's frequent comments that she looked like "Cinderella in denim" had fallen on deliberately deaf ears. Had, in fact, often led to more rebellion. Bess had never actually found the nerve to scalp her head or pierce her bellybutton, yet she knew she could if she wanted to, and knew no one would give her a second glance. Well, maybe the scalped head.

"It's great to see you, Elizabeth," Tom said, effectively slicing through her digressive thoughts. "I had no idea you were in Australia. I'm surprised your father didn't mention it when he sent me down here."

"He probably doesn't know. I didn't tell him, and please, Tom, I'd appreciate it if you didn't either. Father is so . . . so intrusive sometimes."

"Sure, honey, whatever you say. But what are you doing here? It's a long way from home."

"I'm collaborating on a book with an Australian author, and I came down to sort out some of the details." Bess wanted to be truthful without going into specifics. She liked Tom Rossiter, but when all was said and done he was still her father's man.

"Is it going well?"

Briefly, she chewed over his question. "It's shoving my career in a new direction," she said, parroting Geoff's original e-mail plea. "But there's nothing wrong with having more than one iron in the fire. My visa's good for three months, and I've been here almost a . . . what's the Aussie word? . . . fortnight. I guess you could say the collaboration's going well, even giving me an opportunity to see a bit of Tasmania, which is a bonus. So, what are you doing here?"

Tom seemed to hesitate. Then he said, "You know the old man, Elizabeth. He hasn't given me my instructions yet, but he probably plans to market kangaroo coats."

"Cruella Cornwall," she said with a smile and a shudder. "That's from Disney's Dalmatian movie," she explained.

"Yup. I remember when everyone wanted to buy spotted dogs. Why don't you give me your phone number, honey, and I'll take you out for dinner? I'm down here with Gerry Coolidge."

Just what I need, Bess thought. Rossiter was her father's man, but Coolidge was . . . something else again. If Gerald Coolidge saw an advantage in telling her father he'd seen the missing Elizabeth in Launceston . . . but then what could her father do?

"I'd like that, Tom," she said. Only to suddenly grow cautious again without really knowing why. "But my friend's number is unlisted and I never have to use it, so I'm afraid I can't give it to you because I don't know it myself. Where are you staying? I can check my calendar when I get back, and call you."

"I'm at the Casino with Gerry. Do you know where that is?"

"Yes. I ate some oysters there with my friend and another . . . friend."

Tom gave her the room number, adding that he would likely be heading home soon. "Please have dinner with us, Elizabeth. It would mean a lot to me. And Gerry, as well. He's always liked you."

Bess knew exactly what it was about her that Gerald Coolidge liked, but she let the remark pass. "I will, Tom, I promise. Right now I have a ton of work to do and it's about to rain cats and dogs and kangaroos, so I'd better scoot. You take care of yourself, and please remember what I said about telling Father."

"No problem." Rising to get himself another beer, Tom watched Elizabeth exit onto George Street, then disappear.

Gerald Coolidge's reaction to the encounter was predictable.

"You must have horse-shoes up your ass, Tom," he said. "But your timing is rotten. Dinner would be perfect for stage two, when the plan is to get her back to her old man, but first—first, damn it!—we have to find a way to use her to turn Barrett around. And we sure as hell can't have her suspecting our involvement, at least not at this stage."

"I didn't even think of that," Rossiter said. "It seemed like a good idea at the time, Gerry. Give us a chance to pick her brains and find out what's really going on between her and Barrett. I thought we'd take her to dinner, ply her with fine wine, and you could put your talents to work."

"Talents?"

"You know, get some information out of her. You're good at that."

"True," Coolidge agreed, preening like a rooster. "But Elizabeth has always been very stubborn, even when she was under her old man's thumb being squashed like an ant. Obviously, she didn't tell you very much."

"Only that she's down here collaborating on a book. She didn't mention Barrett by name, but since he's a writer it should be safe to assume he's the one she's collaborating with. What did you want me to do, Gerry? Come straight out and ask her? Damned smart that would have been."

"I'm not being critical, Tom. You've done splendidly, as far as it goes."

"Yeah, well, let's just be sure your Sydney thugs don't decide to kidnap the girl right after she's been to dinner with us, okay? We don't want even the slightest suspicion in our direction, and I'd expect Barrett has some fairly good contacts down here. Something we don't."

"You just leave that part to me." Coolidge's agile mind, often compared to a computer by less-than-amused colleagues, could almost be heard to whirl and hiss. "When do you think she's likely to get in touch with you?"

Rossiter shrugged his massive shoulders. "She was almost cagey about not wanting me to contact her, and of course I couldn't let her know we already know where she is and who she's with. But Elizabeth and I have always been friendly, Gerry, and she seemed more than pleased with the idea of getting together, so it shouldn't be too long."

Hunched in front of Geoff's computer, Bess tried to concentrate on Kate, who had to defend her virtue from the brutal and sadistic ship's captain. Bess was also thinking about how soon she might have dinner with Tom Rossiter.

And Gerald Coolidge, if that couldn't be avoided.

She liked Tom, always had. But something kept prodding at her, now that she had said she'd phone and arrange a get-together. One element of the issue was that she did not like Gerald Coolidge, who had always struck her as the slimiest of snake-oil salesman types, despite his immaculate appearance and polished good manners. He was a man with whom she would not wish to be stuck in an elevator for any length of time.

But what it came down to, she kept thinking, was that she resented bitterly this intrusion—intentional or not—of her father's world into her own. She had traveled to Tasmania to get away from that, but now it seemed to have caught up with her.

"And I do not like that!"

"Don't like what?" Geoff said, causing Bess to snap upright with a small cry of dismay. "Have I gone and offended your American verbiage again?"

"I do wish you wouldn't sneak up on me, Geoff. It's very disconcerting."

"Okay, I'll start wearing steel-shod motorcycle boots, or I'll stamp my feet. What's the problem, Bess? It must be fairly serious. I can't remember you getting quite this vehement about my writing before."

"It's got nothing to do with you. Just something personal I'll have to fix."

"Need help?"

She could tell by his expression that it was a genuine offer. "No. No, thanks. It really isn't all that serious. This afternoon I met a guy from back home. He wants me to have dinner with him, and I'm not sure I want to go."

"Seems pretty simple to me. If you want to, you do, and if you don't want to, you don't. Couldn't be simpler."

"I just wish it was," she said with a sigh. "But it isn't your problem, so forget it. What I want you thinking about is Kate, and whether she's going to be able to fend off this sadistic captain. And if so, how? You've gotten her into a pretty pickle here, Geoff, and I really don't see how she's going to survive this voyage with her so-called virtue intact. You haven't given her any sort of escape route that I can see. I mean, she can't very well jump ship and swim ashore."

"Maybe our hero—"

"Tom."

"You named our hero Tom?" Geoff grinned. "After your first boyfriend, I presume."

"How . . . oh, the monkeys. No, that was Tommy, and he wasn't very heroic. He took me to the movies, but I paid him to take me. I wanted to prove to . . . to someone that I could date a popular boy, a football jock. When I wouldn't let Tommy touch my breasts, he asked me to be his girlfriend and I said yes. My steady status lasted exactly ten days. As soon as I refused to pay for movies and hamburgers, Tommy demanded his jock jacket back. Why are you looking at me like that?"

"It's hard to imagine you paying someone to romance you."

"I didn't say romance. Okay, picture a very heavy Shirley Temple with red hair. That was me at fifteen. By the time I slimmed down, Tommy had gotten some girl in trouble. He'd also been kicked off the football team, and my father . . . I mean, his father . . . well, just let's say Tommy's family business went bust. Please, Geoff, can't we talk about your book?"

"Our book. Okay, so where were we?"

"Saving Kate's virtue. I think we decided she couldn't swim to shore."

"A shame they didn't have aircraft in those days."

His second grin proved he wasn't taking her seriously. Bess had exhausted her verbal sparring skills for the day on Tom Rossiter, and she was in no mood for this.

"Fine," she said, flinging herself out of her chair. "Why don't you think about it, and when you know, kindly let me know, because I can't do much more until you do!"

She stomped out of the room, leaving the hapless Kate to the mercies of her creator, then slipped into the back yard to play with Lady. Damn Geoff, she thought, and had to smile. Because she'd just realized that at least half her pique was the result of his too-casual attitude toward her Tom dilemma, and as the demented dog whirled out of the kennel, Bess gave herself a mental kick in the pants. What had she expected? That Geoff would suddenly get all jealous and possessive? And why on earth had she recited some stupid story about her first boyfriend, who wasn't even her boyfriend? She should have told Geoff the truth. That she'd named their hero for Tom Rossiter, the man who'd invited her to dinner.

"Maybe then he'd have shown some interest," she said, for the moment oblivious to the whirling dervish at her feet. Glancing down, she had the most vivid mental picture of a childhood bedtime story about a little boy up a coconut tree with tigers running round the base until they melted into butter.

"What would you turn into, chocolate milk?" she asked the demented dog. "Lady! Pay attention! Sit!" Which, somewhat to her surprise, the dog immediately did, squarely on Bess's foot.

"You're spoiling my dog, but I suppose you know that," Geoff said from the open doorway, and discipline again flew out the window as Lady, exhibiting her usual paroxysms of ecstasy, raced over to sit on his feet.

"You should have bought a Labrador retriever," Bess retorted, throwing back at him the concept he so often threw at Lady whenever the Springer spaniel was driving him to distraction.

"I think maybe we should have hot dogs for dinner," he said with a broad grin, whereupon the dog wriggled with delight and Bess couldn't help but respond with a grin of her own. Anyone hearing the way Geoff talked to Lady might have been forgiven for thinking he hated the dog, except for the warmth in his voice when he called her names and threatened all sorts of dire retribution for her many failings. The fact was, of course, that no dog could be more loved, and as fractious as Lady behaved, Geoff wouldn't have traded her for anything.

"I thought you were supposed to be saving Kate's virtue, Mr. Barrett. Or is such a task too difficult for a mere man? I suppose it is, actually. Am I asking too much, expecting you to set aside the sworn purpose of your gender in order to help create a book that might sell?"

"What's made you so damned cranky? No, don't answer because I suppose I shouldn't even ask."

"Damn straight," she said. "And I can't do much more with 'our book' until you do some more writing, so would you like to get busy?"

"Not just now. I'm tired of saving Kate's virtue. Why don't we take Lady down to the river for a bit, instead?"

"That's not going to get the book finished!"

"No, but it's going to mean I can go to the dog trials next weekend without the bloody dog totally disgracing me. Lady has been missing out since I let you get involved in this book."

"Let me get involved? I would remind you, Geoffrey Barrett, that you practically got down on your knees and begged me to help you with your book."

"Semantics," he said dismissively. "Now go find your gumboots and let's get to it. Time's a'wastin'."

No sense arguing when Geoff was in this sort of mood, Bess thought, and went off to find her gumboots.

That day set the pattern for the rest of the week. Whatever else Geoff did in the mornings, they religiously took a portion of the afternoon to go dog training. Lady was delighted. She could recognize the route to Hobler's Bridge, and also knew that gumboots and a whistle and hat meant it was to be her sort of trip. Every time they got ready to go, she danced round the Land Cruiser, waiting for the rear doors to be opened, ecstatic in her joyous activity.

By Friday the constant repetition was starting to show signs of having some effect. Lady fairly flew through her exercises, running the hundred fifty yards from Geoff to the dummy without faltering, then returning to deliver properly to hand. Except for her habit of wanting to sit on Geoff's feet when she delivered, instead of sitting properly in front of him, she was perfection.

Laughing at the dog's foolish foot fetish, Bess stood beside the river. For quite some time she'd been throwing dummies into heavy cover while Geoff was well down the walking track, working Lady from there.

The next dummy Bess hurled flew higher and farther than usual, landing almost in the water amidst the heaviest of reedy cover, just before the track gave way to a short-cut lawn area beneath and alongside the bridge.

Lady, as expected, dashed down the track and into the cover, bounding in the high, springing leaps of her breed. Then she halted, barking and growling in a manner Bess had never before heard from the sweet-tempered dog. Bess started forward to see what was wrong, only to have Geoff shout at her to keep back in case it was a snake. He was making speed of his own, charging up the track and calling to the dog as he ran. But for all the difference it made, he could have saved his breath. Lady was fiercely upset now, and sounded it.

Geoff had almost reached Bess's side when the cause of the alarm suddenly became obvious. A very tall, tough looking man rose from the thicket where Lady had been spooked, and began to pick his way through the cover towards them. At the same time, he stuffed what appeared to be a handkerchief into his pocket.

"Sorry if I muddled your dog," he said in a friendly enough fashion. "Just . . . uh . . . a call of nature. You understand."

And without waiting to see if they did, he walked quickly toward the parking lot, where a new-looking Holden squatted next to Geoff's Land Cruiser. Geoff watched him go, then gazed down at the dog, who was still bristling.

"Ah well," he sighed. "No sense going on with this now. It'll take my little sausage here the rest of the afternoon to settle down. Funny, though. She doesn't make a habit of getting upset with strangers, except when she's home guarding the yard. Normally, she'd beat someone to death with her tail if she ran into them out here."

"I think she was surprised. I know I was," Bess said, and promptly forgot about the incident until they reached Geoff's Land Cruiser and found the man sitting behind the wheel of his car, obviously in no hurry to leave. He waved casually, then turned away and began looking through some papers.

"Salesman taking a break, I suppose," Geoff said, as they departed for home. "Tough looking sort, though, wasn't he?"

Ten minutes later, the tough looking sort's partner made his way back to the car and jumped into the passenger seat. "Damn mongrel dog," he practically spat. "I thought it was going to have me for tea, until it decided to start in on you."

"Damn good thing you were able to stay hidden," the driver replied. "I told them I was taking a bog. They weren't even a bit suspicious. But I'm beginning to think this is no place to try and snatch the girl. That dog makes it just about impossible." Reaching into his pocket, he dragged out the ether-soaked rag, glanced at it with disgust, then tossed it out the window. "And I'm not happy about using this. I'd rather clip her across the jaw, when the time comes."

"Coolidge said no damage to the merchandise. And I'll tell you straight, I'm not about to get that bloke pissed off with me."

"Coolidge pays well, which is the only reason I put up with

him. If not for the money, I'd tell him where to get off. But a quid's a quid's a quid." Starting the car, the driver proceeded carefully toward their motel, maintaining the speed limit since it wouldn't do to get stopped for speeding. "Don't go all jittery on me, mate," he said, darting a quick glance toward his partner, who was twitching in the passenger seat as if *he* had to take a bog. "We'll lift the bitch next time, and I don't mean the bloody dog."

CHAPTER NINE

The insistent jangle of the telephone sounded more hostile with each repetitive ring, and Bess simply couldn't ignore it anymore. Tearing her gaze away from the computer screen, she toed her chair across the plywood and picked up the receiver.

"Hi there, Colorado, what are you doing for lunch today?" Ida's husky voice had a certain cynical, sardonic quality, even over the phone.

"Did you want Geoff?" Bess couldn't imagine why Ida would be calling her.

"I've already had Geoff, darling." That blatant statement was followed by an almost masculine chuckle, the low pitch bolstering Ida's image as a man's woman, a woman used to dealing with men on their own ground.

"Oh." Bess couldn't think of anything else to say.

"Yes, oh. So, are you game for lunch or not?"

Not, Bess thought, but kept silent.

Ida chuckled again. "How about I come for you in half an hour? No need to dress up. Today we'll go somewhere for the food, rather than showing off."

Frustrated with Geoff's awkward attempts to re-characterize their heroine, anxious to take a break from editing a chapter that was "buggering off" in the wrong direction, Bess found herself agreeing. At the same time, she glanced down at her raggedy cut-offs and wondered what Ida would consider casual attire.

131

Not that it made much difference. As soon as she had set up her apartment in Colorado Springs, Bess had donated all her "respectable" clothes to Good Will. Whereupon, she'd deliberately established a reputation for looking unconventional, even quirky, in a *haut monde* Barbra-Streisand-thrift-shop manner. It was a reputation she preserved and treasured, despite the addition of her designer mini-skirt and top, a birthday gift from Mouse.

"Right . . . see you then." Ida hung up without any farewell, leaving Bess staring at a silent telephone.

It was with a strange sense of satisfaction that she opened the passenger door to Ida's Pajero and saw that her efforts to look offbeat hadn't been in vain. She could never compete with Ida, who was resplendent in a figure-hugging jersey dress that stopped just short of being a top with a wide belt.

Still, Bess had to give Ida credit. The stunning blonde didn't show any reaction at all to Bess's Navy-issue sailor pants and the blue baseball jacket that bore a woeful BROOKLYN DODGERS on the back. Hefting herself up into the high vehicle, wriggling onto the passenger seat, Bess was startled to hear Ida's sudden burst of laughter.

"Is this what you call working gear, Colorado?" she asked. "If you wear this when you share a computer with Geoffrey, we'd best go to Hobart for lunch, and see if we can't find you a chastity belt."

"What do you mean?"

"You look almost as tasty as Gene Kelly in that movie about the three sailors who invade New York."

"*On The Town?* I don't understand."

"Your butt, Colorado. Those trousers are tighter than paint. Hasn't Geoffrey ever been tempted to pinch your butt?"

"No. I told him I didn't like men pinching my butt."

"And he listened?"

"Of course he listened." Bess didn't bother to mention that Geoff had never seen her in these pants. Which, she now realized, molded her buttocks like a second skin. And, for the record, she admired Gene Kelly's rump as much as Ida did, even though Geoff would have given Gene a run for his money.

"Are you wearing anything under that jumper?" Ida asked.

"Jumper? Oh, you mean jacket. A cotton camisole. Why?"

"Ah well, I didn't really fancy a pub lunch anyway. We'll go find us somewhere posh, eh? Show off a bit and give the lads a treat."

"I have no intention of taking my jacket off, Ida. It's a classic!"

"So are you, darling. And you will take your bloody jumper off," she said.

Sounding, Bess thought, like Geoff when she insisted . . . no, begged him to make their "Flower" of Ballarat a tad more sedate. Having fended off the sadistic captain, Kate had suddenly evolved into a modern-day seductress—a modern-day Ida, actually—and although Bess had no objection to what Geoff called "Kate's trollop ploy," this morning he'd gone too far. Unfortunately, by the time Bess discovered the anomaly he'd left for one of his damn business meetings.

Which was another irritant. What exactly did he do? Every time she asked, he side-stepped her questions.

Ida had barely hit the downtown area when her mood suddenly changed. The smile vanished along with her salty small-talk, and she took to keeping a steady eye on her rear-view mirrors.

"Have you been having any more problems over your way?" she eventually asked Bess, yanking the four-wheel-drive around a tight inner-city corner in one savage gesture.

"No, nothing that I know of. We left the bugs in place as you suggested, and we've been circumspect in what we say on the phone or in E-mails."

"Hmmmm. Well, it might be me then. Here, steer this thing for a mini, but do it from the bottom of the wheel so they can't see you're doing it."

With no more warning than that, she let go of the steering wheel and began fumbling in her huge handbag, her manicured fingers emerging a moment later with a cell phone. "Just keep going straight," she said, reaching down to punch in a number. When it was answered, she mumbled into the phone so quietly that Bess could pick up only the occasional word. After a brief conversation, Ida dropped the phone on the seat beside her and took over the driving again, abruptly switching lanes as if she'd changed her mind about something.

"Lunch at the Rosevears pub . . . bloody waste in this sort of gear but can't be helped," she remarked, heading for the West Tamar highway and keeping an eye on her mirrors at the same time.

To Bess, it seemed as if Ida was actually ensuring that whoever was following could keep them in view, although her driving was so skillful it didn't appear that way. When Bess asked, she got one of those incredible smiles.

"But of course, darling," Ida said. "How else are we going to find out what they're up to? And don't you dare glance back! I want everything to look as innocent as possible."

They had barely swung through the roundabout at Legana when a police car passed them, headed in the opposite direction. "Bloody wonderful," Ida exclaimed, stamping on the accelerator. "With any luck at all, we'll be able to high-tail it for Exeter and swing round home on the back roads. The

Rosevears Pub is a fine place with excellent tucker, but I really did fancy somewhere a bit more posh, and now we can manage it." She glanced in her mirrors again. "It's okay to look round now, Colorado. Our 'friends' have just found themselves caught up in a small traffic check, which should keep them busy for a while."

Bess turned to see two men engaged in an agitated discussion with a patrolman.

"You organized that, I take it?"

"They were driving like idiots," Ida replied with a throaty chuckle. "They deserved to be stopped."

Not long afterwards, she and Bess were being shown to a choice view table at Hallam's Waterfront Restaurant. A reserved sign was moved to free up the table for Ida, obviously a well-known and valued customer. Although she certainly hadn't been intimidated—or cowed!—by the exquisite blonde, Bess grudgingly removed her jacket and slung it over the back of her chair.

"As good seafood as you'll get anywhere in town," Ida said. "Your camisole is rather prim, Colorado, even though it shows your breasts off nicely. Still, if you're going to wear those trousers around Geoffrey's office, I suggest you have the oysters."

Feeling self-conscious in her "prim camisole," Bess spent the entire meal fending off Ida's remarks.

"I reckon you're just what the old bugger needs," she said at one point, uttering the words around a mouthful of fresh fish. "You're the right age, you're beautiful, smart, you've got similar interests, and . . . well . . . I guess you can't help being a Yank."

"Is being a Yank such an awful thing?"

"Naw . . . not awful, really. America has such a powerful influence in the world overall, it's only natural people are envious, sometimes even cranky. Don't worry about it, Colorado. As far as you're concerned, I was joking."

Occasionally, Ida could be so blunt that it was hard to decide how to take her. And yet, Bess suddenly realized, she instinctively liked Ida . . . even trusted her.

"Okay, Colorado," Ida said, "let's change the subject. When are you going to trip darling Geoffrey and beat him to the floor? It hasn't happened yet. I'd know if it had by the look in your eye, dear, and although I suppose you've been told this before, I would kill for those eyes of yours. Give us a look at your game plan. It'll give me something nice to go to sleep by, thinking of poor Geoffrey getting what's coming to him. He's already smitten. I suppose you realize that . . ."

She stopped, staring hard at Bess as if trying to memorize her.

"You don't realize it, do you? You think you're the only one who's smitten. Bloody oath, Bess! There's the poor bugger going round with his tongue hanging out and you can't even see it. Did you think he's so close to his damned dog, he pants like that all the time?"

"Ida . . ."

"Yes, I know. You're a very genteel young lady, for a Yank, and I'm making you uncomfortable."

"No, it's not that. I mean, yes, sometimes you make me feel uncomfortable, but I was going to ask you why you invited me to lunch?"

"I could say I wanted to stir . . . tease you, Bess. But the truth is, I don't have many women friends. In fact, I don't have any women friends. I know I can be rough as guts sometimes. It's a hangover from my years as a cleaner, and before that, back home, when I was a courier. Neither are jobs for the faint-hearted, and you get into the habit of using the kind of language you hear around you."

"Stop it, Ida. Your language doesn't bother me in the least. Neither does your directness. It's just that there are things about me I'd rather not share. Can we be friends without the usual this-is-my-life confession?"

"Suits me. I won't share, either. But I am, and always will be, a snoop who ought to know better. Hell, I do know better, but it doesn't stop me mouthing off. And since I got this security business going, I'm afraid my curiosity bump has grown bigger and bigger."

"I'll trade you my eyes for your smile," Bess said.

Ida laughed, a huge, gurgling, throaty laugh that erupted straight from her tummy. "My, my, you are a piece of work, aren't you? I don't envy my darling Geoffrey when you finally get him in your sights."

They had just finished ordering dessert when there was a ring-a-ling from inside Ida's capricious handbag. She grabbed up her cell phone and strode outside to ensure better reception. Watching through the window, Bess could see from the flickering range of expressions on Ida's face that whatever she was hearing, it wasn't exactly good news.

"Sydney heavies," Ida said upon her return. "Standover men of the worst sort," she added, looking at Bess through blue eyes gone agate hard. "Of course there was no mention of them following us. The copper wouldn't have asked, for starters. But this is hardly a tourist destination for standover merchants from the Big Smoke, not at this time of year and not without some appropriate female company, although they could easily enough buy that here, I suppose. Still, it's strange. Very strange."

She sat down, ordered coffee for them both, then turned to Bess again as the waitress moved out of earshot.

"You haven't been up to no good, have you? My first impression was that it had to be me they were following, but now I'm not so sure. We didn't pick them up until after I'd collected you."

"Me? I'm simply collaborating with Geoff on his book. There can't be anything sinister in that. The book is total fiction, not an exposure of any kind. It's set back in the Victorian gold field era."

"And you, personally? Nothing hanging around in your past? An estranged husband?"

"My husband . . . died."

"I'm sorry, Bess. How about a pissed-off wife of somebody you've been . . . ah . . . involved with? No, strike that. You're not the type."

"Thank you, I think. But no, there's absolutely nothing like that."

Briefly, Bess wondered about her father with his worldwide network of informants and spies and industrial espionage people. But that made no sense. Her father wouldn't go out of his way to cause problems just because she'd escaped his corporate-hooker scheme. Besides, by now his "British suitor" had surely targeted another heiress. Bess had often heard War Cornwall compared to Howard Hughes, going after the things he wanted with an insane vengeance. As Father aged, he even exhibited a few Hughes fetishes. But blood was thicker than . . . what? Oil? Diamonds? Kangaroo pelts?

"Geoffrey then?" Ida took a sip of her coffee. "It's the only logical explanation if we eliminate the two of us."

Bess couldn't think of any response because she didn't know enough. What was a standover merchant? A gangster of some sort, she thought.

"Our Geoffrey has fingers in many pies," Ida continued. "He's worth a bundle, which is something else I'll bet you didn't know, and wouldn't care if you did."

Maybe that's why he never talks about his business, Bess

thought. *Maybe he doesn't want me to know he's worth a bundle. Hell, I'd already guessed that from my airline ticket. Maybe his ex-wife took him for a bundle.*

"And where there's money," Ida said, "there's somebody out to relocate it, or steal it, or launder it. Come to think of it, Geoffrey did mention something about a proposed take-over bid he was fighting. Some American asset-stripper that got on Geoffrey's case in a big way and really put his nose out of joint. Yes, that might account for it, assuming what we see on the telly is true and American business tycoons all use hit-men to solve their problems."

Again, Bess said nothing. But her thoughts returned to her father, then, logically, to Tom Rossiter's presence here in Tasmania. Not to mention the presence of Gerald Coolidge, a man without any morals or scruples. Bess gave her head a mental shake. The men who'd followed the car already knew where Geoff lived, so why trail her?

"Well, whatever's going on, Geoffrey has to be told," Ida said. "When we get you home, I'll come in for a few minutes if he's there and see what he thinks about it all. That," she added with a huge grin, "will give you a chance to get out of your chase-me-catch me-root-me gear before the poor man realizes you're serious."

Bess opened her mouth, then shut it again. Protestations wouldn't help, would in fact only energize the locomotive that propelled Ida's one-track mind.

Accept her friendship and ignore her pandering, Bess told herself. *And whatever you do, don't stir the cauldron by asking Ida why she's playing matchmaker. Obviously, she has demons too.*

When they got back to the house, Bess saw Geoff's eyes widen as they strode side-by-side toward him across the expanse of living room carpet.

"My very word," he said. "What have you two been up to, or is it anything I want to know about?" And his eyes flickered like lightning over Bess's camisole. Perversely, she now carried her Dodger's jacket.

"Women's business, darling," Ida replied. "You wouldn't understand, so I won't give you the relative pleasure of failing. Now, take me into the sanctity of your office because I desperately need to talk to you."

Bess changed back into her cut-offs and Broncos tee-shirt, then entered the office just as Ida was finishing her description of the day's events. Geoff looked serious but didn't seem overly alarmed.

"Following your car doesn't make sense to me," he said. "But you're spot-on, I think. They might have followed Bess to get to me. The question is, why? I'm easy enough to find. Are you positive it isn't one of your operations that's behind it all?"

"As positive as I can be, but rest assured I'll be checking that out. And watching my own back. Still, it doesn't feel right to have it aimed at me. I'm certain those blokes picked us up here, or near here, and even though they didn't try anything, or do anything but follow us, it gives me bad vibes. Very bad vibes."

"Me too," Bess chipped in. "I didn't get a good look at them, Geoff, but seeing them standing there with that cop . . . er, copper . . . I had a feeling one of them might have been the guy who spooked Lady, the man we saw down by the river. Except, that really makes no sense either."

"None of it makes sense," Geoff said, "but it will, sooner or later. I guess it means all of us will have to be a little more careful. Rocky, watch how you go. I know your style, and having you involved in something like this worries me."

"Worry about yourself, darling. I have my bloody cell

140

phone, and I'm a big girl. Come to think of it, Colorado should carry a cell phone."

"Good idea."

"Now, I'll be off. Please, you two, be careful and don't do anything I wouldn't do." She looked pointedly at Bess's cut-offs, then made a pinching gesture with her fingers. "Remember what I told you, Colorado, and watch your butt as well as your back."

Flashing Geoff a smile, Ida departed. Disappearing, Bess thought, like a bloody Cheshire Cat.

Many aspects of Ida and Geoff's conversation were being repeated, almost word for word, in Gerald Coolidge's suite at the Casino. The major difference was that almost everybody involved in the discussion was either angry or extremely angry.

"It don't wash," the larger of the two Sydney crims was saying. "There was no reason for that copper to pull us over. None. I wasn't speeding and I wasn't driving recklessly."

"And all he did was check your identification?" Coolidge asked. "He didn't breathalyse you, didn't check over the car for defects?"

"I've already told you we weren't drinking. And why the bloody hell would he check over the car? It was a hire car, bloody near brand new. There'd be no reason to check it over."

"You must have done something to make him suspicious. Cops here don't go pulling over hire cars in the middle of the day without some sort of reason. Maybe he didn't like your looks. Maybe he thought he recognized you from some crime file. Maybe he's an ex-Sydney copper."

"And maybe you're full of crap." The Sydney standover merchant, not at all intimidated by Gerald Coolidge, was fast losing patience with the discussion.

"The first thing we did was trade in the hire car," said the other man, nervously shuffling his feet. "Which isn't going to help the coppers because we also used phony I.D. when we checked into the motel. So they're gonna have a bugger of a time finding us. I mean, if they really do want to find us. I mean . . ." His voice trailed off, obstructed by his fingernails, inserted between his teeth.

"But you used proper identification to hire the original car and for your plane tickets," said Tom Rossiter, speaking up for the first time. "If they go chasing along those lines it won't take them long to figure out who you are, then wonder what the hell you're doing here in Tasmania." Rossiter turned to Coolidge. "I don't like it. The thing's jinxed."

"Don't be stupid, Tom. It's not anything to worry about. And the lads here handled it perfectly, as far as I'm concerned."

" 'Course we did," growled the leader from Sydney. "Just give us a few days to let the smoke clear and we'll take another run at the redhead. And her blonde friend too, if it comes to it. I wouldn't mind cutting me a slice off either one."

"There'll be none of that!" Rossiter's voice held the ring of authority left over from his days on the New York City police force. Now he looked at each of the Sydney men in turn, and made sure they both saw the message in his eyes as well as his voice.

"Yeah, sure," was the grudging reply. "I didn't say I would do it, just that I wouldn't mind."

"Don't even think about it," Rossiter said, his body language making the simple statement into a brutal threat.

"Are you going soft on the old man's daughter, Tom?" Coolidge asked, once the Sydney crew had left the suite.

"Not soft, no. But Elizabeth's always been good to me,

and I'll admit I don't much like this business of dealing with her the way you're going about it. You let scum like that get her someplace where there's no control and you've practically guaranteed rape, or worse." Rossiter's eyes grew bleak. "Using her as a lever against Barrett is one thing, but this is something else again. Also, don't forget, I'm the one who has to deliver her back in New York, and the old man'll be livid if she's returned to him in less than perfect condition."

"She will be, at least on the surface."

"No, Gerry. She will be . . . period. I want you to pay off those thugs and bring in someone who can do this job the way we first agreed."

"And if I don't?"

Rossiter shrugged, the gesture hardly showing against his rumpled suit. "Far as I'm concerned, you're responsible. You don't want to piss me off, Gerry. I know too much. So just do it, okay?"

"Tom . . . Tom . . ."

"I mean it, Gerry. There are better ways to handle your first phase."

Coolidge met Rossiter's eyes directly, then was forced to look away. He hated to admit, even to himself, that the expression in those eyes frightened him.

"All right, Tom, I'll get rid of them first thing in the morning. We can use some of my own people. I have total control over them, and I can assure you there will be no violence, no sex, just a nice tidy nab. And we'll take her someplace she can be detained in comfort. Okay with you?"

"Sure, because I plan to be there. It shouldn't be too hard to arrange it so she doesn't see me or recognize me."

"Dangerous move, old friend."

"Yup, but I guess that's the way it's going to be, so get used to the idea. Nothing bad will happen to Elizabeth, and

I'm going to make damn sure of that."

"Whatever you say. Now, how about you get on with your side of things while I set this up the way you want? It will take until day after tomorrow to bring in my own people because I can't use anybody from Tasmania. This place is too small and word would leak, sure as God made little green apples."

Coolidge waited until Rossiter had left the room, then picked up the phone and dialed the number of the motel where the Sydney men were staying, assuming correctly that they had returned there directly after their meeting with him.

"Rossiter is going to be a problem," he said when the leader answered. "I think it might be a good idea to remove him from this game."

"Rossiter is tough. It's going to cost you."

"That's all right. I've got a company checkbook with room for lots of zeros. Just make sure he's out of the way before you collect the girl, or he'll be more of a problem than he is now."

The voice at the end of the phone didn't hesitate. "Consider it done."

"Hold on." Coolidge's computer-like brain whirred and hissed. If there was the slightest possibility that Rossiter could turn the tables on the standover merchants before the nab, the bloody jig would be up. And hadn't Tom said something about knowing too much? Did too much include useful, perhaps profitable information about the British chap Cornwall wanted to procure for his daughter?

"Don't do anything yet, mate," Coolidge said into the phone. "I've got an even better idea."

CHAPTER TEN

When the front door closed, Bess didn't immediately react. Her head was filled with the theme music from *Rocky* and, for no discernible reason, she pictured the sensual scene in Rocky's run-down apartment, where Stallone had kissed Talia Shire for the first time. No naked bodies, no artistic camera angles, just enough tenderness to make every girl, young and old, breathe a universal sigh, followed by a universal purr.

Finally, something clicked. "Why do you call her Rocky?" Bess asked Geoff. "Has Ida been a prize fighter, too?"

"I don't know, but it wouldn't surprise me. Very little about Ida would surprise me. The nickname is simply my personal acceptance of Ida's own view of herself . . . Ida, woman of stone. She's had more men than you've had hot dinners, and by her own admission is a user and abuser par excellence. Thrives on it, I think, although you'd wonder if she doesn't get awful lonely sometimes in the process."

"A user and abuser? She doesn't strike me as the type, somehow, although I realize she's been around a bit."

"More than a bit. She probably qualifies for a circumnavigation award when it comes to the world of the male species. And yet a better person you'd be hard put to find, when she's in the mood."

He shrugged, as if to flick away some insect of memory. "I have to go out for a while, Bess. I'll bring back something for tea, and don't forget we have to make an early night of it be-

145

cause we'll be up before sparrow-fart if we're to get to the trial tomorrow in time for check-in."

Despite helping Geoff train Lady for her competition in the novice section of the Tassie Cup, Bess had forgotten all about it. And nowhere, thus far, had Geoff made any mention of her accompanying him to the dog trials, which were being held somewhere in the region around Ross, about an hour's drive to the south.

"You mean I get to go too?" And her face must have revealed her excitement at the prospect, because Geoff grinned hugely before he answered her.

"You think I'd dare leave you behind? Lady would piddle on my boots in retribution, not that she mightn't anyway. Of course you're coming. After all, you've been helping with the training ever since you arrived. Just don't expect too much. One of the laws of retrieving trials is that a dog can do everything right in training, then go to a trial and forget what he or she has learned in a matter of seconds."

"Oh, surely not."

"Oh, surely yes. Scientific studies have proven it takes forty-two consecutive correct applications of a specific exercise before you can be certain the dog knows what you want. But I'll guarantee you this, darling, if it's something you don't want a dog to learn, they only have to see or do it once and it becomes embedded in their tiny brains forevermore."

Bess found sleep difficult that night. Part of the reason, she knew, was her propensity for childish reactions to upcoming treats. She had never enjoyed a decent sleep on Christmas Eve, or the night before her birthday. But now there was worse to consider . . . the way her tummy had done a contented little flip-flop just because Geoff called her darling.

Which was ridiculous in the extreme. He hadn't meant

anything by it, anymore than most Aussies meant anything when they called total strangers "love" or "mate." It was simply part of the national speech pattern. And yet . . .

What had Ida said? That Geoff was smitten? What an amazingly old-fashioned and yet somehow comforting, descriptive word. Ida had also said something about how the poor bugger was going round with his tongue hanging out and how Bess couldn't even see it.

Well, sorry Ida, but I can't, she thought, and wished she could see it, even though she knew it was the last thing she should want to see. No good could come of it; Paul had seen to that. Elizabeth Carson Bradley wasn't worth any man's serious attention, and certainly not the attention of someone she truly cared about.

Still, it didn't hurt to dream a little.

Bess didn't dream that night, although she slept so poorly it was hardly surprising. At four a.m., she was gulping down her second cup of coffee, dressed in her Navy-issue sailor pants and cotton camisole. When Geoff wandered into the kitchen, he looked as if he hadn't slept well either.

"Ah . . . coffee," he sighed, and mixed himself a cup before sitting across the table from her. Eyes half-shut, he slowly sipped at the brew. Then he said, "I thought you were coming to the trial with me."

It was the most surprising remark she might have anticipated, but she quickly replied, "I am. Or at least I am if you still want me to come."

"Then you'd better change into sensible clothes. Those white trousers would be filthy before you'd taken two steps, and that . . ." He gestured toward her top.

"Camisole, Geoff. Surely you know what a camisole is. You've dressed Kate in one often enough."

"I only meant there'll be frost on the ground when we get

there, I can almost guarantee it. You get about like that and I'll be bringing home an icicle."

His smile softened his rebuke, but Bess was nonetheless feeling more than a trifle embarrassed as she donned her denim cut-offs, then struggled into an old pair of jeans over the shorts. Her Broncos sweatshirt hid her camisole. When she returned to the kitchen, Geoff, who was dressed comfortably in moleskin trousers and a thick flannel shirt, nodded in what seemed to be approval, and handed her a bulky polo-fleece jacket.

"You'll need this too, I reckon, at least at first. By noon, your camisole might have proven a wise choice, but dog trials aren't fashion shows at the best of times, which is just as well."

"I wasn't making a fashion statement. I just . . ." Bess paused, all too aware that she'd chosen her outfit because Ida had admired it. "I just wanted to be comfortable, that's all."

Lady was her usual rambunctious self, and seemed to know they were going somewhere special. She did her little dervish performance, but cut it short the instant Geoff opened the back of his Land Cruiser.

There was a last-minute check . . . whistle, dummies, gumboots . . . then Geoff looked at Bess and shook his head. "Damn, I forgot about buying a hat for you."

"I don't much like hats," she replied. "And my hair is long enough that I shouldn't need one. Or should I?"

"You damned well should. You've no idea how powerful the Tasmanian sun can be, especially when you're out all day with no shade. Ah well, nothing to be done about it unless somebody's got an extra one we can borrow."

They talked little on the way south, except for Geoff pointing out the few landmarks the Midlands Highway had to offer. When they reached the site of the Tassie Cup, Bess re-

alized that he hadn't exaggerated when he'd said this would
be no fashion show. Dressed in the shabbiest clothing imaginable, most of the people there would have looked right at
home outside an American soup kitchen.

But it was the dogs that captured Bess's attention, and
held it. All breeds of gundog—Labradors, Chesapeake Bay
retrievers, German shorthaired pointers, Weimaraners,
Springer spaniels like Lady, and some she couldn't even iden-
tify—yodeled and barked and stared from a variety of crates
and travel kennels and trailers.

Geoff was greeted by almost everyone they met, and although he politely introduced Bess as his American visitor,
she quickly realized she was of no importance or interest to
this group of enthusiasts. All around her the talk was of only
one thing . . . their dogs, or somebody else's, and what might
be expected from the mainland judge who was in charge of
the event.

Yet even without introductions, everyone, it seemed,
knew who she was, which Bess found somewhat amazing.
People she hadn't been introduced to came up to say things
like, "You're Geoff's American lady, eh?" then stayed to talk
about "that mad bloody dog, Lady" or about someone else's
equally mad dog. After scrutinizing Bess's pale complexion, a
woman managed to procure a hat, a floppy monstrosity with
an equally floppy brim that hid one's eyes. Although she'd
never thought of herself as vain or pretentious, Bess stuffed
the shapeless headgear into her jacket pocket as soon as the
woman was safely out of sight.

Geoff had also been right about the cold. All around, the
tussocks and paddocks were white with thick frost, and the
nearby river was swathed in a fog-bank so thick that already
the competitors were debating if the trial could even start on
time.

Which, eventually, it did. All the novice dogs were re-moved to a blind so the competitors could get a look at the run. There was a bit of last-minute adjustment, and then the first dog was brought forward and the Novice Stake began.

Bess had been warned by Geoff that she would be well down his list of priorities until Lady had been through her turn, and wasn't the least bit surprised when he passed her on to one of his friends so things could be explained while he concentrated on the work to come.

The novice competition involved single, marked retrieves at distances Bess thought shorter than she and Geoff had been using while training Lady.

The rules were simple. A dog was brought to one position, walked off lead at heel to the next, then was expected to sit and watch as the bird was cast and the handler fired at it with a blank cartridge. Bess already knew the basics of the judging, which involved how well the dog behaved, how well it "marked" the fall of the bird, and how straight and quickly it could dash out . . . once commanded to do so . . . pick up the bird, and return to deliver it gently and tenderly to hand.

What she hadn't expected was just how obstinate and un-controlled some of the dogs could be. Most played up horrifi-cally when they were supposed to be walking at heel, one "broke to shot" so quickly Bess thought it would be there waiting to catch the bird when it finally landed, and another "went walkabout" and had a fine wander, totally oblivious to its handler's whistles and screams, before finally coming back without the bird . . . or the slightest sign of contrition.

Lady did the first run, to Bess's inexperienced and thor-oughly biased eye, as well any other dog. On the next run, which involved having to swim through a narrow channel and get a bird from the other side, the spaniel messed about on the shore, looking . . . or so it seemed . . . for an easier way to manage the task. But eventually she retrieved the bird and brought it back without putting it down to shake the water from her drenched fur. Bess knew that would please Geoff, who had mentioned it was one of Lady's failings.

On the third and final run, things came totally unstuck. Lady fiddled around so much at the water's edge that she forgot where the bird had landed, and Geoff had to use whistle and hand signals to direct her. Then she put the bird down on the shore to shake, picked it up, returned to do a perfect delivery, and immediately dashed away to the gallery, where she promptly sat on Bess's feet and refused to move.

"Too little too late, my little sausage," Geoff was heard to mutter at the wriggling dog, once he'd walked all the way to where Bess stood, biting her lips to keep from laughing along with everyone else. Geoff put Lady's collar back on, then shook his finger at the dog in mock indignation. "Hot dogs tonight for tea, and you're going to be the main course, you mark my words."

"Geoff, I'm really sorry . . ." Bess began, only to be cut off in mid-apology

"Not your fault, darling. If this bloody little dog hadn't done that, she'd have found some other way to stuff things around. She's a Springer spaniel, aren't you ladykins? And who'd be silly enough to love a Springer spaniel, eh?"

Which gained him nothing except that Lady promptly sat on his feet, her little rump solid there while every other part of her wriggled.

"Listen, Bess," Geoff said, after they had enjoyed a lunch purchased from the catering tent. "I've been roped in to work a bird thrower this afternoon for the All-Age. Do you think you can handle this idiot dog? Actually, just tether her in back of the Cruiser with the door open. She's tired enough to sleep most of the afternoon. We could have gone home, but I reckoned you'd want to see the really good dogs work, so I said I'd do this. Okay with you?"

Bess was happy enough to agree, and watched Geoff head off with one of the large, complicated catapults over his muscular shoulder. She tethered Lady and took the few moments of total privacy to shed her jeans. She had earlier removed the heavy jacket, then her sweatshirt, as the sun broke through and warmed the dog trial area to the point where it might have been midsummer. Now it was even warmer, so she braided her thick, unruly hair, fished a barrette from her shorts pocket, and clipped the braids to the top of her head. Almost instantly, she felt cooler.

She watched the first run of the All-Age, and part of the second, then went to check on Lady, whose slumber triggered a similar reaction in Bess. Spreading out a car rug from the Cruiser on the ground directly behind it, she bunched up the jacket as a pillow and lay down in the warm sunlight . . . just to rest her eyes.

And woke up two hours later with the certain, instinctive knowledge that she was in trouble. Sure enough, a touch at her shoulders told the story. She was thoroughly sunburned both front and back, including her legs, and it would get significantly worse before it got better.

"Bloody oath," she muttered, and almost smiled at her own use of what was, to her, a very specific Australianism . . . but an appropriate one. She carefully slid her jeans back up over already tingling legs, then slipped on the over-sized sweatshirt, wincing at its weight across her shoulders.

During the drive home, one in which Geoff was more voluble than usual, Bess was, if anything, far less so. There was good reason; she was too busy swallowing down the urge to be very sick to her stomach and praying they might make it home before she was forced to succumb.

She spent so much of the trip with her eyes closed and her jaw clenched that she didn't notice the increasingly worried look on Geoff's face. But when they reached home and the Land Cruiser was parked, she couldn't help but flinch when he took her arm to help her disembark.

"Ah," he said, and immediately released her. But she was hardly in her room, staring sadly and guiltily into the mirror at the evidence of her stupidity when there was a knock on the door.

"Are you decent?" Geoff asked.

"No, I'm not," she replied. Wearing panties and camisole, she strode toward the door, planning to lock it.

Too late. The door was pushed open and Geoff stepped in, his gaze roving over her blotchy body. His eyes held no hint of passion, only a weary acceptance of a problem he had obviously anticipated.

"Decent enough," he said, reaching out to take her gently by one wrist. "Now come along like a good girl. I've run you a nice cool bath and you're going in the tub if I have to throw you in. Understand?"

She did. The look in his eyes was fierce, piratical, somehow angry without hostility. Geoff meant every word, and Bess allowed herself to be led into the main bathroom, where he gently helped her lower herself into the enormous tub he had filled with water that felt like ice.

"It's nowhere near as cold as it feels to you," he said grimly. "Bloody hell, Bess, what do you Yanks use for brains? A complexion like yours and you haven't got the sense God gave a brown dog. I'd best get a doctor over here."

"Oh, no. Please, no. It's not as bad as it looks, honestly it isn't. I've done this before, as you can well imagine. And . . ."

Then she was choking and his fingers were like brands on her skin as he hoisted her dripping from the water, rushed her next door to the loo, and gently but firmly held her fevered forehead . . . the same forehead that should have been protected by an ugly hat brim. Slumped forward, anchored by Geoff's strong hand against her ribcage, Bess endured further humiliation as her stomach rebelled, again and again and again.

When she had nothing left, she sagged weakly against Geoff, who half-carried her back to the tub. Where she discovered through now-clear eyes that her camisole and panties were superfluous; could in fact have been nonexistent. Not that Geoff appeared to notice. He no sooner had her settled in the water than he asked if she could cope for a few moments, nodded at her acceptance, and stalked out of the bathroom. Moments later she could hear his voice on the phone, and felt even more mortified when she realized he was seeking advice from Ida. He made another call, this one in a harsh, direct, no-nonsense voice, and then he was with her once again.

"Doctor!" And his expression dared her to refuse.

"It isn't necessary!" Bess didn't know if she was lying or not, but having voided her stomach she knew the rest was only sunburn, and that it would pass, could be dealt with. What she wanted most just now was for this man to leave her alone and to stop looking at her as if she was some sort of foreign object floating in his tub.

Because there was no sign of interest or lust in Geoff's eyes. She could see only sadness and compassion. And anger. His gaze traversed her modest breasts and the tuft of auburn between her thighs as if they didn't exist, had no relevance. But when he looked at the blotchy sunburn on her shoulders and legs, she fancied she could see her pain in his eyes.

A ringing of the doorbell interrupted his survey of her shame, and he excused himself and went to answer it. Excused himself! Bess could hardly credit her own reactions . . . one moment the man she loved was observing her almost naked body without a hint of interest, and the next he was excusing himself as if they were residents of some luxurious drawing room.

She looked down and saw, for the first time, how such a thing could be possible. What a mess she was in, and her sunburned body was far from the worst element of it. The man she loved! The thought echoed through her mind like a funeral dirge, which in a way it was. She could accept her love for Geoff, but nothing beyond that, she knew, could ever work. She was damaged goods, and he deserved better, even if she dared to assume he might return her feelings. She would never be any good to a man like Geoff. He needed totality, a woman complete in every respect, who could walk through life beside him and hold her head high with the pride he deserved. And she wasn't that person, could never be.

"I don't think you're going to like this much," he said as he strode back into the room, hands and arms filled with bags of . . .

Ice! She didn't, couldn't, believe it, until the first shards bounced off her reddened skin like sparks as Geoff dumped one bag of ice into the tub. She shrank from it as if the ice was blood in the water.

Geoff ignored her, opened another bag, and dumped. "If you're too damned stubborn to have the doctor, which you might well get anyway, damn it, then you'll have to live with this. We're going to cool you down and then, my dear possum, you're going to get carted off to bed and drowned in anti-sunburn cream. And by all that's holy, if you're not one helluva lot better come morning, it's the doctor's office or the hospital for you and no room for arguments. Now, move back a bit."

Bess obeyed, all too aware of the way the move thrust her breasts inside her loosened camisole above the scanty protection of the water, but also aware that Geoff wasn't looking, didn't notice, or didn't care.

He left the bathroom and returned with a thermometer, which he waved in front of her face, demanding that she open her mouth and accept it. By now her teeth were chattering so hard she could only shake her head from side to side.

"Just do it, Bess," he said. "And stop trying to look modest because I can tell you with certainty that if you are blushing, it sure as hell doesn't show through the sunburn. Besides, if you don't mind me saying so, you're about as appetizing as a scalded cat. So just put this damned thermometer under your tongue and stop playing silly buggers, okay?"

He persisted long beyond what Bess thought was reasonable, alternately adding ice to the bath and taking her temperature until he'd reached some compromise he didn't bother to explain.

"Right. Up and out of there. Time now for the fun part," he said.

Leading the way to her room, he removed her sopping-wet camisole and stripped back the covers on the bed.

"Face down first, I guess," he said. "And then, if you're a very good, very cooperative young lady, I'll let you put this goop on the front of you all by yourself."

Again, Bess obeyed. Not that she had much choice. And she was no sooner flat on her face then she could feel Geoff's fingers slathering some sort of cream along the nape of her neck. Within moments she was almost purring. Geoff had hands that would have put a professional masseur out of business. He slowly and gently worked the ointment into her shoulders, then down the nubbly line of her spine and out to the sides in strokes that felt like feather touches against her inflamed skin. Somehow, the treacherous sun had sneaked inside the loose cotton of her "prim" camisole. And if she hadn't been so vain, she'd have tied the bodice ribbons tighter. Or worn a different, more modest, more functional top.

Geoff worked his way down her back, seeming to take an inordinate amount of time at the tender dimples above her buttocks, his touch somehow managing to work the ointment not just into her skin, but right through the center of her body. She felt her insides begin to melt, felt a fire totally different from the sunburn flaring up from long-dead coals inside her.

She sighed, heard herself sigh. Purred, heard herself purr. Felt her body stretch like that of a thoroughly satisfied cat. Heard Geoff's voice in her mind . . . *appetizing as a scalded cat* . . . and stopped stretching, stopped purring, went rigid against his fingers, which paused, but only for an instant.

Moving to the back of her legs, he worked his way up first one, then the other, gently smoothing in the sunburn cream as his fingers worked other magic on Bess herself. When he touched the sensitive skin at the backs of her knees, she felt her insides go all mushy again, felt herself almost doing a Lady wriggle. And when he reached the top of her thighs, his fingertips only a millimeter from the questionable protection of her panties, Bess had to forcibly demand that her body remain still so she wouldn't reveal the effect he was having on her.

"Right. That's my part of it done," he said. "Assuming, of course, that you're sure you can manage the front by yourself. And that you promise me faithfully to do it, and do it now, no drifting off to sleep before you've got this stuff worked into every place it's needed."

She nodded, knowing that her eyes that had gone somnolent and sleepy at the very mention of the word. And at the pleasure, the sheer bliss of his touch.

"See that you do. I'm going down to beat that bloody traitorous dog within an inch of her young life, and if I come back and find you asleep without having put on heaps and heaps of this cream, you'll get the same treatment. You won't want tucker, darling, not the way you're feeling. But Lady does, although the fickle wee bitch doesn't deserve it." His grin belied the gruesome aspect of his words; he wasn't really upset with the dog and both of them knew it. "I'll look in on you later, and in the morning I'll give you a decent brekkie if you feel up to it."

And he was gone, the door closing softly behind him.

Bess slathered the front of her body with his magic antisunburn potion, then sprawled on the bed, arms and legs spread out to allow as much heat as possible to dissipate from skin already forgetting the coolness of the bath. Lay there, staring up at the ceiling as the room seemed to revolve around her, spinning her toward sleep that she feared to approach because of the dreams she knew would be inevitable. She tried closing her eyes, had to open them again to defeat the nausea that seemed to surge up out of the darkness, and finally just let herself drift, her mind no longer either awake or asleep, nor caring or even aware . . .

Idly, she lifted one hand to touch at her breasts, then moved it lower to trace designs across the now-dry satin of her panties, feeling the simmering inside her as it threatened to erupt, to join the fire that raced across her skin. A fire left over from Geoff's fingers. She knew it without having to think about it, wasn't thinking anyway, merely drifting in a half-awake, dreamlike fantasy as the ceiling slowly spun before her eyes.

Was she spinning?

Or the bed?

Her hand slid beneath the satiny fabric to even smoother skin, and she closed her eyes and allowed her fingers to roam at will, fueling the flames inside her, sending tendrils of ecstasy racing through her already over-heated blood. Eventually, she fell into a deep slumber as fantasy gave way to proper dreams.

Geoff peered into the room some hours later and raised an eyebrow as he took in Bess's position on the bed. In spite of the provocative position of her hand, she looked like a collapsed puppet, uncoordinated, disjointed. And soon, despite the fire beneath her skin, she'd be cold . . . the night air had already cooled the room. He shook his head and very gently laid the sheet over her drowsing figure. Then he returned to his office and began to work on the latest spicy scene for "The Deflowerization of Kate." No. What had Bess decided to call their book? The Flower of something . . . Ballarat? Bloody hell! Maybe he should change the title to "The Sunburned Flower of Ballarat."

It came as a surprise to him, although he later wondered why it should have, that the scenario sprang to life almost full-grown, and he knew without question that Bess would have difficulty describing his spicy scenes as staid and Victorian.

CHAPTER ELEVEN

Ida stormed in the next morning as Bess was glumly staring at a platter of bacon and eggs. The slender blonde wore ragged jeans and a sweatshirt that had clearly seen better days. Her face was shiny, devoid of makeup, and her hair lacked some of its usual perfection. Yet she still managed to exude an air of profound sexuality, along with a sense of discipline and command.

Geoff was instantly banished to his office, just before Ida poured herself a cup of coffee and straddled a chair across the table from Bess.

"Bloody oath, Colorado, you don't do things by halves, do you? I suppose it never occurred to you that you could get Geoffrey's attention without going to these extremes."

"It was a desperate ploy," she said, striving for humor and wondering if she sounded as mirthless as she felt. "I can't write the words 'Dammit, Geoff, focus on me' while I'm editing our book. Even if I could, it wouldn't be as effective as looking like a cooked lobster and puking my guts out in the loo."

"Or is that part of the plan?" Ida said, ignoring Bess's attempt at wit, and her sour mood. "Get him in a situation where he can touch you, but only under very specific circumstances? On the other hand, you're not going to be feeling terribly romantic for a fair old while, or at least not in any position to do much about it."

Which finally drew a grin from Bess, who had wakened

feeling as if her skin had turned to some brittle form of armor. Who had clambered from the bed with all the alacrity of a geriatric tortoise. Who had staggered into the bathroom to throw water into a face that stared back at her from pain-filled, haunted eyes. Truthfully, she had only fragmented memories of the evening before, of Geoff's hands manipulating her body, manipulating sunburn lotion into places she could hardly believe he had touched.

Within minutes she was being shepherded upstairs to her room and ordered to get her gear off so a proper inspection could be made of the damage, and so direct and casual was Ida about issuing the orders that Bess never so much as thought to argue.

"Ooooh," said Ida when Bess slipped off the silky wrap which had been all she could bear to put against her skin this morning. "Ooooh, darling, normally you'd get no sympathy from me for self-inflicted wounds, but I've been there myself and I know only too well how you feel. Happily, I also have a magic remedy that will make it at least bearable, I hope. But first, I think, a quick bath. Okay? You wouldn't be able to stand a shower, so it's back to the tub. I'll slip down and get another cup of coffee. Shout for me when you're done and I'll smooth some of this stuff on the parts you can't reach. Of course, Geoffrey will have to continue the treatment over the next few days. Not that I expect you'll mind, but after what you put him through last night I think the poor, brave lad needs a day to recover."

Feeling like a scalded cat again, Bess ran a tepid bath, but stayed in it only long enough to very gently wash away whatever potion Geoff had applied the night before and cool herself down in the process. Then she shouted for Ida, who bounded up the stairs with a huge, unidentifiable bottle in her hand.

"Don't ask me what this is, Colorado, because I don't know, don't want to know, and wouldn't tell you if I did know because I'd be too busy trying to get the patent rights. Now, assume the position, as they say in all the best cop shows, or lie down. And don't fret. I'll let you do your own front, just like I assume Geoffrey did last night. The difference is that I won't mind."

Whatever was in the potion, Bess could feel the effects almost immediately.

Then, rising and twisting her face to one side, she could see that the angry crimson color had faded from the backs of her legs.

"Right," said Ida. "The rest is up to you. And when you're done, I suggest you put on something that's pure cotton. That silky stuff may feel cool, but it isn't. I'll go boil the jug again, although you really ought to stick to water for a day or so."

"Water? My God, Ida, Geoff was right about you. You really are a woman of stone. Keeping me from my caffeine is about as mean a thing as I can imagine."

"On your head be it. Speaking of which, how is your head this morning? You seem okay to me, but are you dead set positive you didn't get a touch of sunstroke along with the rest?"

Bess shook her head, and immediately regretted it because it sent the ends of her hair flying across her shoulders like a cat'o'nine tails, each individual hair whipping the sunburn with a signature of its own.

When she returned to the kitchen, she found that Ida had eaten all the bacon and half the eggs. Nor was she looking one whit guilty about it.

"Liquids, all you can manage for the next few days," she said. "Send the boy out for some of those liquid breakfast things that athletes advertise and lazy buggers actually drink.

Lots of good stuff in them, even if they don't give you enough bulk. I'd advise meusli for that, instead of this decadent rubbish. I cannot imagine what Geoffrey was thinking of, but he's only a boy, after all."

To which Bess had to grin. Despite her knowledge to the contrary, Ida seemed more like a mother than a former or current lover. Rocky . . . woman of stone . . . user and abuser . . . all probably true in their way, and yet Bess found her almost a soul mate, without understanding why.

Geoff stayed in his office even after Ida had gone, and it wasn't until lunch time that he emerged, declaring himself to be starving and wondering if Bess dared brave the world outside because he'd already cooked once that day and wasn't in the mood to do any more *chef a cuisine*.

"Especially for someone who won't even eat it," he added, softening the complaint with a slow smile. Then he glanced at his watch and muttered a curse.

"Are you late for another business meeting?" Bess knew she shouldn't ask, but her mouth seemed to have become unhinged. "Just what exactly do you do at all those meetings?"

"Earn a living, my dear child."

"Yes, okay, but how?" A sudden thought occurred. Inside the seafood restaurant Ida had mentioned something about gangsters from the Big Smoke, and laundering money. Could Geoff be involved in drug trafficking? What kind of drugs? On all the best cop shows, as Ida would say, the drug of choice seemed to be angel dust, or heroin, or ecstasy, or . . . damn, she was letting her imagination run away with her. And yet Geoff still hadn't answered her question.

"With all due respect," he finally said, "my business interests wouldn't concern you."

"Au contraire, Barrett. I was once personal secretary to a

ruthless business tycoon. In fact, he's called War . . ." She paused to cough behind her hand, once again reminding herself that she didn't want to talk about her father. "Warhorse, that's what he's called. Because he dabbles in politics," she finished lamely.

"My, my, waitress and personal-tycoon scribe. What haven't you done?"

"I haven't played professional assassin for a crime syndicate, at least not yet. However, if they put out a contract on a certain smug Aussie, I might reconsider. Honestly, Geoff, did you think I evolved from my mother's womb a full-fledged romance author? Now, please tell me why you were cursing at your poor watch."

He thrust the undoubtedly offensive object under her nose, but all she could see were numbers and a date and the fact that his arm was beautifully bronzed. Sure, she thought, he bronzed while she scalded.

"Isn't it working?" she asked, guessing that his ire had been directed toward a defective product, knowing how he felt because she had several Mickey Mouse watches that were inoperable. In fact, Mickey seemed to die the day his warranty ran out. She'd tried Minnie Mouse because women tended to live longer than men, but Minnie had only ticked for two additional weeks, following her warranty date.

"It's working all too well," Geoff said. "Look at the bloody date! We have to go and we have to go now. The Deloraine Craft Fair is on this weekend. It's the finest craft fair in Australia, probably in the southern hemisphere."

"But . . ."

"No buts about it. You may be one of the walking wounded, but you simply can't miss this. And if we wait until tomorrow they'll be starting to pack up and all the best stuff will be sold. Damn, we should have gone on Friday, but I forgot about it entirely. And yesterday we had to watch Lady mess up at the dog trials."

He insisted she looked perfectly fine as she was, in a light cotton blouse and turquoise harem slacks, studded down the sides with fake jewels. The turquoise shade highlighted her eyes, he said, while the fake rubies paid tribute to her sunburn. Bess contemplated a career as professional assassin again, especially when she flinched at the task of sliding her feet into sandals and heard him laugh.

Less than an hour later they were parking amongst hundreds of other vehicles outside the community sports complex at Deloraine, a small community to the west of Launceston. Here, each year, the local service clubs combined to stage what had, according to Geoff, become the major craft fair in Tasmania, if not the entire country.

"And the really good part of it is how they organize things," he had explained as they drove. "You pay at whatever venue you can find parking near, and then go from venue to venue on a free bus service, getting off when and where you like, picking up the bus again when you're ready. I usually walk most of the way; it isn't that big a town, after all. But today we'll use the bus because the less you see of the sun the better, I expect."

And he made sure she saw as little of it as possible, not least by insisting on spending what was, to Bess, an outrageous price for a hand-painted pure silk parasol, displayed at the first exhibits venue they approached. It matched her eyes exactly, and set off the clothes she had on to absolute perfection. That was Geoff's excuse for buying it, and he refused to be dissuaded.

Bess accepted under protest, but not too much protest, because she had fallen in love with it at first sight herself. Besides, it gave her something to do with her free hand while the other held the purse she dared not rest by its strap on either shoulder. The alternative had been to find, as she had in City Park, that Geoff just naturally took her hand whenever the opportunity arose, and the effect it had upon her was discomfiting.

Geoff put up with this state of affairs for a while without comment or any attitude that suggested he didn't appreciate the shield he had, himself, provided, then got round it by carrying the parasol whenever it wasn't needed. Bess was outwardly wary but secretly pleased, and hid her own smiles of pleasure each time her small hand disappeared into the grip of his much larger one.

They spent the entire afternoon wandering the various venues, discovering a vast similarity of taste as they viewed woodwork and wood carving, paintings and pottery, and a variety of other crafts that ranged through the entire spectrum of creativity. Their only disagreement, in fact, rose from Geoff's insistence that he would buy her something to remember Tasmania by, something uniquely Tasmanian and unique in and of itself. Which to Bess's eye meant only one thing . . . expensive. And this she was determined to avoid. The parasol alone was too much in her eyes. She also silently confessed that she didn't want something to remember Tasmania by, since that would be an admission that this was, after all, merely a working holiday that would all too soon come to an end.

Her three-month visitor's visa meant that she must return to Colorado, but it was a prospect she didn't want to face up to or even think about until time forced that upon her. And her apprehension was not eased by the fact that Geoff wanted to buy a piece of jewelry and kept insisting she try on rings. He avoided the inevitable junk jewelry stalls, and seemed to know with instinctive certainty which were exhibits by good

166

local crafts people. He also knew, she quickly found, what he liked and what he didn't.

The only saving grace was that he appeared to be in no great hurry about buying anything. They wandered through every venue, some fifteen or sixteen in all, Geoff taking his time and, Bess suddenly realized, protecting her from undue bumps and scrapes when they were negotiating the crowds. He used his own bulk to ensure—or at least try to—that nobody pushed against her in the crush at some of the most popular exhibits, and especially when they walked along the seriously crowded streets.

And he held her hand whenever it could be managed. And she loved it, though she dared not show it, much less tell him so. There was such a feeling of security, or being wanted, in the way he seemed to gather her into his own aura. At one point, as emotions overwhelmed her, she had to excuse herself and visit the loo, just so she could release a tear or three.

He fed her. There was nothing all that fancy to be had at the various venues, but, remembering Ida's advice, she drank great quantities of herbal tea and feasted on ice cream and a variety of fancy Tasmanian-made chocolates; so many sweet goodies that she was glad in the end to have missed breakfast.

Geoff ate hot dogs. Gleefully, he told Bess he had driven to Deloraine before dawn so that he could sell his perfidious Lady to the vender.

Eventually, however, they had exhausted the exhibitions and Bess herself, without any decision being made about her Tasmanian keepsake, and she professed her exhaustion in hopes she could replace Geoff's insistence with concern for her tiredness.

They returned to the Land Cruiser, which had been sitting in the hot sun long enough to demand that the air conditioning be turned on immediately, and Geoff was in fact backing out of his parking space when he muttered something to himself, drove back in again, and told Bess he had forgotten one thing he'd promised himself to buy.

"You stay here where it's relatively cool," he said. "I won't be long at all, because what I want is just inside the main pavilion." And he was gone before she had any chance to agree, disagree, or argue.

He told the truth, because he was back in what seemed only a very few minutes, clutching several large bottles, gaily wrapped, with stickers declaring them to be from the Lark Distillery. Bess remembered seeing the exhibit, and timidly tongue-tasting some of the exquisite bush liqueurs sold there.

"Can't go home without this stuff," Geoff explained. "I try to get some here every year, and from the distillery in Kingston, south of Hobart, whenever I run out. Absolutely splendid liqueurs, although in your condition you won't be finding that out for a bit. All you need is an overdose of grog on top of that sunburn."

"You're a spoilsport," she retorted, despite knowing he was right. Truth to tell, she wasn't much of a drinker in the first place, and could just imagine the effect a combination of liqueur and sunburn would have on her.

She was almost asleep in her seat when they finally got home, and more than glad there was no need to go out for dinner, or even cook up something. Half an hour later she was sprawled across her bed within three warm thoughts of being asleep, when Geoff's brisk knock at the door brought her bolt upright.

"You can argue until you're blue in the face, Bess, but I am going to renew your sunburn medicine if I have to sit on you to do it, so make up your mind how you want it done," he said when she attempted to stave off an experience she both feared and desired.

But this time Geoff's application of Ida's special remedy was vastly different from Bess's fragmented memories of the night before. Now his movements were almost brusque. His touch was as sure and indeed as gentle, but the attitude behind that touch had changed. He smeared the oily lotion across her back, even undid her bra strap to make it easier, but there was no sense of that wondrous, lethargic caress she thought she remembered. His hands on her legs were gentle, but they didn't linger near her crotch, didn't alter the pattern of their touch when they reached the hem of her panties.

His hands returned then to her back and shoulders, rubbing in excess vestiges of the oil, and suddenly she could feel the change, could feel it as surely as if his fingers were shooting sparks. His hands moved upward, cradling the nape of her neck, fingers gentle as a kiss along the soft and bony areas behind her ears.

Lying with her face half-turned toward the side of the bed where Geoff was kneeling, she felt her very bones go limp, felt again that strange softening in her tummy. And without thinking, half-opened her eyes to see that whatever was happening to Geoff, it didn't involve softness in the part of him she could see only too clearly. His groin throbbed, the fabric of his trousers straining against the evidence of his thoughts. And even as she saw that, she felt his touch begin to alter yet again, felt his fingers tremble as they moved away from her neck, back to her shoulders.

She heard him sigh, breathe deeply, then push himself back into control. Felt that control re-enter his fingers. Heard him sigh again as he lifted his hands from her, lifted himself from the edge of the bed.

"I'll leave you to deal with the rest," he said, and if there was really a tremble in his voice it was hidden in the terse way he spoke. "And thank you for coming with me today. It was a

169

wonderful time made even better because of your company."

She barely got out her own words of compliment about the afternoon before he was gone, the door closing silently behind him. No warning this time about making sure she applied lotion to her front, no promise of breakfast in the morning.

Just . . . gone. Except, he wasn't. His touch was still with her, lodged in her mind like a splinter.

She applied the lotion carefully and thoroughly, despite being so tired now she could barely keep her eyes open. Then she collapsed again on the bed and didn't wake until sunlight through the window brought her slowly up out of sleep, slowly up out of a dream she couldn't remember upon waking, but was certain had been exotic, erotic, and thoroughly pleasant.

When she joined Geoff in the kitchen, things were just as they had been several days before. He informed her it was her turn to prepare breakfast, which they both considered the only meal she was capable of cooking, and that only if it was cereal drowned in milk. He poured her coffee for her, made the usual small-talk over the morning Examiner and the news therein, then asked politely if she felt well enough to join him in the office so they could work on the book together.

"I'll just toss in a load of laundry and be right with you," she replied, and when she entered the office some few minutes later he was already staring at the computer screen, his fingers flying across the keyboard.

She slid into her own chair, then rolled herself so she could look over Geoff's right shoulder and watch his words as they emerged on the screen. It always seemed a magical process to her, even when the words were her own, but doubly so, for some reason, when they were his. He was a furious typist, often making errors and muttering insane and profane things when he had to go back and fix them.

Bess had originally found it amusing that while she dealt with errors by moving the cursor behind the letters and hitting the back-space key, Geoff did just the opposite. He moved the cursor ahead of the offending letter and used the delete key. Now she was so used to watching him do it, she hardly noticed unless he added vocal impetus to the process.

"Right," he said suddenly, lifting his hands away like those of a concert pianist. "We have to go back a fair bit to pick up where you and I left off the last time. Do you want to take over now, or would you prefer to stay where you are and shout your objections in my ear?"

"Oh, that, definitely," she said, catching his mood and falling into it. "It's a far better way to get my points across than making changes and then having to sit here and explain them all to you." Which gained her a savage grin as he turned to meet her eyes, only inches away.

"You're a hard taskmaster, Bess. There are times you make Ida look like a cream-puff by comparison, which is saying something, believe me."

"So what are you going to call me? Stony? I'll have to ask Ida if she can sing? We could tour together, call ourselves 'The Gravelettes.' "

Geoff's voice held gravel of its own as he scoffed, "More like The Rocky Horror Show," then ducked in an exaggerated motion as she pretended to try and knock his head off. "But you never told me you sing, Bess. Do you? In tune and all that?" He didn't wait for a reply, just kept on speaking. "So what sort of stuff do you sing? And when are you going to sing for me? I'd quite like that, I think. I've never had a girl sing just for me . . . to me."

"Believe it or not, I was once a singing waitress. But I haven't sung many Australian songs, Geoff, except for

'Waltzing Matilda,' which everybody knows."

"They won't in another generation," he said with surprising bitterness. "Bloody politicians and their political correctness. Go anywhere in the world and people recognize 'Waltzing Matilda' and react to it with great good pleasure. Half the people here in Australia don't know the words to 'Advance Australia Fair,' and don't care anyway, but they all know 'Waltzing Matilda,' chapter and verse." Then he paused and gave Bess a lop-sided smile. "Bloody hell. What brought that on? I thought I'd climbed down off that hobbyhorse years ago."

"It's obviously something you feel very passionate about," she said without trying to provoke him further. She'd been able to feel his anger; it had radiated from him like the heat from a fire, almost frightening in its intensity and passion.

"Yes, well, it's my long-held philosophy that there is nothing in this world so perfect that it can't be totally buggered up by a little political intervention."

"I totally agree," she said, thinking of her father's political connections. "Now, why don't you scroll back to where we left off so we can actually get something constructive done today?"

Soon she and Geoff were back to their usual arguing and bickering like children over this word or that, this phrasing or that, and the seemingly endless differences between Australian and American spelling and word usage. Then they came to the first of their heroine Kate's erotic adventures on Australian soil, and Bess suddenly found it difficult to breathe. It was as if the room had shrunk, become airless, and she felt her throat constrict as if she were choking.

Because this scenario was absolutely nothing like the ones she had criticized and chided him over, earlier in the book. This scenario was dynamite!

It began from the point of view of Kate's soon-to-be lover, being tended by Kate after a flogging he'd earned while protecting her from another member of the crew. And in some ways, Bess thought, it mirrored how Geoff might have felt if she had treated his sunburn rather than the other way around. He must have written it after she'd fallen asleep night before last because it was all about touch, about gentleness. Yet it also included the hero's frankly male physical reactions, which Geoff had then subtly twisted until suddenly the reader was in the heroine's mind, Kate's mind, feeling not what she felt, seeing not what she saw, but totally, intimately aware; a part of what she wanted to feel and see. The touch of her lover's fingers on her body, everywhere on her body, and in it. The feel of his breath against her breasts, against the round softness of her tummy, the furry center of her womanhood. And the touch of their bodies as they joined, still in Kate's mind, but so physically exquisite in the writing that the reader would have no doubts, could only join and indulge in the raw power of the scenario.

Bess neared the end and found herself reacting as she knew the reader would react—assuming they could push this past whatever editor had to deal with it. Kate had retired to her narrow, primitive bed and lay there, lost in the mysteries of the love she thought she felt and the physicality that threatened to devour her. Lay there, fully clothed, as would have been the situation in that era. A callused hand, driven by Kate's own fantasy, traveled up beneath her skirt, fingers moving in a slow, sensual dance that ended, eventually, in Kate finding physical release. And soon after, the release of sleep, much needed sleep if she was to survive the rigors of the days ahead.

Bess read through it as if in a trance, half her mind thrilling to the beauty of the writing, the sheer eroticism so brilliantly constructed. But the other half of her mind was in shock, suddenly frighteningly afraid that Geoff had somehow learned to invade her dreams, for where else could he have found this sort of overall inspiration? Certainly it hadn't been in him a few days earlier, when his attempts at such intimate writing had been clumsy at best and masculinely inept at worst.

"Are you all right, Bess?"

Geoff's voice penetrated the fog of her thinking, but she knew somehow that the question she'd just heard was not his first. He had asked it at least once before, and she must have replied, but this time her mind had been too numbed.

"Yes. I . . . I'm fine," she finally managed. Lying, because she definitely was not fine, was not even close to fine. And then she couldn't take any more, didn't dare stay here in this claustrophobic situation with herself, much less with Geoff. "I . . . you'll have to excuse me. I must have overdone it more yesterday than I thought. I've got to go now. Sorry."

She fled to her room, both her body and mind in a turmoil such as she had never imagined possible. If Geoff could decipher her dreams, maybe Mouse was right. Maybe Geoffrey Barrett was Lucifer.

CHAPTER TWELVE

Tuesday morning gave Bess the excuse she wanted to get away from the house, away from Geoff, away from the book, away from everything.

She decided she'd seek the relative asylum of the library, because if Geoff's approach to the historic accuracy of their book did nothing else, it presented her with a valid excuse.

Every time they got into "Flower of Ballarat's" history part, umpteen levels of research emerged like soldier ants from the framework of the story, and Geoff's approach tended to drive Bess into fits of fury.

"I thought it was my job to nit-pick," she had cried earlier this morning, barely shifting into gear after two cups of coffee, only to find him making lists of things that still needed checking. "I swear you'd test the patience of a saint, Geoffrey Barrett. How did you ever get your other books written? You spend so much time checking out obscure references, I'm surprised you had time to write. Do you honestly think your readers care what color neckwear some totally irrelevant character wore when your fictional . . . fictional, damn it! . . . ship was attacked by pirates?"

"I care. And how do I know if it's relevant until it's been checked?"

Bess had no choice but to stifle her temper and apologize. She was a professional too, and she agreed with the old journalistic edict that you might use one percent of a given set of facts, but you had to know one hundred percent in order to use it right.

And today she was actually pleased that his research demands had given her the reason she so desperately needed to get out of the house. Absent, so to speak, from the pattern Geoff had established. Looking at her when he thought she wouldn't notice. Sighing to himself when he thought he'd gotten away with it.

Brow beetled, Bess trudged down St. John Street, only half aware of the passing vehicles and pedestrian traffic. Yesterday had been little short of torture for her. Her sunburn, combined with the incredible sensitivity she felt whenever Geoff so much as looked at her, was just too much to endure.

Today she had opted for cotton shorts and a light cotton tee-shirt as being the least abrasive on her still-tender skin. The shirt boasted the words SISTERS IN CRIME, an organization Bess supported with pride, even though she wrote romances. Through Sisters in Crime, she'd met a local Colorado Springs author named Denise Dietz; a woman who not only resembled Bess physically, but who had managed to successfully survive some serious angst of her own.

Hadn't Denise hooked up with an Australian for the purpose of co-authorship? Yes. Bess remembered a post Denise had sent to their Novelists Inc. authors' loop: " 'Tis a collaboration made in heaven and hell."

So how would Denise-the-mystery-author handle this present situation?

Bess could have e-mailed her friend, just to chat, perhaps commiserate, only she'd never memorized . . . or written down . . . Denise's E-mail address, which included the name of one of her book characters. Ellie? Ingrid? Calliope?

Left to her own devices, Bess was about half sure she would simply grab a cab to the airport and flee. Flee

Launceston, flee Tasmania, flee Geoff, flee her own confusion and torment. But that would go with her no matter where she landed, and she knew it. Furthermore, her professional ethics wouldn't let her run. She'd taken Geoff's money, or at least accepted him paying for her trip, which was the same thing. And now she had almost two full months in which to make good her part of the bargain. Except that her part of the bargain had become iffy. The erotic scene he'd written was so much better than anything she could even imagine doing herself, she honestly felt her inclusion as imported expert on the sensual elements of their book was little more than a devilish jest.

"Maybe the whole damned thing is a joke of some kind," she heard herself saying aloud, and looked around to see if anyone was listening. But she was starting to feel exactly that, despite the fact it didn't make much sense. Certainly she had something to offer; her knowledge of American history and speech patterns. And she had to admit that in those places where their collaboration had worked best, the writing fairly flew. It was good writing too, better than either of them could have done alone. Or was it?

That question continued to plague her during three fruitless hours in the library. She managed to find most of what Geoff had demanded, but none of her own needs were fulfilled because of the American specifications. Finally, frustrated to the point of being angry, she took stock and realized that hunger and thirst were destroying her logic.

So she marched to the nearest place she could remember that would provide a decent lunch and a blessed beer, and having got both she perched at a seat near the window, where she could watch the human traffic pass by. Which was something she usually enjoyed, until one pedestrian—this one inside the pub—managed to lurch against her table, spilling most of her beer into the remains of her nachos.

"I'm sorry," said an unfamiliar voice from an unfamiliar face. "My fault entirely. Dicky ankle, I'm afraid. You must let me get you another beer. Draft, was it? Or something else?"

"No, please, don't bother." Bess might as well have spoken to the wall. The tall stranger wouldn't accept no for an answer. He insisted on getting her another beer, even a new lunch.

"I was all done with my nachos, but I guess a beer would be okay," she said, hoping this wasn't some pick-up situation. And was quietly pleased when the man brought her a new glass of beer, repeated his apology, then hobbled off to sit halfway across the tavern with his back to her.

She resumed her people-watching, sipping at the new beer as she did so and wondering what sort of draft he might have ordered for her. Not the same one she'd started with, that much was obvious. It was lighter in color than the dark Australian beers she'd come to enjoy, and it had a flavor that paled by comparison.

Ah well, more important things to worry about, she thought. Like returning to the library for another session. She tossed back the rest of the glass, took a final look out the window, and leaned down to pick up her handbag.

And was falling into the handbag, bonelessly, helplessly, when she half-heard the stranger's voice saying something about too much sun, too many beers, and her husband being on his way. "There he is now," Bess heard, just before her ears stopped working.

"Now was that slick, or was that slick?"

His hobbling gait gone, slouched in the back of the hire car with an unconscious Bess cradled against his shoulder, the second of the Sydney standover merchants smiled in appreciation of his own talents. It was, in fact, the first time since his arrival in Launceston that he didn't feel as if a bomb was about to go off.

The driver growled approval without bothering to look over his shoulder. "Better than slick," he finally said. "You got her out of there so smooth I doubt anyone will remember you, or her, an hour from now. Except maybe for the color of her hair. Damn, she's a looker. Pity Coolidge is being so hard-nosed about her not being put to use while we've got her."

"Since when did you start listening to Coolidge? I thought you hated his guts."

"I do. But I got him on the cell phone while you were staging the lift, and our fee just doubled. So let's be nice to him, for now."

"Fine with me. What about Rossiter? Weren't we supposed to take care of him before we got into this?"

The driver shrugged. "Don't worry, Rossiter will get his. Fact is, we're supposed to slide by and collect him on our way to the place you organized. Where is it again? Deloraine?"

"North of there a bit. Perfect for this. Not a neighbor in sight or sound, no likelihood of visitors, council inspectors, or anything else. Just a nice, quiet little hobby farm hidden away in the bushes. Couldn't be better."

"For you, maybe. I'd be happier if it was right here in town somewhere. But it's tough in a pissy little town this size. Every bastard knows every other bastard, or they're related. I'll be glad to get back to the Smoke, I can tell you that."

"Yair, me too. And will you slow down? We've got all the time in the world. She won't come good for a couple of hours yet, and all we have to do is collect Rossiter. 'Ent that what you said?"

The driver nodded. "In the casino parking lot. No worries

about being noticed. We'll hardly have to slow down."

"Fair enough, but what the hell are we gonna do with him? He's a big bugger, and rough as guts."

"If the two of us can't handle him, big or not, we should be looking for jobs as barmaids." Pausing for a traffic light, the driver turned and gazed at Bess. "Bloody oath," he said, the words half growl, half sigh. "Just look at those legs, would you? Even with that sunburn, I'll bet it would be fun to get between them."

"The sunburn's her problem," said his companion, reaching for his groin in a gesture deliberately made crude by the smirk on his lips. "Here's my problem, and the sooner we sort out Rossiter, the sooner I can get it fixed."

"Not bloody likely," said the driver, erasing the smirk so quickly it might not have existed. "Sorry, Davo, but this sheila's not for you. Or me either, come to think on it. Coolidge probably wants her first."

"Bugger that for a joke. We'd have to show him how."

"No, Davo, at his prices he's entitled. That's why we're back to plan A, with Rossiter along to keep an eye on her. We'll get our turn with him right enough, but Coolidge wants them both kept sweet in the meantime. Seems Rossiter knows something Coolidge don't. And the girl might, too. Anyway, it's hands off for now, so don't give me any problems on that score."

There was no time for further argument as the hire car swerved into the driveway of the casino and slowed long enough for the rumpled figure of Tom Rossiter to slide into the front passenger seat.

"She okay?" The words emerged from Rossiter's lips before he had the door closed, and the look in his pale, washed-out eyes made it clear there could be only one answer he wanted to hear.

"Right as rain," was the reply from the back. "She'll be out of it for at least another hour and a bit, and maybe half an hour after that, before she knows what day it is, much less what's going on."

"Right," said Rossiter. "Then let's get wherever the hell we're going. I don't want her to see I'm involved in this so we need to get her secured. Then we can sort out with Coolidge exactly how he wants to handle the rest."

That remark drew a snicker from Davo, but since Rossiter didn't know the reason for it, he merely shot a filthy glance over his shoulder and said nothing. The rest of the journey was made in silence, out along the Bass Highway, a quick swerve through Deloraine, then north along the river to the isolated hobby farm.

Bess was removed from the vehicle, carried by Tom Rossiter as lightly as if she'd been an infant, and placed on the cot in what must originally have been the farm house laundry. Tom noted with satisfaction that the small building had running water, a toilet, a door that locked from the outside, and no windows.

"She'll be comfy enough in here," he said, glaring around the small room as if to warn off any unseen danger. He carefully spread a car rug over the girl's recumbent form, made sure there was a small mug of water available for her awakening, then followed the others outside and watched as the door was locked.

"So how does it play?" the chief of the Sydney crew asked, as he sprawled in the lounge room and gestured for his companion to bring some grog.

"We wait for Coolidge. He's got some tricky scheme all worked out that should have this wrapped up in just a day or so." Rossiter absently reached for the beer being offered to him. "Coolidge should be here pretty soon, along with

181

Rambo. Until then we just wait."

"Too bad we didn't grab her when she was with that blonde sheila," Davo said, almost talking to himself. "Least we'd have the blonde to amuse ourselves with while we waited." His caw of laughter filled the room as he shot a glance at his companion, known . . . only half in jest . . . as Jack the Ripper.

"Too right," Jack growled. "But I suppose we could make do with what we've already got. What did Coolidge say to you about that, Rossiter? Still a case of don't mess with the merchandise?"

Tom Rossiter's reply was explosive, considering he neither moved, nor seemed to stiffen, nor raised his voice. The explosion was mental, almost psychic, and intense. "Your call, friend," he said, his voice almost a whisper. "Guess it depends on whether you want salt on your sausage when I feed it to you. Of course I only offer you that choice because you seem to be in charge. Your sidekick here would have to take his without seasoning." Then he turned to look at the lesser of the Sydney duo, and his eyes were death personified.

"Easy, mate." Jack spoke to both men, but his eyes never left those of Rossiter, who had turned again to concentrate on him. The tension in the air, enough to warm the beer, faded at the sound of an approaching vehicle. "That'll be Coolidge. So let's just settle, okay? There's a lot of money riding on this."

Coolidge entered the modest farmhouse and glanced around with a sneer on his lips that suggested he might have to lower his fastidious standards. Behind him, bent almost double under a load of electronic gear, stood Coolidge's favorite bootlicker and computer expert. Rossiter thought Rambo looked as if he was desperately searching for a way to pick at the scars on his face and carry his equipment at the same time.

Brushing away the proffered beer, Coolidge sat himself in the cleanest of the easy chairs, then ran an appraising eye over the assembled crew. "It obviously went all right. Is it safe to talk here? The girl is . . ."

"Still out cold, and locked in that old laundry out back," Jack said. "She can't hear anything, can't see anything, and will be there whenever we want her."

"Good. So how about you and your mate take a little stroll in the fresh country air? Because I need some private words with Mr. Rossiter here."

Coolidge waited until both men could be seen from the open window, walking cautiously through the farm yard. Then he turned to Rossiter. "All right, Tom, let's go back to the beginning of all this. Rambo can get his gear set up while we talk, but I want to know everything there is to know about your mission here before we make a move toward contacting Barrett."

Rossiter patiently ran through his discussions with Cornwall, his search for Elizabeth in Colorado, and his subsequent trip to Australia with instructions to return her to New York and her father's control.

"Okay, but what's the Englishman got to do with it?"

"I haven't the faintest idea, Gerry. Like I told you before, it sounds as if the old man is trying to sell her into some sort of corporate marriage or something. Makes no sense to me."

"Me, either. Elizabeth would never agree to that, and even with all his pull, Cornwall can't make her attend a marriage ceremony. I mean, she can't very well accept a wedding band and say 'I do' if her arms are bound and her mouth is taped. What the hell does he have to bargain with?"

"How should I know, Gerry? The old man doesn't go

around explaining his decisions to me. Or to you either, I imagine. But I'll say this. He's getting nuttier every day."

"I suppose you don't know anything much about this business with Barrett, either?"

"Only what you do. Barrett has the controlling interest in Tascalypt Enterprises Limited, whatever the hell that is. Something to do with essential oils of some kind. Anyway, the old man has been trying to pry it loose from Barrett for nearly three years now, and he's getting damned sick of waiting."

"Damn it, Tom, even I know that much. But why does the old man want it? That's what I can't figure. I've had all Barrett's business interests checked out six ways from Sunday, and this essential oils outfit doesn't make any money, never has made any money, and from what I've found, never will make any money. So why is Cornwall hell bent on obtaining the company?"

Rossiter slumped lower in his chair and sipped at the beer can buried in one huge hand. "I don't think you'll like the answer, Gerry," he finally said. "And I won't swear it to be true, either. But my take on this is that the old man just can't stand not having his own way. Simple as that. There was some very minor discovery by Barrett's outfit a few years ago, and that's when this all started. But as you say, there's no commercial, logical reason now. Except the old man thinks he's Howard Hughes, wants the damn company, and he's out to destroy anything or anybody that dares to challenge him."

"Figures. Don't get me wrong, Tom, I'm planning to crush Barrett. I just wish it made more sense. I thought maybe you knew something I didn't."

"What makes 'more sense' is to get this over with, collect our reward from the old man, and start hunting up a new job. Anyway, that's the way I see it."

"Will you take his daughter back to him, first?"

"Yup. Only thing is, I'm going to make it easy on her. I'll beg her, if that's what it takes, but none of this dragging her back by the hair. If that's what the old man wants, he can come do the job himself."

Coolidge stayed silent for a long moment, then glanced over at Rambo, who nodded that yes, he was ready to go.

"Okay, Tom," said Coolidge. "Here's how we do this. Rambo will send Barrett an E-mail through a blind shunt. Barrett won't be able to trace it back. We're going to tell him that we have his American visitor, and if he wants her back safe he has twenty-four hours to put all his shares of his oil company on the market. No ransom money, as such. No negotiations."

"And you've got it all organized to have those shares bought up in a series of blinds and double-blinds, so that when Cornwall finally gets them there won't be any way to tie him into this. Or us, either."

"Right. When we get our money, the old man gets his company. Are you happy with that?"

"Far as it goes. How can you be sure Barrett will check his E-mail today, or even this week? He starts getting worried about the girl not coming home for dinner and he mightn't check for days."

"He'll check, because once the message is sent we're going to phone him and tell him to check."

Rising to his feet, Coolidge walked over to where Bess's purse had been dumped on the kitchen bench. He casually rifled the contents, grimaced at a cell phone which he quickly pocketed, then grunted approval at whatever else he'd found.

"Perfect," he said. "Here's a list chock full of research data. My guess is that she visited the library. So we tell Barrett we lifted her from the library. If he still doesn't believe us, we read the list. That ought to be enough to kick-start him into doing what he's told." Once again, Coolidge looked around the room, his features expressing acute distaste. "Are you sure you've told me everything you know, Tom?"

"About what?" Rossiter's eyes narrowed. "Were you planning to keep Barrett's company all to yourself? Did you think it might be worth more than the old man's gratitude? Speaking of which, how do I collect my share of the money?"

"As soon as I get it, you get it, minus a cut for our Sydney friends. And I do apologize for keeping them on the job, Tom. I totally agree they're sewage, but I couldn't find any others who'd travel here on such short notice. In any case, I wouldn't cheat you out of your money because I want to live long enough to enjoy mine. So, is it okay to proceed with my plan?"

Rossiter sipped again at his beer, eyes on the floor. When he finally spoke, there was no uncertainty in his voice. "Okay. And in the meantime?"

"In the meantime, she stays where she is. We keep her well fed and watered. The Sydney crew can take care of that. And once this part of the job's done, you can take her straight to New York if you like. There's no sense delaying it, and no logic in returning her to Barrett just so we can go through all this trouble again. Does that work for you, Tom?"

"As long as I'm here to keep an eye on things. I wouldn't trust those Sydney thugs within ten feet of her, nor this little scumbag either." Rossiter nodded toward where Rambo stood with a set of headphones covering his ears.

"Oh, you'll be here," Coolidge said. "You can be sure of that!"

CHAPTER THIRTEEN

Geoff stood staring at the telephone receiver, holding it at arm's length and eyeing it as if it was a seven-foot tiger snake ready to strike. In the sudden silence following the brief message he'd just received, he could hear his own heart thumping like a frenzied jungle drum, and he had to fight for breath, fight even harder to maintain control.

"Go check your E-mails," the voice over the phone had said. "Then do what you're told and do it right, because your little American redhead is depending on you."

The subsequent closing of the connection had not been . . . as some vestigial element of Geoff's shocked brain kept insisting it should have been . . . a thunderclap. It had been worse, far worse. A subtle, hardly audible click that underscored in his mind the seriousness of what he'd just heard.

Go check your E-mails. It took him three tries just to get the proper icons on the screen, something he could normally do with his eyes closed. And when he picked out the message: SNATCH, Geoff almost wished he could keep his eyes closed. He didn't want to read it, couldn't not read it, and when he had, could only read it over and over and over again, the words pounding in his head as if being thumped in from the outside with a piece of 4×4 timber.

Geoffrey Barrett,
Your American house-guest is not, as you might surmise, at the library doing research. She is now aiding

us in our attempt to persuade you to co-operate in a certain business matter.

You will immediately call your broker and put on the market every single share you hold or control in Tascalypt Enterprises Limited.

Failure to do so will result in significant risk to your redhead's health and physical well-being. She is in good hands, but capable hands. Get the picture?

There is no need to reply to this message and no sense in attempting to trace it. So just do what you're told and your house-guest will thank you for it.

The rest of the E-mail included the library list Geoff had given Bess this morning.

With shaking fingers, he grabbed up the phone and punched in Ida's number.

Her advice was simple and to the point. "Just do it, Geoffrey darling. Do it now. Without explaining one damned thing to your broker. That might be very important later. And then stay there, because I'm on my way. Do you hear me, darling? Stay there! Is that clear? Do you promise?"

He promised, then began making the required telephone calls after having formulated the most likely excuse he could conjure up for his sudden decision. It griped him to ask close friends and business associates to follow his lead. They couldn't lose, really, but the principle irked.

It took him less than twenty minutes, all up, and another fifteen before Ida swept into the house, where he had been pacing like a caged animal.

"So it was you all along," she said without preamble or

greeting. "Damn, I should have known, or at least guessed."

"I don't give a damn who it was. I just want . . ." Whatever he'd meant to say next was cut off by the wave of one manicured fingernail before his eyes.

"What you want is miracles," Ida snapped. "Now, give it all to me again, right from the beginning, as close to word-for-word as you can remember."

He managed to struggle through that exercise, aided by the fact that his computer still had the words on the screen. Ida stood rock-still, and read the message as he spoke.

"Accent," she said brusquely.

"What? Oh, the phone. Australian. Not Queensland, not Adelaide, probably not Melbourne, definitely not Tasmanian. Rough voice, male, mature, and totally confident, which is what worries me the most."

"The Sydney crims who followed Bess and me."

Her statement was rhetorical, yet Geoff fought to make his memory cooperate, to over-ride the panic he felt growing up out of his guts. The man by the river had spoken only briefly, but hadn't his voice sounded similar?

"Yeah, Ida, likely," Geoff replied. "More than likely. Didn't Bess say she thought she recognized one of the crims?"

"Yes. Okay. Now to the tricky stuff. You want the coppers?"

"I want Bess back here safe and sound and unharmed; that's what I want." He was almost shouting, could feel his voice rising as his control began to slip. "If it takes cops, get cops. If it takes every bad bastard either of us knows or can find, get them. We have to do something, Ida, and I don't even know where to start."

"With a cuppa," she said, sadly shaking her blonde hair and staring at the floor as if unable or unwilling to meet his eyes.

189

Which frightened Geoff even worse than the phone call. Anything that could disrupt Ida's rock-hard veneer was terrifying, had to be terrifying.

"Please, Geoffrey," she continued, "just go and boil the jug, would you? I have to make some calls and you'll only distract me."

"Use your cell phone, then. I don't want this one here tied up."

Ida waved him away, toward the kitchen. Yammering into her cell phone, she hovering while he boiled the jug, threw in the tea bags, and somehow managed to get some cups down from the cabinet without dropping one.

She made one call, five, a dozen. Geoff lost count, couldn't keep track, and was hardly surprised. He felt as if he'd been kicked in the guts by a very big boot.

"Okay," she finally said, pointing to the kitchen table like some old-fashioned school marm insisting a recalcitrant pupil sit. "First off, the plan is simple but complicated. You put the shares on the market, and they go round and round until nobody can find them anymore, and then they pop up where, I assume, you didn't want them to be in the first place. No way of tracing that, not really. And no way to stick the eventual holder with any of this if you do find him. Right so far?"

"I don't have to find the bastard. I know who's behind this, even if, as you say, it may never be provable. But I know, Ida, and once we get Bess back I'll go to New York and have it out of his hide!"

"Never mind that right now. Bess is the only issue, and that's when the bad news comes up. No ransom note, no indication of when you get her back, or how, and no real guarantee, darling, which is what worries me the most. Also, there's probably no sense in trying to track down the source of that E-mail. It could be anywhere—"

"Mouse!"

Geoff roared the name so loudly that Ida almost dropped her cup, and before she could put it down on the table he was up and rushing for the office.

"We aren't going to get any more phone calls from them," he said, his voice strangely calm. It wasn't a question, really, yet he looked to Ida for confirmation. Once again, she somberly shook her head.

"Right then." And he was in his chair, fingers moving like lightening across the keyboard, no clumsiness now. He punched on the appropriate keys, found Mouse's E-mail address where Bess had—thank God!—stored it, and quickly typed in his own message above the one from the kidnappers.

"Bess lifted from library, see below. Business blackmail. Price paid. Can you trace the following? Now, damn it! Spare no expense, Mouse, but drop everything . . . EVERYTHING! . . . because she may be in danger and we are totally buggered."

Geoff hit the send command, then cursed and called back the message long enough to add in his telephone number and Ida's cell phone number. Then it was off into the ether and the hands of the gods, because by Bess's description of Mouse and his working habits, only the gods knew when he might get the message.

In the end, it took less than five minutes. But it seemed like five days to Geoff, as he sat and waited for the ringing of his phone.

"What the hell are you doing down there, you sonuvabitch?" Mouse, like Ida, didn't believe in idle chatter.

Geoff did his best to explain, but it was like trying to talk to someone who spoke a foreign language. He couldn't even understand half the profanities, and there were plenty of those because Mouse, clearly, was mad as hell. Ida, in the end, grabbed the phone away from Geoff and began all over from the beginning.

But not before doing a bit of screaming herself . . .

"Just shut up and listen, you little turd," she raged. "This is Bess we're talking about here. So take your temper out on someone else or I'll reach through this damn phone and fix you so you won't be able to spawn baby mice, and I mean ever! Have you read Stuart Little? Well, I'm telling you now that I'm a bad-assed Templeton. Capiche?"

Whereupon, things seemed to settle down. Geoff, ears still ringing, grabbed in vain for the receiver as she abruptly terminated the call.

"No sense in you talking to him, darling," she said. "I don't know how you got on his wick so thoroughly, but trust me on this. You do not want to talk to Mouse. Clear? It bloody well better be, darling, because if we need him before this is over, I want him on our side, not all bound up in angst because he hates your guts. He now calls me Templeton and he calls you—"

"Lucifer. Yes, Bess told me." Geoff took a few moments to let the sense of it all seep into his fevered brain. He felt totally exhausted, wanted only to lie down and go to sleep, then wake up to find it had only been a dream in the first place.

"You can talk to him by E-mail, I guess, if you promise to read any message you write at least three times before you send it. Promise?"

"Of course I promise. Damn it, Ida, I didn't come down in the last shower, you know."

"In this situation, darling, you might as well have. You're very little more than a bloody liability, and except for your financial status, which I hope is healthy in case we need that, you're worth about as much as a politician's promise. But at least you had the sense to call me, which is about the only thing in your favor. Now, can I have one more cuppa? And then I have to get on the move."

"You want a cuppa, you make it!" he shouted. "So you have to get on the move, do you? And what the hell do you expect me to be doing?"

"You? Why you get to do the fun stuff, darling. You should be able to handle it, big macho type like you. It seems hard, I know, but it can't be, really, since women have been doing it for years and years. You get to wait, Geoffrey darling. And stuff your cuppa up your jumper while you're at it!"

Bess dumped out the water in the mug.

Even in her nauseous, head-splitting confusion, she could recognize a potential threat when she saw it. The sink taps might be safer, certainly worth the risk.

Getting to the sink was punctuated by a stop to use the convenient but filthy toilet nearby. Then, three mugs of wonderfully cold water later, her confusion gave way to sheer terror.

She had the vaguest of memories about the lame man in the tavern, the spilled drink, the replacement that had obviously been drugged. But afterwards . . . nothing. Nothing until she'd wakened, dizzy, foul-mouthed and shaky, beneath a car rug that surely didn't belong here.

Wherever here was.

It made no sense. A kidnapping? Inside a pub in the middle of the day? In Launceston? Why? She had no tangible value she could possibly think of, unless someone planned to blackmail her father. Or Geoff.

Seated on the edge of the cot, nervously eyeing her sunburn and wishing she'd worn something a bit less revealing, she allowed her concern to grow. Hadn't Ida mentioned at some point that Geoff was extremely wealthy? Just the thought of being a pawn in some sort of extortion scheme against him caused bitter bile to rise in her throat.

She cowered in a fresh outburst of terror when the lock clicked and the door was yanked open so a voice could demand, "Get over to the far wall and stay there. Face the wall. Shut your eyes and keep them shut, if you know what's good for you."

Bess did it. And did it more quickly than she could ever have thought possible. That rough, grating voice held a menace she'd never heard before in her whole life.

She had only just reached the wall and lifted her hands to cover her eyes when there was a mighty thump, followed by the slamming of the door and the amazingly quiet click of the lock. Bess didn't move. Didn't dare to move, until, eventually, she could do nothing else. The strange quality of the room's silence finally forced her to turn around.

At first her blurry eyes saw only a disjointed heap of rags on the floor inside the doorway, but when she blinked it became something worse. Bess stalked it, cautiously, throwing away her trepidation at the last possible moment when she saw, beneath the mask of blood, the battered face of Tom Rossiter. He had landed on his stomach, but his face was turned to one side so that he could breathe.

If he breathed at all.

She rushed forward to kneel beside his body, hands outstretched as she tried to find the courage to turn him over, to see what other damage had been done. Not that it mattered. He was surely dead.

"I'm . . . all . . . right." The words were barely audible, but caused bubbles of fresh blood to burst from his smashed and swollen lips.

"Tom, what happened?"

"Keep it down." His voice was coming clearer now, or she had lost enough panic to let her hear. "Not 's bad 's it looks. I think I fooled 'em . . . maybe. Hope so . . ."

His voice faded again.

"Tom," she whispered, afraid to speak in a normal tone lest she scream. "Just lie still. Don't try to move. I'll get some water, clean you up."

"No, pleas-s-s-e." The sigh burbled out with more blood as he tried to raise his head. "Have to . . . leave me like this. Have to . . . just get me . . . drink . . . thassall. No . . . clean. No . . . move me."

Getting the drink into him was tougher than she could have ever imagined. He was essentially belly-down on the floor, and he was twice her weight. She managed it in the long run, but ended up with his blood all over her and her hands shaking so badly she dropped the small plastic mug.

"Good . . . don't . . . worry. They'd expect you to try and help. But thass enough. Now lean close an listen, 'cause I have to tell you whass goin on before I pass out again . . . if I'm gonna."

It took him time, and much backtracking through slurred words she couldn't follow, but eventually Bess knew all he was trying to tell her. Knew how he, too, had been drugged.

"Muss've been same dose as for you," he said through a groan. "Forgot I'm bigger. Don't matter, long's they think I'm out of it. Had to fake it some, let 'em think hurt wors'n I am."

Bess understood he had let himself be drawn into the kidnapping solely to protect her, and that he'd been beaten down and kicked half to death without the slightest chance to defend himself. They had waited until the drug took effect enough to weaken him. And while they might have given him the same dose they'd given her, they'd filtered it into more than one beer so Tom could hear them laughing while they beat him. Whereupon, he only half-pretended to pass out cold.

"Damn it, Tom," she said. "You could have been killed. But thank you, so very, very much."

" 'S okay. Done some bad things for your old man, but not crap like this. He's nuts, 'lis'beth. Not sane no more. Have to figure way outa here . . . worry 'bout your father later."

"Out? Tom, you can't even stand. How can you even think about getting out? There are . . . what? Four of them? Look what they've already done to you. You need a doctor, not an escape plan."

A rictus of a smile flickered redly, then died. "Firsh things firsh," he said, gesturing for more water. With that inside him, his speech seemed to clear along with his thinking, although he made no move to try and get up.

"Look 'round," he said, "an see what you can find for a weapon. Leg off the cot, maybe. That damn water mug's useless, but check inside cupboards, there, behind toilet . . . for plunger or somethin'. Hurry. We may not have much time."

She didn't need much time. The old laundry was too small to hide much of anything, and whatever might have been available had obviously been cleared out in preparation for her confinement. Prying a leg off the cot proved impossible, and there were no slats to be ripped out. But then, way at the back of the bottom shelf in the cupboard, she found what looked like a length of broom handle, doweling actually, about three feet long.

Rolling up on his good hip, Tom managed to tuck the piece of doweling alongside him, hidden by his bloodied clothing but right at his fingertips. "When they come," he said, "you have to fight. Scream, kick, make all the fuss you can." He grimaced. "Didn't want them to touch you, Elizabeth, but if you can distract them it would be good. Know what I mean?"

Bess knew, just as she knew that even without Tom Rossiter there to help, assuming he could even get to his feet, she would have screamed and kicked and done anything else she could think of to protect herself.

And would have failed, in the end. Still might. If they'd only left her purse with her, she'd have had some sort of weapon . . . a nail file, a pair of manicure scissors, the purse itself. Bess couldn't help it, acutely detested herself for it, but the tears came and she couldn't stop them any more than she could stop the fear that threatened to make her soil herself.

"Elizabeth! Look at me!" Rossiter's voice groaned through his smashed mouth. "I'll get you outa' this, I prom—"

An almost-silent snick of the door lock interrupted his words, and Bess retreated to the far corner of the room as the door was eased open.

The first voice Bess heard, coming from just outside the slightly-opened door, was one she didn't recognize. It was young, light, whiny, and didn't sound like either of the two Sydney standover men she now knew she had already met; one while she and Geoff trained Lady; the other in the pub.

"Mr. Coolidge ain't gonna like this. You'll be in big trouble if he finds out, and Mr. Coolidge ain't nobody to be stuffin' around with."

There was the muted sound of a slap, still outside the door, and a new voice, this one harsh and grating. "Put a sock in it, boy, or we'll drop your daks and make you into a Long Bay bitch. But if you're good, and I mean really good, we might let you in for thirds."

Bess couldn't understand the Long Bay remark, although the threat and promise was obvious enough.

Tom Rossiter clearly understood the reference to Sydney's notorious Long Bay Gaol. Through half-shut eyes, he saw Rambo pushed into the small room, ahead of the two much larger Sydney men. Rambo entered the room in a rush, almost tripped over Rossiter, then found himself being shoved to one side as Davo and Jack swaggered in, both of them fixing their gaze on a cringing Elizabeth, after a casual glance at where Rossiter lay unmoving.

"Looks as if all your Christmases have come at once," Jack said. "You should be smiling, girl, not huddling there against that sink."

Which drew a growl of assent from his companion and a wide-eyed, panic-stricken gasp from Bess. She tried to cringe further against the sink, deliberately not looking at Tom. She knew he needed all the attention focused on her, on her fear, and that required no acting at all.

"You . . . you're surely n-not going to d-do this," she stammered. "That little creep is right. Coolidge will have your heads on a platter if he so much as hears about this."

It was false bravado, and it showed. Both men laughed and sauntered closer. Bess fought for mental balance, then physical balance, poising herself so that she had one foot almost weightless, ready for a kick if the opportunity presented itself. Both men were now past Tom's still unmoving form, but in a room this size that brought them almost within touching distance of Bess.

"Come on, don't be shy," said the larger of the two men, and his eyes flared into those of the devil as he reached out with one large hand to seek her hand.

"Get away!" Her voice rose into a shriek as she tried to move back where there was no more room to move. The man merely grinned, and it was suddenly Paul there grinning, suddenly the epitome of her marital humiliation all over again. Bess sagged, then caught at the edge of the sink as she turned partly away from the men, defense forgotten in her sudden need to vomit.

"Aw, the bitch is gonna spew," said the younger man.

As if she starred in some drama and that was her cue line, Bess turned to the sink and watched her system void all the water she had earlier consumed. But then, somehow, it seemed as if the worst of her terror had flowed out in the revolting tide. She turned back toward the men, fear forgotten, turquoise eyes flashing, ready now for battle.

And watched Tom shamble to his feet, rocking toward the two unsuspecting men, the length of doweling upraised in one huge paw. He lurched forward, swinging the slender piece of wood like a baseball bat, and the younger of the two men dropped as if pole axed when it struck his temple.

A yowl of surprise and terror erupted from the whiny, pimple-faced man, but it was drowned in the pure roar of animal rage as Tom reversed his swing and clipped the other, older man a lick across the brow that brought an instant rush of blood down over one eye. Another switch in direction, and the doweling smashed the man's nose, although the effort almost brought Tom to his knees.

And then it was on for one and all. Bess could only watch helplessly as the frenzied thug leapt toward Tom, but was driven back by savage, rapier-like thrusts that took him in the throat, ripped the base of one ear, and drove into his stomach. Tom growled like a savage beast at each blow, but she could see the growls and grunts were due more to the pain he was inflicting on himself than anything else.

It was over in less time than the two men had used in threatening her. Tom turned as Pimple Face tried to flee out the door, and his huge hand dragged the weedy youth backwards and flung him past Bess, half into the sink. Clouting Pimple Face senseless, Tom folded to his knees, exhausted.

"Keys," he managed to spit out, gesturing toward the unconscious Sydney thugs. "Try the bigger bloke since he did the driving. Hurry, Elizabeth, they won't be out of it long."

She had to steel herself to reach into the older man's pockets, and did so in mortal terror that he would regain consciousness. Somehow, she yanked free the keys. Then she tried to help Tom through the doorway.

"Minute," he said, his voice as ragged as his clothing and his bloodied face. Using the doweling as a foreshortened cane, he lurched close enough to deliver each of the Sydney men a truly vicious kick to the face, then another, before turning to Bess. "You go . . . get the car started. You'll have to drive 'cause I can't."

"Aren't you coming with me? Let me help . . ."

She got no further. Tom glared at her, his pain-wracked expression imploring her to leave. She bolted through the doorway, into the yard, yet her ears became her eyes as she listened to the distinct, never-before-heard but unmistakable sound of a bone snapping like a rotten branch beneath Tom's shoe. She thought she heard the sound again when she was halfway to the car, but couldn't be certain.

Literally throwing herself into the driver's seat, she turned to see Tom reeling toward her, barely able to keep his balance. He reached the hire car, got the passenger door open, then almost fell in, his voice preceding him.

"Can't go yet. Your purse . . . inside the house. Get it. Quickly Elizabeth . . . I can't last much longer."

It took her only minutes, but even that had clearly sapped Tom's strength. He slumped in the seat beside her, huddling over the pain of his broken ribs, fresh blood seeping from his facial wounds.

"Turn right, after driveway," he groaned. "Go until Deloraine, then left to—"

"I've been to Deloraine and can find my way from there," she interrupted. "But I don't know where the hospital is."

"No hospital. Just get us back to Barrett's and stop worrying about me. I've been through worse than this and lived. Promise me, Elizabeth, Barrett's first."

Bess started to argue, but noted the raw emotion in his battered eyes and shut her mouth. She had seen Tom Rossiter in action now, and she thought it best not to upset him any more than she had to. Not because she feared him, but because she feared his own savage nature might yet kill him, especially if he was opposed.

"Promise," he insisted.

"Okay, yes, I promise."

"Don't speed," he added in a voice that was almost a whisper. "I don't want cops in this, not yet, maybe not ever."

She didn't bother to reply, just tooled the hire car out into the narrow road and headed south. She was quarter-circling the Deloraine roundabout in fifteen minutes, and Tom had been unconscious for thirteen of them. He never moved as she drove quickly but carefully, well within the speed limit, all the way to Launceston and Geoff's house.

And sanctuary.

CHAPTER FOURTEEN

Both Geoff's Land Cruiser and Ida's Pajero were there in the driveway when Bess plunged the hire car to a halt. From the backyard, Lady barked frenetically, then bayed gleefully, as if she were a coyote rather than a dog.

Ida and Geoff ran outside before Bess had barely placed one quavering foot on the ground. Geoff said nothing. He merely spread his arms, a cloak of protection into which Bess hurled herself without a second thought. It was left to Ida to open the passenger door and peer in at the gory, wounded mess that was Tom Rossiter.

"Bloody oath, Colorado, you don't do things by halves, do you?" she said. "Come on, make my day and tell me you did this all by yourself."

"That's my friend, Tom Rossiter. He rescued me. And he needs a doctor . . . a hospital," Bess said, her voice muffled because her face was buried against Geoff's chest, her ribs aching from the strength with which he was holding her against him.

"No . . . no hospital . . ." Rossiter's voice was barely audible, but the authority was there, even if the volume was not. "Looks . . . worse than it is," he gasped. "Maybe need doctor . . . but not questions."

"All right, darling, we'll do it your way," Ida said. "But should we be getting rid of this car while we're at it?"

"Yup. Wipe it down good. Get rid of it. Airport parking lot best. As for me, just get me somewhere . . . few days to recover . . . worse than it looks."

Ida fiddled in her handbag and came up with her cell phone. "I want two people at Barrett's house twenty minutes ago," she said. "And I want Doc at my place in fifteen minutes. No names, no pack drill."

When she turned to Geoff and Bess again, her eyes were as hard as her reputation. "This is my business now. You two sort yourselves out and I'll talk to you about everything tomorrow, unless sooner is needed. Colorado, you must be all right or you wouldn't have made it this far, but leave the rest to me. Okay?"

Bess managed to nod from her refuge in Geoff's arms, then allowed herself to be led toward the house, unable to stop her trembling, unable to totally come to terms with the last few hours. Tom was badly injured no matter what he might say. But with Ida in charge, Bess thought, at least he wouldn't be worse off.

She and Geoff hadn't reached the doorstep before one of Ida's company vehicles slid round the corner and into the yard. Ida's gritty voice issued instructions.

Entering the house with Geoff's arm around her, Bess halted in genuine shock at the apparition that stared back at her from the hall mirror. Even Geoff's presence wasn't enough to offset the horror of seeing this creature, auburn hair a mane of disarray, turquoise eyes wide with anxiety and torment. Her tee-shirt and shorts were bloodied, and the evidence of Tom's injuries was smeared all over her arms and legs.

"I have to get cleaned up," she said to Geoff's image, which stared at her from beside the stricken figure that was her but not her. Stared with pale, ice-green eyes that seemed to swirl with emotions, eyes that flickered from pain to anger to outright rage, then back to compassion again. All within an instant.

"Of course you must," he said, and gently turned her away from the mirror, holding her tightly as he guided her to the staircase, then up the stairs to the doorway of her room.

"I think a shot of liqueur wouldn't go astray either," he added, releasing her on the threshold. "I'll bring it up and leave it on the dresser for when you're ready. Are you certain you're all right, Bess? Bloody oath but you're white as a sheet. I don't want to come back and find you collapsed in the damn shower."

"I'm fine, really," she lied. "But yes, a drink would be wonderful. And maybe some food, later. I feel like I . . ." The rest was too much to bother trying to say. She turned away and stumbled into her room, vaguely aware of Geoff closing the door.

Whereupon, she flung off her stained clothes, heedless of where they landed, brushed her teeth until her gums practically bled, and gargled with peppermint mouthwash. Then she luxuriated beneath the warmth of the shower's flowing water, leaning back to let it stream across her breasts and stomach. Even the sting of the water against her still sunburned thighs was something to be relished, as was the rich smell of the shampoo she quickly worked into her tangled hair, then used as a general cleanser as she patiently and gingerly washed herself from top to toe and back again.

The bloodstains fled down the drain, but the mental stains were harder to erase, and Bess found herself scrubbing at her thighs and between her thighs, refreshing the shampoo over and over again with quick swipes at her hair. When the tears began, she hardly even noticed, and the shower rinsed them from her face as quickly as they fell. At first. But then her soft weeping matured, strengthened, and suddenly she was shaking like a leaf, her voice howling in pain and shock, and the entire shower cubicle was moving, distorted by her blurred vision, and she had to reach out to try and steady the walls, steady herself against collapse.

And then other arms were there to steady her, and Geoff's voice, tense with alarm, sounded in her ears. "My God, Bess." And his moan echoed her own as he gathered her into his arms, heedless of the water that soaked his clothing, heedless, it seemed, of anything but her need to be held, to be comforted.

"Your clothes," she managed to say, only to feel his chest expand against her cheek as his unsteady laughter boomed into her ears.

"I'm not made of sugar, you silly American wench," he said, his voice too loud and also, strangely, as shaky as she felt herself to be. There were peculiar tremors in that voice, even more peculiar ones in the arms which held her so closely against him.

"Turn around," he ordered, after what seemed like an hour in which her own tremors eased and her breathing steadied. She obeyed, bracing herself between Geoff and the wall of the shower cubicle as he worked his fingers gently through her hair, rinsing away the remaining shampoo and easing the tangles as he slowly, patiently, combed her hair with his fingers.

It was a strange, almost magical sensation, not only vividly erotic, but comforting. Then his strong fingers gathered round her waist, lifting her, moving her into the furthest corner of the cubicle, where she still faced the wall.

"There has to be a limit to ridiculousness," he said, his voice huskier now. "Can you stand up by yourself? Just a nod will do."

Bess could manage the nod, but wouldn't have trusted herself to speak. And then simply could not speak as her ears recorded the unmistakable sound of sodden clothing striking the bathroom floor.

"Better," he said, voice soft in her ear. "And since I'm here, and wet already, might as well finish the job, I reckon. Hand me the soap, would you?"

Bess groped in the soap dish, and somehow contrived to reach behind her and give the scented soap to Geoff. Then she shut her eyes in acceptance of this madness, this unbelievable situation, as she felt his fingers gently begin working the suds across her shoulders. He used increasingly intricate patterns and designs, his hands roaming across her fevered skin with the gentleness of a mother bathing a child.

But the skills in those hands were anything but motherly. They seemed to find every erotic, tender, sensitive place that existed beneath their touch, and . . . it seemed to Bess as she swayed against Geoff's manipulations . . . places she had never realized were so sensitive.

She shivered with delight as his fingers caressed the dimples above her rump, shivered with anticipation as his hands slid almost casually across the swell of her behind, then down her legs to pause momentarily at her ankles before beginning a return journey upward that had her gasping with surprise and expectation.

"Clean enough?" He didn't wait for a reply, didn't even seem to expect one. His voice crooned on, soft as thistledown, soft as his touch on her skin. "Reckon you'd better be, because I expect we'll be out of hot water pretty soon. So, my little foreign collaborator, it must be time to get dry, but first . . ."

Bess found herself being gently turned around, and despite her still-closed eyes was aware of him replacing the soap in its dish, then flicking across the taps so that the curtain of water ceased. One of his blessedly tender hands touched lightly at her waist, tugging her slightly closer to him, as the other hand reached out to touch beneath her chin, lifting her face, somehow daring her to open her eyes and look at him.

"Bess . . . oh, God . . . Bess . . ." It was half sigh, half caress, never completed because his lips were closing it off against her own, both of his hands behind her now, featherlight against the swell of her hips, iron-strong as they drew her closer and closer against the muscular strength of him.

His lips were undemanding. They touched and probed and teased, but didn't seek to overwhelm her. His kiss was the least of her distractions anyway. His fingertips played a lover's waltz along the nubbles of her spine and his erection, throbbing a counter-tempo against her belly, managed to be in tune with his kisses, in tune with his fingers, in tune with Bess herself, all at the same time.

She yearned to take her arms from around his neck, to reach down and feel that throbbing against her own fingers, to feel the size of him and the sheer maleness of him with her hands. But she didn't, because suddenly he was holding her away from him, shifting her so he could turn and lift her through the shower cubicle doorway, stepping carefully as he moved toward the bed. Her bed.

She looked into his eyes then, and saw lights that held all the devilment of the buccaneer image she had always given him, but also lights so warm, so gentle, so totally magical that she had to close her eyes again for fear of being blinded. And then, a single kiss and she was being gently placed upon the counterpane of the bed. Opening her eyes, she looked up to see him standing there, gazing down at her with a soft smile on his lips.

"Lie still a moment and try not to go to sleep," he said, his smile widening. "I want to pat you dry and get some more of Ida's sunburn oil on you. And then . . ."

The grin said it all, and Bess couldn't contain a timid grin of her own, which stayed with her the entire ninety seconds he was out of the room, having strode away so natural, so comfortable in his nudity that she almost forgot about her own. By the time she remembered, that, too, was far too late to worry about.

"Turn over on your face," he said, kneeling by her bed. "This shouldn't take long, although if I get to enjoying it too much . . ." And, again, his smile was infectious. Bess rolled over on her tummy and let herself be drowned in the magic of his hands as he carefully applied the oil, rubbing it in gently but thoroughly from her ankles upward, driving her crazy with desire.

In some place, like the sensitive skin behind her knees, he prepared her for his touch with kisses and flickering caresses of his tongue. Yet when he reached the inner tops of her thighs, he was fastidious about applying the oil delicately but precisely, without even a hint of the erotic elements she expected.

His kisses returned to those dimples at the base of her spine, before his fingers began to play with the nape of her neck. His lips were warm, but she shivered briefly before the purring began. He massaged her neck with fingers and lips until she was literally boneless, could only sprawl like a rag doll and luxuriate in it.

"Turn over." His lips brushed at her ear as he spoke, but the choice was left to her because suddenly he wasn't touching her at all. Bess lay still, her drugged mind fighting to make sense of it. Then she let instinct guide her, and she rolled over onto her back and met his eyes. This was now, this was the moment, and he was going to let her choose. So she did.

And positively glowed at the smile which greeted her, more than glowed as his gaze wandered from her eyes to her sunburned shins and back again, each look a touch, each touch a caress. And then he was pouring sunburn oil into his hands and reaching down to her ankles, shifting onto the bed until he knelt between her feet, holding her with his gaze as he began all over to touch her into insensibility with his fingers, his lips, his very being.

Bess could only lie back and wonder as his hands worked their way upward, sometimes following his lips, sometimes tracking alone into unknown territory with the surety of a frontiersman. Once again, he managed to bypass the core of her, at least with his touch. Yet his avid gaze devoured her, and the quick flit of his tongue across his lips brought a gasp of longing to her own lips.

He had no need to put sunburn oil on her breasts, but his lips revealed a need of their own, as did his slick, gentle fingers, and now Bess had to close her eyes, to let the sensations flow over her, into her, as he kissed and licked and sucked each nipple to a throbbing mound of delight. Then he shifted from his position above her, leaning over to lay down the sunburn oil as he lowered himself beside her and sought her mouth with his own, sighing her name as he kissed her, between the kisses, through the kisses. At the same time, his hand moved to explore her body.

His kisses became firmer, his tongue searching now through her mouth as his slick fingers continued, teasing, tantalizing, thrilling her body into spasms that were not yet orgasm, but hovered on the edge as he brought her nearer and nearer to the edge, before retreating and giving her respite but no release.

Bess couldn't hold back any more. Her hand managed to find some vestiges of sunburn oil before sliding down the muscles of his chest, searching carefully until his erection was within her grasp.

"Bess," he moaned. "Don't start that, but don't stop. Don't . . ."

The small amount of oil she'd captured lubricated as she instinctively grasped him harder, fighting his own instincts, suddenly desperate to keep him from exploding then and there.

"Please, Geoff," she sighed, feeling her success and an unexpected pleasure. She released him, only to reach out again, touching him with wonder, letting her fingers trace along the strength of his erection, letting her ears delight in his ragged breathing, her eyes delight in his body. "Now . . . please . . ."

"Oh . . . yes . . . now . . ."

He came into her slowly, gently, lovingly, his eyes locked on her own as if he could read through her eyes any possible problem. Bess felt a tinge of uneasiness as some remote part of her mind floundered over the size of him, then forgot it in her body's quick, delightful surge of acceptance.

She heard herself gasp, saw the fierce pleasure in his eyes, then gave herself entirely to the sensation of his movements, the running buildup to the crescendo that trilled through her entire being. Her legs locked around him and her muscles clenched and unclenched, beyond her thoughts, beyond all control as she tried to squeeze the magic, tried, it seemed, to absorb him into her piece by piece, and then, after the explosion of his climax had matched her own, drop by drop.

He made no attempt to leave her when it was done, but stayed inside her, letting the fingers of one hand trace magic as he stroked the hair away from her eyes, kissed away the tears she couldn't keep back. Happy tears.

"Ah, Bess," he whispered, and lapsed into silence, seemingly content just to look at her, to touch her so terribly gently, and occasionally to twitch within her.

Then he kissed her, and it was such a slow, languid kiss it

seemed destined to send her purring. Until there was another twitch within, and suddenly the kiss was roused and rousing, and her breath shortened as she responded, and she panted with surprise and exultation as he released her mouth to dip his lips and tongue to the peak of one breast, then the other.

Bess let her own hands roam along his back, into the hair at his nape.

Then she clutched at the muscles of his buttocks as she felt him growing again within her, twitching, throbbing, but growing, filling her with sensation after sensation.

Without warning, he rolled over, taking her with him, keeping her with him, steadying her with his hands until she was sitting upright, now in total control, able to use her own muscles to soften or strengthen the effect of him.

She closed her eyes and gave herself to that power, letting herself rise and fall slightly as she tested it.

Until . . .

She heard, clear as if someone had turned on a stereo, the "tlot-tlot; tlot-tlot," the "horse-hoofs ringing clear" from the Noyes poem, and her eyes flew open, half expecting to see Geoff's eyes behind a highwayman's mask, a cocked hat on his thick hair.

But all she saw was that fierce, buccaneer's grin, and the flash of pure pleasure in his pale green eyes. Except she was more than half-sure he had heard the hoof music too, and the sheer absurdity of the thought forced laughter into her throat and a quicker, more savage rhythm into her movements. And then he was laughing with her, and she bared her teeth and let herself go, abandoning herself totally to the rhythm within her, riding him to the tune of their shared laughter until both cried out in ecstasy and she sagged to the circle of his waiting arms.

"I knew you'd be a laughing lover," he said a lifetime later, as they lay in each other's arms, replete, passion-spent, both nearly asleep.

"I'm glad one of us did," Bess managed to reply, suddenly shy. Not in any way ashamed . . . that, she thought, might come later . . . but no longer feeling brazen, either. It was shaping up for Cinderella time, she thought, and laughing or not, a pumpkin is a pumpkin is a pumpkin when midnight comes.

"You had to be a laughing lover; it's the only kind worth having," he continued, eyes closed, thankfully not looking at her although one arm cradled her against him. "But now I have to remind you, dearest Bess, that there is a time for everything, and I suspect we're well past the time for feeding you. Your tummy's been telling me stories for the last half-hour."

And he howled with joy when she pulled away from him in not-entirely phony embarrassment, and he laughed louder when she flung a pillow at his back as he grabbed up his still-sopping clothes and departed the room, shouting that he'd have his own shower now, in his own room. And if she was damned lucky, he might then condescend to fry some water.

Frying water, Bess thought fondly, was his intimate but sometimes annoying way of describing her cooking skills, or lack thereof, as opposed to his own, which were awesome. She knew she should move, but remained where she was, unwilling to abandon the scene of such wondrous, unbelievable pleasure. Bad enough that she would eventually have to leave it all behind, but for now . . .

"Tucker time!"

Slipping into her cut-offs and Broncos sweatshirt, she tripped downstairs just as Geoff slid perfectly baked potatoes onto their plates, followed by huge rounds of choice filet, not only wrapped in bacon but pocketed with oysters as well.

They ate together in a silence that wasn't strained, but seemed from her viewpoint to be too comfortable. It would be too easy to get used to, and there was no sense in that. Geoff needed more than she could ever provide, although he mightn't realize it for the moment. But Bess knew it, and dared not make more of this than there already had been.

He'd even gone so far as to make proper, percolated coffee, and was pouring it when Lady barked to announce a visitor. Geoff strolled to the door in time to admit Ida, who stalked into the room like an avenging angel. She curtly accepted Geoff's offer of coffee, her attention focused on Bess.

"Well, Colorado, your Tom Rossiter will live, but only because he's too damned stubborn and stupid not to. Still, I think you can take it as a given that he won't be going back to work for your father again."

"I should certainly hope not," Bess started to reply, only to have Geoff interrupt in a voice that demanded attention.

"I thought you told me your father was dead."

"If I ever get within gun range of the bastard, he will be," Ida raged, her voice icy with an anger Bess had never seen in her. "If Rossiter is right, then Dover Warren Cornwall is as mad as a cut snake and rich enough to be just as bloody dangerous. He kidnapped his own daughter, Geoffrey, just to force you into selling out to him. And putting the job in the hands of a mob of slime that came too damned close for comfort to raping her, or worse. That's why I totally mean it when I say . . ."

She got no further. Even Ida, woman of stone, wouldn't have dared continue in the face of the astonished ferocity that blazed from Geoff's eyes. He glared at Ida, enforcing silence, ensuring silence, then turned his gaze on Bess, who felt as if he lashed her with whips of ice.

"You're Warren Cornwall's daughter?" he asked, as if he still didn't believe it.

Bess tried to meet his eyes, but couldn't hold it together. She had to drop her glance, had to try and find some words, any words, but couldn't do that either. She could only sit there in shattered silence.

"Well, hell, Bess," he said, his voice dripping with despair and contempt and betrayal. "Doesn't that just about say it all?" Then he marched to the door, his anger pounding out through his feet. "Damn all women! Fickle, lying, cheating bitches, the lot of you! Damn it!" And his voice seemed to echo every step. "Dammit . . . dammit . . . dammit . . ."

Even after the sound of the door slamming, even after the faint trill of his whistle for Lady, Bess could hear Geoff's words, and they burned into her brain with the cadence of Noyes' poem . . . *tlot-tlot, tlot-tlot, dammit, dammit, dammit.*

CHAPTER FIFTEEN

Geoff's words were still ringing in her ears when Bess entered her room, shed her clothes, stripped off the bed's counterpane, and crawled beneath the sheets.

Then crawled out again to don her oversized Goofy nightshirt, stagger into Geoff's office, turn on the computer, and write Mouse a brief E-mail. Before Ida had left, practically at Geoff's heels, she'd offhandedly suggested that "Colorado might want to reassure the bloody rodent."

Bess didn't even try to guestimate the time difference. However, Mouse's response came within minutes, as if he'd been impatiently waiting by his computer.

"I'm so glad you're safe," he wrote, "and I like that Ida-Templeton person. But if you stay with Lucifer, you're playing with fire, and I wash my hands of you."

Paws not hands, Bess thought, swallowing the urge to laugh hysterically.

Instead, nearly blinded by tears, she stumbled into bed, where, physically exhausted, emotionally drained, she fell asleep. She awoke the next morning, dripping with perspiration but unable to remember her dreams, and soon found that Geoff had not bothered to come home. His bedroom was empty, his bed hadn't been slept in, and the ethereal, auburn-haired nude in the painting seemed to mock Bess's anguish.

Packed up and ready to leave, Bess waited for Geoff's return. She could have been gone much earlier, except her pain had evolved into anger.

Ironically, last night she'd discovered a gift from Geoff under the dinner plate that held the remnants of her baked potato. A jade Tasmanian tiger hung from the end of a slender gold chain, and Bess remembered admiring the exquisite piece of jewelry at the Deloraine Fair. Geoff had probably bought it during her visit to the loo or, more likely, when he purchased his bottles of liqueur.

Why hadn't he given it to her right away? Because of her sunburn? As delicate as the piece of sculpted jade was, he knew it would irritate the sensitive skin at the base of her throat. He was always so thoughtful!

And, this time, so wrong! She needed to explain away his accusations. If he didn't believe her, so be it.

Yearning to showcase the tiny tiger above the peasant blouse she'd tucked into her long patchwork-quilt skirt, Bess merely placed the necklace inside her purse. She was sitting over her umpteenth cup of coffee when she heard the door open and the scuttle of Lady's paws on the polished floor. The dog slid round the corner, floundered for footing, then lunged toward Bess.

Geoff was only a few heartbeats behind, and arrived as the spaniel was busy sniffing at Bess's luggage. Walking into the kitchen with the rigid stride of a cautious, angry predator, he halted to survey his domain from halfway across the room.

"Do you think you're going somewhere?" His voice was low, level, calm and totally menacing, as cold as his eyes and even colder than the block of ice in Bess's stomach.

"It doesn't seem very good sense to stay here, under the circumstances," she replied. "Although, for the record, I want to say a few things before I leave."

"You'll have plenty of time to say them." He marched forward to loom over her. "Because you are going nowhere, Elizabeth Carson Cornwall, until you've done what you came to do, which is help me write our book."

"Elizabeth Carson Bradley, not Cornwall." She forced herself to stare up at him, forced herself to look as if she wasn't being intimidated, and she desperately tried to keep her own voice calm and cool. "And you, Mr. Geoffrey Barrett, must be out of your mind if you think for one minute that we can continue to work on our book after—"

"Me being led down the garden path? After me being used? After me being totally, ruthlessly betrayed? Being made to betray my investors . . . my friends? Is that what you're trying to say? Save it, darling, because if you eat it, you'll stain your teeth. All you need to remember is that I paid to get you here and here you will stay until I've had my satisfaction. And I will. Mark my words, I will." His pale eyes bored into her own, then broke away to roam the contours of her body. "One way or another," he said, and the message was clear as window glass.

Bess shriveled up inside. Couldn't help it and didn't care. In those angry eyes she saw traces of Paul. In that angry, controlling voice, she heard her father running her mother's life, her life, everybody's life. She took a deep breath and held it, playing for time and winning.

"I did not know of your dealings with my father," she said, choosing her words as carefully as ever she had chosen words. "Not in any way. Nor did my father send me here. It was your idea, in case you've forgotten."

"And how convenient for you. I'm sure you had your father on the phone thirty seconds after my E-mail. You told him you'd play it cool and refuse my offer until I begged you to come to Tasmania. Less suspicion that way, you said. The airfare was a bonus, I expect. Good work, Elizabeth."

She shuddered. "Don't you dare call me Elizabeth! Your premise is ridiculous and you know it. No, I take that back . . . you can't even imagine how ridiculous it is. I've never done anything to jeopardize your business dealings with my father. Except to get kidnapped, or do you believe that was some sort of scam, too?"

"No, I don't," he replied, surprising her. "I think you either began to regret your stool-pigeon role, or you asked for more time. Then your father became impatient and told his pack of bloody crims to speed up the process."

"He wouldn't have told them to kidnap me. Damn it, he's my father! It's a strange set of circumstances, I'll admit that much, but I repeat, Geoff. I did not have one damned thing to do with any of it. I didn't know you were involved with my father. If I had known, I never would have come here."

"Sure thing, darling. That's your story and you stick to it. Although how you can, now that everything's out in the open, I simply can't imagine. Because that's maybe the worst part of all. How much of a fool you've taken me for and how much of a fool I've been. Sort of buggers a man's faith in himself, a thing like that. Still, I'll get over it with time. And with a bit of help from your mate Rossiter, I might just show your father that taking on some people with his kind of tactics can be expensive."

"I hope you do," Bess said, and although she was speaking more to herself than Geoff, she instinctively knew he'd heard her.

Whether he could begin to understand was a different story, not that it mattered anymore. There was no way she could confide in him now, not about her having accepted his invitation to escape her father, and certainly not about the events that had led up to that decision.

In his present state of mind, Geoff was probably more than

prepared to see her in a corporate whore role, she thought, only half aware that he had moved away from her and was pouring fresh coffee. For both of them. Could this be some sort of signal that hostilities were on hold, at least for the moment?

She didn't have to wonder about that very long. Geoff plunked the coffee down before her, turned, picked up her bags, and headed toward the stairs. He got halfway there, then stopped and shook his head.

"Hell," he said, "you got them down here, you can get them back up again. Be good exercise for you, because you're going to be spending a lot of time without any from now on. I expect every possible waking hour to be spent at the computer working on finishing our book." A sneer was in his voice as he dropped the bags like sacks of rubbish and walked back to sit down in front of his own coffee cup. Lady, attuned to the bad vibes, scrambled round to huddle at his feet, then looked from one human to the other as if waiting for yet another explosion.

"Whatever you say," Bess said, relieved in a way to have the confrontation over with, praying that it really was over. "I suppose you want me to give you my airline tickets and passport, just so you can be sure," she added, hating herself for what she considered a purely feminine remark.

"Bloody hell, Bess, don't talk nonsense." Geoff looked up at the ceiling, as if unable to believe he had made such a contradictory remark. Bess could hardly believe it either, and was almost comforted when he grudgingly said, "I'll take your word that you'll stay out your term. Whatever else, you've been totally professional about the book. I can't fault you on that."

"How magnanimous of you." Although it was the closest thing he'd said yet to an apology, and obviously closer to an apology than he had intended, she felt even angrier than she'd felt before.

She stared into the coffee she no longer wanted, then surged to her feet and tipped it down the sink. Sitting here wasn't going to accomplish anything, and since leaving now seemed out of the equation, she might as well get to work. She didn't bother wasting even one glance on Geoff as she picked up her luggage and headed for her room.

Then she marched straight back downstairs to the office, somehow managing to ignore the whirling dervish round her feet. As always, Lady sought attention, only this time she was frustrated at not receiving it.

"Go piddle on someone else's shoes," Bess finally said, closing the office door, blocking the dog's attempt to enter. Then she physically kicked Geoff's chair aside, dragged her own in front of the silent, almost mocking emptiness of the computer screen, and fired the cursed machine into action.

And there she stayed for three solid days, accomplishing, by her own standards, about as much as she could have accomplished by watching television or washing her hair. Words came, words went. Phrases came, phrases went. It seemed after a while that she was merely going through the motions, that she could write whatever she wanted to write, because the next step was to hit the delete key.

Worse, she began to develop headaches, and they were not the relatively minor type she was used to from long hours before the screen. These were, she suspected, severe stress headaches. Or, perhaps worse, migraines. Finally, on the afternoon of the third day, she could stand it no longer. Swallowing a couple of pain-killers, extracted from a vial she'd discovered on a shelf in the loo's medicine chest, she retreated to her room and sprawled out on the bed with a cool cloth across her forehead. Her mind was so dulled by the pain that sleep was impossible. All she could do was drift in and out of the edges of sleep, never quite getting there, but never far away.

Until the argument began downstairs.

The first words to penetrate Bess's fog were: "Tom Rossiter."

Geoff's tone revealed disbelief, and Bess managed to distinguish yet another "dammit," then mumble . . . mumble . . . mumble . . . and finally: "Don't be stupid, Ida." By which time she had rolled off the bed.

Ignoring the searing pain in her head long enough to tiptoe to the partly-open door, she huddled and unashamedly eavesdropped.

"Bloody oath, Geoffrey darling, I do wish you'd stop being so obtuse. Rossiter saved your girl, in case you've forgotten."

"She's not my girl. She's Warren Cornwall's girl. Or have you forgotten?"

"Bugger all men! She's Cornwall's daughter, which she can't help any more than you can help being your father's son. Really, Geoffrey, did that little chit of a child bride of yours root your feeble male brain to the point where you can't see the truth when it's out there in front of you?"

"Leave her out of this! She's got nothing to do with it!"

"Nothing to do with it? Your delightful child bride led you down the garden path, dropped you in the shit, took you for half a bloody fortune, and totally destroyed your faith in yourself, not to mention whatever common sense you might have had where women are concerned. And you dare say she has nothing to do with it?"

"Ida, you're getting very close to the edge here. I won't warn you again!"

Bess would have shut up upon hearing that unmistakable caveat, growled in a voice that, until recently, didn't even remotely belong to the man she thought she loved. She'd have shut up and run a mile. Ida was clearly made of sterner stuff.

"Put a sock in it, darling. You've never hit a woman in your life and you sure as hell aren't going to start now. So stop with the empty threats. All I'm telling you is that Tom Rossiter swears blue that Colorado didn't know what was going on, couldn't have known. And if you won't take my bloody word for it, go talk to him."

"May I remind you that Tom Rossiter is Cornwall's man?"

"Tom Rossiter is his own man, just like you are. Only better, because at least he's man enough to see the truth when it comes up and bites him in the bum. God save me, Geoffrey, but I've never met anyone so stupid and stubborn as you."

"That's a load of old cobblers, Ida. You've seen the evidence. Once is an accident, twice might be a coincidence, but three times is a conspiracy. There are too many inconsistencies about this whole damned business for me to ignore it. A lot of people got screwed around in this, may I remind you? People who trusted me, friends who trusted me."

Ida's snort of derision was like that of a spirited horse getting ready to kick, and Bess had a mental picture of Geoff turning away to protect his family jewels.

"And who still do; depend on it. Okay, Geoffrey Barrett, boy wonder. If you're so clever, tell me what the hell Colorado is still doing here? Come on, let's have an explanation. And one that's plausible, please."

"She's doing what I brought her here to do, working on my damn book."

Even to Bess's pain-wracked ears, there was a distinct note of uncertainty in Geoff's voice. Followed by what seemed to be an awfully long silence, in which Bess tried, but couldn't imagine, the expression on both unseen faces.

"Ah . . . but you're a trusting soul, aren't you darling?" Ida finally said.

"What the hell are you on about now?"

"Where is she working on this wondrous epic of a book, Geoffrey darling? I mean, is she up there in her little trundle bed with a laptop computer? Or down on a bench in City Park?"

"She's using the computer in the office. What's your point?"

"Ah . . ."

There was another of what Bess might have called a pregnant pause, if she'd been able to think straight enough to remember the word pregnant. Or pause, for that matter. She seemed to be hearing the entire conversation through cotton wool, and while the words were clear enough, some of the nuances kept escaping.

"Will you stop with the bloody ahs, Ida? They don't tell me anything, they don't ask me anything, and they don't bloody well accomplish anything. Okay?"

"Okay. But please answer this, darling. If your Yankee is so devious, so cunning, so much her father's corporate whore, then what in the name of all that's holy are you doing leaving her alone day after day, hour after hour, in your office, with your computer, with access to all your records? Aren't you afraid she'll call her father and—"

"There's nothing on that computer but the book! I downloaded all the records and took them to the office before I left her in there alone."

There was a hint of smugness in his voice now that ripped through Bess's headache like a hot knife.

"Geoffrey darling, you're full of—"

"Are you calling me a liar?"

"No, darling, a fool. The same fool you've been right

223

along, as far as Colorado is concerned. I would have thought your child bride taught you something, but it seems you've only got to see a pretty face and your brains fall out of your pecker. Come with me."

Their voices faded as Ida apparently led Geoff toward the office. Bess found herself trying to recall if there was anything on the computer that would make this entire situation even more ridiculous, but her mind wouldn't work. Mouse's E-mail address was there, of course, along with a few others. She hadn't bothered with her laptop since arriving, except to download the few things she thought she might need. During the past three days . . . in fact, since her arrival in Tasmania . . . she hadn't attempted to open any other file but the book itself. Despite her curiosity over what he did for a living, which by now he would have added to his betrayal list, Geoff's business files were none of her business.

"Okay, so I didn't wipe the stuff properly. So what does that make me?" Geoff's voice echoed up the staircase again, followed by Ida's self-satisfied laughter as they moved back to the kitchen, and, Bess presumed, coffee she wished she could share.

"A halfwit, darling. But you're only a boy, after all." That was followed by more throaty laughter. "And it probably doesn't mean anything anyway, because I couldn't have done what I just did if one of my boffins hadn't shown me how. I'd bet you London to a brick that Colorado couldn't find your files either. In fact, she wouldn't have even tried!"

"Wrong! She's Warren Cornwall's daughter! She probably has a degree in computer science, along with one in corporate—"

"Corporate what, darling? Corporate whoredom? Or were you going to at least be somewhat charitable and say corporate espionage? Come on, fess up to Ida. But if it's the first, you'd best move away, because while I know you won't hit me, there's nothing that says I won't hit you."

"Why are you suddenly so keen to take her side? All you've done is tease the daylights out of her since she got here. Colorado this and Colorado that, and . . . hell, you were nicer to my ex wife the one time you met her."

Ida's laughter was shriller than usual, and Bess half-thought she could detect a brittle note in it. But the laugh didn't last long enough before sliding into a sort of purring snarl.

"Your ex was a slut. And don't argue with me about that, either. I'm the one who proved it to you in the end, remember? I was nice to her because of you, darling. And . . . well . . . okay . . . she needed somebody, anybody to be nice to her. Colorado doesn't. She's learned to live without that sort of crap if it ain't fair dinkum."

Lies, Bess thought. All lies. She needed Geoff to be nice to her, even needed Ida to be nice, if it came to that. All she'd learned about being alone was that while she might have to live with it forever, she'd never like it. Especially now.

"That's not the issue anymore, Ida. I'm not talking about disliking Bess. I'm talking about not being able to trust her."

"Ah . . ." This time Ida wasn't being provocative or looking for answers. Even from a distance, Bess could feel the ice in that single word. "So what you're trying to tell me, Geoffrey, is that you like her just fine but you can't believe her. Is that about it?"

"Damn it, Ida! Will you quit with the when did you stop beating your wife questions?"

"Sure. Just as soon as you quit being such a dickhead. By the way, did Colorado happen to tell you what Tom Rossiter was doing here in the first place?"

There was a marginal silence, followed by Geoff's, "I

didn't ask her. Why the hell would I?"

"I haven't the faintest bloody idea, but I'm sure it wouldn't be because you actually wanted to know something factual for a change. Just as well you didn't ask, because she couldn't have told you. Not wouldn't, darling, couldn't. Because she bloody well didn't know. But I do. Now, would you like to know, or would it strain your puny male brain to try and absorb something accurate, something that isn't tied to your damn ego?"

"Ida, if you were a man . . ."

"If I were a man, you'd listen to me. At the moment I think I'm closer to being a real man than you are. At least I don't go about harassing an innocent girl, just because I can't see past my own overblown ego. Shut up and listen, or I'm going to walk out of here and let you wallow in your own shit. Do you hear me? You'd better, because in case you hadn't noticed, darling, I am starting to get very, very angry."

Geoff's reply was too low for Bess to catch, but Ida showed no such reticence.

"Tom Rossiter was sent here to find Cornwall's daughter and to take her back to New York with him, hog-tied if necessary. To take any steps that were needed, so long as they worked. Kidnapping, dope, a trip back roundabout through the Arab Emirates or the South Pole, just so long as he got her back undamaged and in one piece."

"Don't be stupid, Ida. Where's the logic in that? All Cornwall would have had to do is pick up a phone and she'd—"

"What? Run like a rabbit? Which is what she did when she left Colorado to come here? It might be bruising to your inflated ego, darling, but at least half the reason she came to Australia is because her father was trying to force her to go back to New York. Where she did not want to go! So she came to you, instead, poor innocent cow!"

"But why? There isn't a skerrick of sense in that."

Had Bess imagined it, or was there a subtle softening in his voice? Maybe even a hint of genuine doubt?

"Rossiter doesn't know all the details," Ida said. "Something about Cornwall wanting to line Bess up with some Pommy bastard as the bait in a corporate deal. Rossiter says Cornwall has lost it, gone halfway round the twist."

"Maybe Rossiter won't tell you all the details. Did you ever think of that?"

"Trust me, darling. Rossiter would have told me."

Ida's voice had changed in timbre. Geoff might not have noticed it, but Bess certainly did, even through her throbbing headache. Any woman would.

"Speaking of which," Ida continued.

And suddenly the voice belonged to a different Ida, this one smooth as silk, seductive as money, the words after "which" so soft Bess couldn't hear a single one, not that she needed to. The message was in ten-foot-tall letters.

"Damn it," Geoff protested. "Stop that!"

"But why, darling? Afraid Bess'll hear us? I thought you said she'd gone to bed with a migraine?"

Ida's voice purred like a tiger facing a tethered goat. Bess could imagine the blonde licking her lips, tongue slicking through the contours of her smile.

"Bloody hell, Ida, quit it!" Geoff didn't shout, but Bess heard every word.

"That was a test, darling, and you just failed," Ida said. "You don't want to root me, not that I would have let you. So how long have you been rooting your little Yank?"

His answer was barely audible, totally incomprehensible to Bess, but apparently clear enough to Ida.

"You bastard," she said. "You rotten, stinking drongo!

Colorado's father treated her like some sort of corporate call girl. She married one of his flunkies—and a nasty piece of work he was, according to Rossiter—who didn't turn out well enough for the old man's plans, so they framed him and he ended up shooting himself right in front of her. You didn't know that either, did you, Mr. holier-than-thou Geoffrey bloody Barrett? And when her father tries to start the same game all over again, she does a runner, here, to you, somebody she thinks of as a colleague, maybe a friend. And what do you do? You know damn well what you did, you right royal twit. You rooted her . . . which hardly surprises me . . . and then treated her like bloody shit. Just like her bloody father! God save me; you both want bloody shooting."

Thanks to the clatter of high heels, Bess could follow Ida's progress all the way to the door. It wasn't until she heard the door slam with an intensity that reverberated throughout the house, that Bess realized her own position and laboriously made her way over and into the bed. She even managed to shut her eyes, just before she felt Geoff ease open the bedroom door and peer in at her.

"Bess?"

His voice was a whisper. She could ignore it, and did, forcing herself to breathe evenly, to pretend sleep, to control her trembling. Until he turned and left, softly closing the door behind him.

Whereupon, Bess remembered something she'd heard a long time ago. Maybe her father had said it. Maybe Mouse.

When remedies do not match your problem, you modify the problem, not the remedies.

CHAPTER SIXTEEN

Some miracle had destroyed her migraine, was Bess's first thought upon awakening. The morning sun streamed through her window and her mind was crystal-clear.

Even better, she found after a long shower that Geoff had gone somewhere and taken Lady with him. Just as well, she thought. It would be a shame to ruin the day with another confrontation, and she knew she'd crack him over the head with his electric jug before she'd endure his caustic contempt again.

She savored her make-shift breakfast of left-over pizza and coffee, then went into the office and searched through Geoff's telephone index until she found the number she wanted. Then she waited with growing impatience until a familiar voice answered.

"Ida? It's Bess. I need to talk to Tom Rossiter, in person. Do you think he's recovered enough?"

"Is Geoffrey there?"

"No. No, he's . . . well, I don't know where he is. Dog training, maybe, since Lady's missing as well. Geoff was gone when I awoke, and there's no note or anything."

"Fine. I'll pick you up in fifteen minutes. And if Geoffrey does happen to come home before I get there, wander down the street a few houses and wait for me. I don't want to waste my time trying to ram some sense up that man's . . . nose."

Tom Rossiter looked, if possible, ten times worse. His face was horribly swollen and his bruises were a sickly, blue-green-yellow combination. What it must look like along his ribs, chest and back, Bess could only imagine, but it wasn't a comforting thought. His huge hands, resting outside the bed sheets and an incongruously feminine pink comforter, showed new scars over the old ones.

"Tom, I have to thank you," Bess said.

"Not necessary, Elizabeth. I'm just sorry I didn't twig to Gerry Coolidge earlier. It might have saved us both a lot of problems."

Twig? Bess allowed a tiny grin to stretch her lips as she glanced at Ida then focused on Tom again.

He winced after shifting position too quickly, and seemed to overhang the ends of Ida's distinctly feminine bed. In fact, the whole room was a tribute to the adage: What are little girls made of? While there was no sugar in sight, spicy potpourri scented the room, and everything nice imaginable . . . from lace to ruffles to peacock feathers . . . served as decoration. Ida's bedroom was an interior designer's fondest dream. Or worst nightmare.

"A thank-you is necessary," Bess insisted. "You know as well as I do what you saved me from, but I think you also know a lot of other things about what's been happening. I would wait until you're up, but—"

"He's already up," Ida interrupted, flashing Bess an enigmatic smile that could have meant anything. "He just isn't out of bed yet."

"Enough, woman." Rossiter's voice subtly changed tempo as he looked toward Ida. "I think Elizabeth and I need to talk privately, so perhaps you'd go make us some coffee."

"But Rossiter, the doctor said you were to avoid stimulants."

"Yeah, well, if you forget about the coffee when you see him, I won't tell him about any other stimulants. Okay?" He grinned a typical Rossiter grin, as rumpled as his suits. "Now be a good little girl and do what you're told, for a change."

Bess stood there in astonishment as the blonde meekly nodded and left the room. Who was this Ida? Certainly not the virago who had nearly wiped the floor with Geoff yesterday.

Tom wanted to start at the beginning, and Bess sat through his recitation in silence, letting him piece together what he knew with what he suspected as he recounted his journey from New York to Colorado, back to New York, then to California and Tasmania. He told her about her father's irrational rages, and about the apparent—and, in Tom's opinion—illogical arrangement Cornwall had made with the Englishman. Tom told her all he knew about his own instructions and trek in search of her, then, finally, the Coolidge deal.

"For which I apologize, Elizabeth. I didn't realize that Gerry is nearly as far off the rails as your old man, and I certainly didn't believe he'd allow his thugs to do what they tried to do to you. Especially since I'd warned him, more than once."

"So, in a way, Geoff was right. Coolidge was using me as a lever, on my father's orders, to force Geoff to put all that stock on the market."

"I honestly don't think it was on your father's orders, honey, which isn't to say he wouldn't have given that order. He would have, no question about it. But I'm fairly certain Gerry never told your father he even knew you were here. The name of the game was to use you for his scam first, blackmail Geoff, then kidnap you again so I could take you back to New York. I don't know what else to say, Elizabeth, because I was just as guilty as Gerry."

"No, you weren't. Not really." Bess was granted a welcome respite when Ida returned to serve them coffee, and she took that time to think. Then she invited Ida to stay and hear the rest. "Tell me about Paul, Tom. All of it, because I need to know all of it."

Rossiter blanched and shook his huge head, but managed to raise a hand to wave Ida away as she surged forward, her concern obvious.

"I'm okay," he said, then focused on Bess again. "Your father didn't much like you marrying Paul, Elizabeth. But he let it go, thinking he could mold Paul into the sort of corporate husband he wanted for you. He gave Paul that new position and helped him out financially, but in the end . . ."

"Go on, Tom, please. In the end, what?"

"Maybe your father pushed him too hard, but . . . hell, Elizabeth, in the end Paul just wasn't good enough. He didn't have the guts and he didn't have the brains. He just wasn't . . . good enough. That's all I can say."

"Oh, no. No, Tom, you can say a lot more than that. Let's have it out in the open, because I have to know. And you have to tell me. Because if you don't, even Ida won't be able to protect you. No matter how much I owe you, I'll have it out of your hide."

"Saints preserve me from all women!" Rossiter raised his paw like a NYC traffic cop. "Okay, honey, but remember I'm guessing at some of this.

"Once the old man decided Paul Bradley wasn't going to cut the mustard, he started getting paranoid about it, putting even more pressure on Paul. Then, when you got pregnant, your father decided he didn't need Paul anymore. It was the heir he'd wanted in the first place. So he arranged for Paul to be set up. Gerry Coolidge did most of it, but I had a hand in it, and I won't deny that. We adjusted some of the books so Paul would get left holding the bag. I'm talking years of prison time, and Paul wouldn't have lasted six months inside a prison. Your father knew Paul would—"

"Damn it, Tom, this is . . . was my husband you're talking about! And my own father arranged this? Ordered it? Sanctioned it? My father did this to his own child, his own grandchild?"

"Pawns! Corporate pawns!" This time it was Ida's voice that broke the ensuing silence.

And Rossiter's that continued. "Once he had his heir, and from the way he spoke there was never any question in his mind that it would be a boy, he didn't need Paul anymore, and sure as hell didn't want him around. Your father told me Paul was too soft, would contaminate the business."

"So my father got rid of him. Might as well have taken out a contract on him. In fact, that's what he did. He drove Paul to suicide, forced him to take out a contract on himself." The words popped out as Bess thought them, but they struggled for a foothold in her mind. It was simply too incomprehensible, too crazy for words. And too obviously true.

"Nobody intended him to shoot himself, Elizabeth. Nobody even thought of such a thing. He was just supposed to . . . go away."

"And then, after I lost the baby, my father let me go off to Colorado to recuperate, but when this British businessman came along, he started the whole game all over again. Same game, just different players, except for me. His daughter. His brood mare. His corporate whore."

"You sound like you blame yourself for this, and you shouldn't." Rossiter shook his head. "Paul Bradley was not a nice person, Elizabeth. We found out . . . a lot of things about him. Later. Your old man's intelligence network must have been wonky when he hired Paul in the first place, because I doubt he'd have had him in the building if he'd known what we eventually came to know."

"He was my husband!"

"He was a bad bastard through and through, with a long, bad history of using and abusing women, among other things. A manipulator, just like your father, but worse, in his way, really . . . well . . . twisted. He was a control freak and he . . . well, I'm surprised you never realized this—although I'm just as glad you didn't—he liked to hurt women. Physically, emotionally, any way he could. He was a piece of shit, Elizabeth. A nut case; you're well rid of him and lucky he did what he did before he started in on you. Which he would have, sooner or later."

Rossiter's angry voice halted as Bess choked down the horrible bile of sudden realization, trying desperately to keep her face from revealing her pain. She gulped, swallowed, gulped again, praying she could contain herself.

This time the silence was complete. Rossiter looked shamefaced and contrite. Ida looked strangely immobile, for Ida. And Bess could only stare at the wall above Tom's head and wonder if she wasn't losing her mind . . . if she could keep from losing her breakfast. Until . . .

"Could you kill my father for me, Tom? Once you're better, I mean? And don't tell me you don't deal with such things. I know—"

"You know about strong-arm tactics and maybe extortion. But I'm no killer, Elizabeth, despite the fact that I'm as tempted as you are. However, your father isn't really responsible, or at least I don't think so. He's nuts. Sick."

"He's evil! That's what he is, what he's always been! Evil!" Bess shook her head, auburn mane of curls flying everywhere as she fought to keep the tears from overwhelming her, fought for the control she knew she must have.

And found it. "All right then," she said, meeting Tom's

eyes once again. "Tell me how to get revenge. How to get even."

Rossiter, for some strange reason, looked over at Ida, then back at Bess, before he slowly replied. "What is it they say? Revenge is a dish best eaten cold?"

"It's a dish best not eaten at all," Ida said, drawing Bess's attention with the icy bitterness in her voice. "Colorado, this is not a place you want to go. Trust me."

"It isn't what I want to do that's the issue. Don't you see what my father's done? I'm just as responsible for Geoff losing out on that business deal as if I had been a part of it all, right from the start."

"That's bull and you know it."

"It's not! If I hadn't been here, none of this would have happened. It couldn't have happened."

"Listen to me, Colorado, and listen up good. Revenge will only cause you more hurt and more pain. I know. I've been there. And let me tell you this for nothing, while I'm at it. You don't want to end up like me!"

"What's so wrong with you?"

Bess and Rossiter stared at each other as they realized they'd spoken in unison. Ida didn't even bother to answer their question.

"If you two are finished," she said, "I have things to do and Rossiter needs his rest. Come on, Colorado, I'll drive you home."

Impulsively and somewhat gingerly, Bess gave Tom a hug. "I forgive you," she whispered, "but I can never forgive my father."

She and Ida were halfway to Geoff's when Bess, having endured the blonde's stoic silence as long as she could, finally said, "I know you thought it was time for Tom to rest. But are you really busy, or might we just go somewhere and talk?"

Ida shot her a glance that could have been curious, angry, bitter, or a combination of all three, then savagely yanked at the wheel of her Pajero.

Turning off at the Sixways, she drove down into the Punchbowl Reserve, then part way up the other side to where a small parking bay allowed them to converse with relative privacy.

"So talk," she said, reaching down to switch off the engine.

"Would you tell me more about what you said . . . about revenge?"

Ida's laugh was brittle black bitterness. "What's this? Confession time? Just two good old girls together? Forget it, Colorado, I don't need that anymore."

Bess stayed silent, determined to out-wait Ida if she could. Only when those manicured fingers reached again for the keys did she finally let out a breath and admit to herself she was no match for this woman of stone.

"I once told you I wouldn't share personal confessions, Ida. But do you know what my husband's last words were to me before he shot himself? Do you know what he did to me before he shot himself?" Her voice was rising, and Bess could feel it, hear it, but she couldn't stop it anymore than she could stop the bitter bile that rose with the words, into her throat, leaving a bad taste.

"He beat me. He smashed me with his fists. He killed our unborn child with his fists because it was a girl. Because he wanted a boy. Because he knew, I realize now, that my father wanted a boy. And when Paul finished beating me, he raped me. He treated me like a paid whore. And he told me I was the worst 'wife' in the world. Except he didn't mean wife. He meant . . ."

The tears came then, but Bess choked and chewed them

236

back, shaking her mop of curls and battling for control. When she continued speaking, it was through clenched teeth.

"It was all my father's doing. My own father. He made me into a whore, Ida, and by God if I'm going to be one, I'm going to be a rich one. My father has the money and I'm going to make him pay. I don't know how yet, but I will make him pay!"

She closed her eyes against the tears again, holding back the moans that fluttered in her stomach like frenzied bats. And when she finally opened her eyes, it was to meet two eyes that looked like blue chips of stone.

"Did Geoffrey treat you like a whore?" Ida asked bluntly.

"Did Geoff tell you about . . . us?"

"No! Geoffrey would no more do that than fly to the moon, and you'd know that, Colorado, if you were thinking straight. But I'm older than you and I'm older than Geoffrey, and I've been places you've both never been and I hope you never go. No one needed to tell me you two finally got it together. It's written all over both of you like a rash. Now, answer my question. A simple yes or no will do, since I'm not real interested in the details, if you don't mind. Did Geoffrey Barrett treat you like a whore? Ever? In any way?"

Bess tried. She really did. But the answer stuck in her throat, grasped with painful claws at her tongue, and wouldn't leave her lips. Ida sat patiently, then rolled down her window, lit a cigarette, and made a great show of smoking it.

"Okay, Colorado, stop torturing yourself," she finally said. "I already knew the answer. I just wanted to know if you thought he'd treated you that way, in which case I might have dropped you off at the mental ward instead of taking you home. So, whose opinion are you going to take? That of a damn loser you were silly enough to marry? Worse than loser, from what T . . . Rossiter said. Or that of the man you love?"

"Geoff doesn't know about Paul. I mean, the rape and suicide. I've never told him. I've wanted to tell him at least a dozen times, but now I can't." Bess didn't trust her voice anymore. Looking down, she watched tears stain her linen slacks. Then, raising her face, she gazed imploringly at Ida.

"What you want me to say is that he won't ever know, at least not from me. So all right, he'll never know from me. But he'll have to know from you, for your own sake. You've got to tell him, Bess, if you're going to have any future together."

"We won't have any future together. It's impossible. It's never been possible."

"Ah . . ." It was one of Ida's all-encompassing, say-everything-and-nothing ahs. Then she reached for the ignition. "Because you're intrinsically flawed; damaged goods. How silly of me not to have seen that. Ah well . . . I'm running out of time, Colorado, so it's home again for you and back to work for me. Whole damn thing is out of my ball park now anyway."

Ida drove back through the Punchbowl and through a variety of side streets until she could see Geoff's driveway, empty, so she drove right up to the door and let Bess out of the car.

"You're a good girl, Colorado, no matter what you think," she said in farewell. "Stupid, but good . . . or you will be when you grow up. Don't lose touch, and remember, you're tougher than you think."

Bess felt anything but tough as she let herself into the house and went straight to her room to change clothes. Then, wearing jeans and an old Beatles tee-shirt, she returned downstairs and stared at the blank face of the computer.

"First things first," she said, and set about composing a complicated message to Mouse. That done, she sent it, then wiped it from the computer's memory. Calling up the file she'd titled "Kate's Confession," she began to work her way through a scenario written out of context. She—and Geoff, for that matter—rarely wrote out of sequence. However, this particular scene was vital to the book's heroine, and the story itself. It involved a lengthy confession. The hero, now renamed a more formalized Thomas, was the recipient of Kate's declaration about her pregnancy, and . . .

Once this portion was completed, Geoff could finish the rest of the book with his eyes shut. So Bess had deliberately been delaying her best efforts, mainly because she'd wanted to delay the imminence of her departure.

Now, her fingertips fairly flew over the keyboard. Her fingers were linked to her mind, but working almost faster than she could think. The words seemed to pour out like individual droplets merging into a stream, a river, a cascade of words and emotions she couldn't halt. She didn't pause to edit, didn't pause for anything, merely let it flow.

Suddenly, the cadence and rhythm of *The Highwayman* was in control, and Bess, still typing furiously, swayed in her chair to the music in her head.

Kate flinched as Thomas grasped her arm. She knew he meant to console her. In fact, his grasp had none of the passion he'd shown a few minutes earlier. But Kate simply couldn't help herself. Memories of Paul invaded her mind; memories she'd managed to hide, the same way she'd been schooled to hide her legs beneath her voluminous petticoats. However, she wasn't wearing petticoats now, and her mind was suddenly as naked as her body.

"My God, Kate, what's wrong?" Thomas asked.

"I want . . ." she began, then took a deep breath before continuing in a rush. "I want to make love, I need you to love me, except you don't know about . . . about Paul Yeldarb."

"*Who the bloody hell is Paul Yeldarb?*"

The voice Thomas used was as cold as Paul's voice had been that long-ago December twenty-fourth, when he'd entered Kate's bedroom and locked the door. She had been wide awake because she never enjoyed a decent sleep on Christmas Eve. Too much excitement. Too much anticipation.

She'd always been half in love with Paul, who was twelve years her senior and her father's protégé, so his presence didn't disturb her. In truth, having just turned eighteen, she was convinced his visit meant a proposal of marriage. Which she'd accept, even though her father had become dissatisfied with Paul's business acumen. Father oft grumbled that Paul wasn't resourceful or intelligent, had no foresight and lacked gumption.

San Francisco was thriving. Paul could easily secure another position, especially since he was so attractive. He possessed a pleasant, exceedingly light voice, and had always treated Bess like royalty. Paul had risen in the ranks to become one of her father's bookkeepers, yet in Kate's opinion he deserved a position that was better suited to his congenial demeanor.

Looking up at him from her bed, she hoped her smile would encourage him. But his face was so contorted, she found herself blurting something far different from what she'd meant to say.

"*I'll speak to Father, Paul. I know he's been treating you horribly. And undeservedly, I might add. You know Father listens to me. I'll insist on some changes and—*"

"*Changes? It's too late for changes.*" Paul lifted her from the bed, stood her upright, and the voice she had thought exceedingly light screeched in her ears. "*I have a better idea,*" he said with a sneer, as one clenched fist followed the other into the softness of her belly.

When Paul's rage could no longer keep her upright, Bess collapsed to the floor, her face branded by slap marks, her eyes blinded by tears, her stomach a well of roiling, heaving pain. Almost immediately, she began to gag.

"Don't you dare spew, bitch," Paul threatened, "because I have other plans for you."

Momentarily, he looked contrite, or maybe Kate only imagined it. She wanted to scream, had wanted to scream from the start, but his blows to her belly had dried up her voice and she could only whisper, "What plans?" just before she released the roiling contents of her stomach. With her head lowered, she couldn't determine his expression, but she envisioned it to be one of disgust, and she desperately hoped he wouldn't renew his abuse. She wanted to tell him that she wouldn't tattle, that her father would never know about this, but her belly convulsed again.

Impatiently tapping his foot, Paul waited until she'd finished. Then he grasped her about the waist and carried her, arms and legs dangling, halfway across the room. When he finally put her down, she was on her hands and knees . . . like a dog.

"I told you not to spew," he said in his death wind voice. "But I suppose it doesn't matter, so long as you clean up your mess after I leave. Not the maids; you! Do you understand me, Elizabeth? There will be no evidence of tonight's activities, not even your foul, revolting vomit. And if you dare vomit again," he said, his tone suggesting that she'd spewed on purpose, "I'll slap you senseless."

Kate managed to nod before the final degradation began. She was only vaguely aware of her nightgown being thrown back, but she was all too aware of the violation that followed. And with the greatest effort of her young life, she contrived to swallow the bitter bile that rose in her throat.

When it was over, when she lay in a dazed heap, Paul patted her curls and said, "Your father wants an heir, Kate. We will be wed as soon as your belly begins to grow."

Paul's plans had never come to fruition. Upon learning that Bess was with child, her father had sacked Paul. Whereupon, Paul cornered Kate in the stables.

"You would have been a lousy, loathsome wife," he said, "which

241

your father's bootlick will discover soon enough. Did you hear me, Elizabeth? You're a lice-ridden, despicable cow! Worse than a cow, underneath the covers, where you've no talent at all."

Then, pulling a pistol from his belt, Paul shot himself between the eyes.

Kate had miscarried during the earthquake. With the ground rumbling and buildings exploding all around them, an elderly woman, a stranger, nursed Kate through the painful ordeal. The woman even ripped her own petticoats into strips so that Kate would have rags to staunch her blood.

"My baby was a girl," Kate told Thomas, finishing up her confession in tones that said she had obviously failed there, as well. Then, with a sense of trepidation, perhaps even dread, she waited for his reply.

"That was then and this is now," he said. "I don't love you any less, or any more. I just . . . love you."

"You cannot love me," she cried. "Don't you understand? I'm filth!"

And with that, Kate fled from the room and the house, hearing but not hearing Thomas's urgent shouts to come back.

Bess was just about to begin properly reading and editing when she heard Geoff's Land Cruiser pull into the driveway. Blindly, she reached out to save the scene.

By the time Geoff entered the office, Lady orbiting round his ankles, Bess was back at work on the main portion of the book, and she forced herself to look up and at least attempt to be pleasant.

"You've had a busy day, Lady," she said to the dog, who rushed over to try and leap into Bess's lap, all four feet skittering on the plywood, tail whirling like a demented weathervane.

"Sit!" said two voices in unison, and the dervish dog

242

plunked her rump on the ground, then looked anxiously from face to face, certain she'd been ganged up on, but not sure who was now the boss.

Bess would have laughed. Wanted to laugh, but didn't dare meet Geoff's eyes to see if he shared her impulse. So she kept her own eyes downcast and her mouth closed.

"You about finished for the day, Bess?"

Geoff's voice was calm, totally unrevealing. Except, she thought, and then cursed herself inwardly for thinking it, too polite. "I wouldn't mind stopping, if that's what you're getting at," she said. "It's been a long day. I got heaps done, but I ended up deleting most of it," she fibbed.

"Well my day's been just the same," he said, surprisingly soft-spoken. "What say we go buy a steak and a beer somewhere, maybe that Lone Star restaurant. It's so American it gives me the bloody shivers, but they do a splendid steak and the line-dancing and music are worth at least half the price."

"Okay," Bess replied, her stomach growling approval. "At least I won't have to change, which is just as well. I absolutely must wash clothes tomorrow."

"Leave tomorrow for when it comes. Go find some shoes and we'll leave as soon as I give Lady her tucker."

They drove in silence to the Lone Star, and sat in almost-silence throughout most of the meal.

"Tomorrow I must drive to Hobart for the day," Geoff said. "I assume you'll be all right by yourself."

It wasn't a question. It was, like nearly everything else that passed between them, a sort of do-si-do, a mental and verbal line dance. Try to keep the rhythm, try to stay in step, but never, ever, really touch. And be aware that in different countries, different cultures, different circumstances, the line dance to a given piece of music isn't always the same.

They arrived at the restaurant as strangers and went home

as strangers, but when Bess slipped her tense, weary body beneath her eiderdown quilt, she knew exactly what she had to do.

Tomorrow. He'd given her the day, and she would make the most of it.

CHAPTER SEVENTEEN

The striking young woman who marched into the offices of the Dover Warren Cornwall conglomerate was a far cry from the waif in faded jeans and Broncos sweatshirt who had flown as directly as humanly possible from Launceston to Melbourne to Los Angeles to New York. And, in strict disobedience of all logic, she had traveled with no more than a purse and a laptop computer.

It was much easier, and much faster, dealing with customs that way.

As a bonus, due to the time difference, she had landed at LAX three hours prior to her take-off from Melbourne. Meaning, she'd gained more than one day.

Elizabeth Carson Bradley was power-dressed to the nines in a British racing green suit that set off her hair, an autumn-rust blouse that matched her hair, and all the accouterments that cried out: *Here is a woman to be reckoned with!*

Jet lag be damned. It had taken her less than half a day to visit a series of expensive boutiques.

"I would like to see my father, please," she said, having negotiated her way through a host of new employees who didn't know her. Now, finally, she faced her father's final bastion, Miss Dragonian. And well named too, Bess had always thought. This woman of mixed-ethnic descent was truly—and had been right from the start—the dragon at the gate to Cornwall's inner sanctum.

The great man emerged from his office like a bear leaving

his hibernation den, and it was all Bess could do to keep from spitting as she allowed herself to be smothered in his welcome, to be hugged and held away for inspection, then hugged again.

"You look wonderful," he said.

As well she should, she thought. He was paying for it. She had used Geoff's return ticket as far as L.A., but from that point on she had splurged with the company credit card she'd never before used. It had paid for her flights, her meals, her hotel and her clothes.

"But I wish you'd come back a bit earlier, Elizabeth. I really did want to put you together with Reg Bingham, the British chap I phoned you about. Did I tell you he's met the Queen? And Fergie? And Prince Charles, of course. Bingham was very disappointed when he couldn't find you in Colorado Springs."

Bess held her breath, then let it out slowly. Fought for total control, and found it. Crunch time, she thought, and carefully chose her words.

"Not as disappointed as I was when your idiot employees totally ruined my situation in Tasmania, Father," she said, forcing a strength she didn't feel into her voice. "When did you start hiring fools? I had him all but hung out to dry, and then your bunch of fifth-rate mafioso had to come along and ruin it."

"What the hell are you talking about?"

Cornwall's expression told Bess he knew exactly what she was talking about. She watched him open and close his mouth several times, looking like a grounded fish.

"I'm talking about Geoffrey Barrett and his control of the Tascalypt shares you craved. The ones you got, I assume, but almost got me raped in the process. Raped, Father! And for what? I could have had the stock up for sale in another week.

246

By the way, have you managed to acquire the majority you wanted?"

"I managed to acquire them all," Cornwall said, staring at his daughter and wondering how he could have missed seeing this new Elizabeth. She was exactly the heir he'd always wanted. Strong, confident, ready to face up to anything, even him! A strange sort of pride surged through him, blotting out her rape statement, blotting out any misgivings, blotting out all logic.

"Good," she said, turquoise eyes flashing. "Considering what I had to endure because of your meddling, you won't object to turning them over to me, will you?"

In her eyes, Cornwall saw something he'd never dreamed he'd see . . . raw, naked power. His daughter was himself, many years ago, and he felt as if he was poised on the steps of heaven.

"And while you're at it, Father, why don't we stop this game-playing and simply give me control of the whole box and dice? I'm going to inherit anyway, so why don't we get the paperwork done while I'm here? Then I can get out of your way and let you run things as you wish, until . . . well, let's not go there. I'm sure you have years and years ahead of you. I certainly hope you do. But it's time I had voting control too, at least for the various blocks of stock that are in my name and Mother's name, willed to me. Shall we start by fixing that little oversight?"

"Certainly, Elizabeth," he replied, fighting for time and aware that both of them knew it. "But how did you find out about this Barrett thing? I didn't even realize you knew the man until—"

"I was your very private secretary for . . . how many years? Do you think I'm so simple-minded I wouldn't have made a few contacts along the way? People who could keep me informed of what's really happening here? This is my inheritance, as you've always been so fond of reminding me when I didn't obey you. And what a bloody awful mess you made with Barrett, Father. He has fingers in pies that are worth a million times more than that little Tascalypt outfit. Patents worth billions, and I was within an inch of getting them, before your goons took a hand."

"I'm sorry, Elizabeth, but I didn't—"

"Speaking of which, I suggest you withdraw that odious Gerald Coolidge from his southeast Asia posting and put him someplace suitable to his talents. Have you got a sewage disposal company handy? That man would have been the first . . . and I want you to be totally clear about this, Father . . . the very first to have raped me. He wanted to, and he was shaping up to do it. Or did you order that, as well?"

"No! I swear! All I wanted was to get you back here so we could—"

"Talk? Well, we are talking, aren't we? And you didn't even have to ask. But, in your words, I want Gerry Coolidge's balls for bookends, and I expect you to get them for me. Is that perfectly clear, Father? I want his head on a plate. I want him rotting in some pestilent third-world jail, assuming you can't have him maimed for life."

"It will be done, Elizabeth. You have my promise." Cornwall could feel himself shrinking into his executive chair, while his daughter, now suddenly a weirdly familiar stranger, stood four-square in front of his desk and looked at him, daggers shooting from her eyes.

"I think it's time you got the 'dragon' in here so we can make a start on this paperwork, don't you?" that daughter asked, her voice silk-smooth, her attitude carved from the finest steel.

Miss Dragonian never so much as raised an eyebrow as she

took down Cornwall's instructions, nor did she flinch at Bess's instructions about where to transfer the relevant information about the Tascalypt shares. She did, in a polite, professional manner, ask for a repeat of the banking and trading details, and the number-specific information Bess provided as to where all this information should go. But not once did she seek to catch her long-time employer's gaze.

"You can stay here and run things, Father," Bess said, after Miss Dragonian had departed to key the details into her computer. "You can even indulge yourself with your newest merger, the one you're trying to set up with that 'British chap.' But get this straight, Father. I am not a part of that deal, nor will I be. I am not your corporate whore."

"Really, Elizabeth, you never were."

"Then I'd truly appreciate you explaining Paul Bradley to me. From the very beginning to the very end. And don't bother lying about it, because I know enough to catch you out if you do."

"Explain? What do you mean, explain? He was your husband, Elizabeth, and the father of your . . . I'm sorry . . . your child."

"A girl, Father. Did you know that? A girl, not the boy you and Paul could have groomed to take your chair the way I've done. Without much grooming at all, thank you. Remember Paul? My husband, whom you pushed and prodded and pried at until he couldn't take any more. My husband, whom you and that slime-ball Gerald Coolidge maneuvered into a situation where he shot himself rather than admit he'd been done like a dinner." The Australianism caught her by surprise, and Bess had to pause and think before she continued.

"My husband, whom I loved." And it all started to come apart with that lie. She had thought she loved Paul, but by comparison to the way she felt about Geoff, it hadn't been love at all. Hadn't been anything, really, except a reaction to a show of affection. And even that affection had been tinged by her father's poison.

Cornwall hadn't gotten where he was without a sense for vulnerability. He caught a whiff of it here with his daughter, and leapt to the scent like a man half his age. "Elizabeth, I swear to God I didn't know about the baby's sex," he said with a salesman's surge of false emotion. "And it wouldn't have mattered anyway. I mean . . ."

"You mean that you would have disposed of Paul anyway," she said, rocking back and forth on her stiletto heels and wondering what in God's name had possessed some idiot designer to even imagine such a concept as stiletto hells. Surely a man had designed them.

Suddenly, the ludicrousness of it all threatened, and she shook her head, afraid that jet-lag and emotion would overcome her before this was done.

"Now really, Elizabeth," Cornwall said, his voice full of mock indignation. "I admit that certain steps were taken to make sure Paul didn't exceed his position, nor go beyond his limited capabilities, but—"

"Don't you lie to me, Father! Don't you ever, ever, even try to lie to me!"

The shouts escaped before Bess could clamp her mouth shut, the emotions surging inside her too strong for total control. She took several deep breaths. "You set Paul up, you did it deliberately, and you were glad when he died. You know it and I know it. And you've always tried to use me as a corporate whore, a business bargaining chip. Please don't bother trying to lie your way out that one either, because it won't wash.

"Now, I'm going to tell you something and I want you to listen to me very carefully. I want you to visualize these headlines. 'Tycoon's Daughter Nearly Raped in Takeover Bid— Daughter Says Father Ordered It.' Visualize it well, because if you don't start playing this game by my rules, you're going to be reading those very words, or worse words, maybe even something about Paul Bradley, whereupon your empire will come crashing down like a house of cards.

"And remember, Father, I'm an author. The publishing business might be in merger hell, or merger heaven, but how much of an advance payment do you think they could scrape up for a tell-all book about the great Dover Warren Cornwall, written by his daughter? We're talking extortion, illegal stock transfers, possibly even murder. I could put my book on the Internet, charge for every download, and there'd be millions of them, Father, because I'd use the money from my company stocks to rent billboards on Times Square and Sunset Boulevard and buy a full-page ad in every newspaper and magazine. Hell, I'd even buy a spot for this year's Superbowl. How about my book as a TV movie-of-the-week? Am I making myself perfectly clear?"

"Yes. But Elizabeth, you're also making far too much out of—"

"A father who drove my husband into killing his unborn child? Are you going to tell me you didn't know that Paul beat me so badly before he shot himself that I lost your granddaughter because of it? And you weren't there in Tasmania when Gerry's heavies came this close to raping me." She spread her thumb and first finger apart, noting with surprise and satisfaction that her hand was steady, not shaking. "You weren't there, but it was your conniving and your orders that took it that close, and you're going to pay for it one way or another."

"Elizabeth . . ."

"And while we're talking about payment, Father, I want

you to call the dragon back in here and order a retirement package put together for Tom Rossiter. A very generous package, if you please, one with enough cash involved so that he'll never have to worry about money again. Three million would do it, I think."

"No, Elizabeth."

"Headlines, Father. Keep thinking about those headlines and my tell-all book. The article is written and ready to go, so you can forget about trying to silence me. If anything happens to me, the balloon goes up and you go with it. I'm not your daughter for nothing. I know how to use extortion and blackmail as well as you do. Don't you ever forget that. Now, do you get the dragon in here or do I? And let's make it *five* million, while you're at it."

This time, when Miss Dragonian entered the office, she looked at Bess with new respect and somehow managed to ignore Cornwall without actually seeming to do so. Only she and Bess were acutely aware of the change in attitude, the undeniable deference to his daughter. And while Bess hated the role she was playing so beautifully, she couldn't stop now.

"I want everything hand-delivered to my hotel before the day is out, Miss Dragonian, complete with proof of deposit to Tom Rossiter's account. You handle the company's banking details, I presume?"

The affirmative reply came from Miss Dragonian. Cornwall slumped in his huge office chair, visibly faded as he fought to keep his daughter from doing what he had always wanted her to do. Her stubborn strength was proving more than he could handle, especially when she seemed so willing and able to stifle his every maneuver.

Bess ignored his stuttered statements as she dealt with Miss Dragonian, but she kept an eye on him, unsure whether he really was as unstable as Tom Rossiter had said. Although he showed no obvious sign of madness, it wouldn't hurt to be prepared.

In the end, it proved a fruitless exercise. He might be as mad as the proverbial Hatter, but the spectacle of his daughter seizing power in such a brilliant and blatant fashion had him so stupefied, he clearly didn't know what to do next.

"I expect you're going to try some counter-punch the instant I'm out of the door," Bess said to the shrunken figure, once Miss Dragonian had again left the office. "But I warn you, Father . . . don't! I know where all the bodies are buried, and I've covered myself every possible way there is. If anything . . . *anything* . . . happens to me, or to Tom Rossiter, or to anyone I'm associated with or care about, you'll be dying in jail. Or the gutter. Or both, for all I care."

She took immense delight in staring her father down as she let silence fill the room. She took even more delight in the way Dover Warren Cornwall seemed to have shrunk, seemed incapable of even appearing to fill the executive chair he sat in. She tried to feel pity, but had none. During her flights back from Australia and across the breadth of the United States, she'd found herself remembering how her father had dominated her mother's life, dominated his daughter's life. He had been a control freak of the worst possible kind, manic with his own power and totally uncaring about anyone, including his own family.

Now, any effort to feel compassion emerged only as contempt. It wasn't what she wanted, but it was something she knew would wane with time, and perhaps with enough time, would disappear entirely.

"I won't see you again," she said. "Which is just as well. Because if I do, it will be because I've had to come back here to whip you into line. Not a pretty thing to think about, is it Father? But just because I'm not here every day, please don't

253

get complacent. I'll be watching the way our conglomerate is operating, and if it turns out I have to destroy it completely to stop you from doing something reprehensible, I'll do that without a second thought. Believe me, Father. Either I'm going to inherit a company that's a tribute to proper business style and ethics, or I'm going to sift through the ashes without a single tear."

She stared coldly at the silent, shrunken figure across the desk from her, then turned away and marched to the door. She had her fingers on the handle before the coup de grace sprang to mind, unbidden but so perfect she couldn't resist.

"And make damned good and sure you keep your filthy corporate fingers off Geoffrey Barrett," she said, turning as she spoke so that she could see the effect of her words. "I'm carrying the next generation of the Cornwall dynasty. Barrett is the father. He doesn't know because I haven't decided yet if he ever will, but one thing I have decided, Father. You will never, ever, have the chance to kill this grandchild because you will never, ever see this grandchild."

She faced the door again. "Have a good day," she called over her shoulder, and fled, her stiletto heels clacking.

The monstrosity of the lie struck her before she had reached street level, while she was still inside her father's corporate headquarters. Had she gone too far? No. Her so-called pregnancy was merely one more link in the safety chain, one more thing to help keep her secure, along with everyone she cared about.

Back at her hotel, Bess sorted out the paperwork she'd brought with her, hooked up her laptop to the computer link in the room, and within minutes had all the information Mouse would need flashing through cyber-space. He had the capacity to rework the Tascalypt stock transfers, returning them to Geoff without a paper trail, or with one so convoluted it would take a dozen accountants a dozen years to sort it out. How Geoff might go about dealing with the company from there, she neither knew nor cared. Her part was done.

She then prepared the envelope in which Tom Rossiter's retirement package could be sent to Tasmania, in care of Ida's security firm. The thought of Tom's face when he saw the financial aspects of the package gave Bess her first genuine smile of the day. Her growing certainty of a long-lasting relationship between Ida and the burly ex-cop brought another, this one even broader, and she was ready to roll when the courier delivered the paperwork.

Ten minutes later she was en route to the airport, Rossiter's package in the mail, Mouse in control of all other details, and herself with a plane to catch.

Soon she'd be back in Colorado, rebuilding her life for the second time.

CHAPTER EIGHTEEN

"I swear to God, Rocky, if you had anything to do with this, I'll cut off Tom Rossiter's private parts and feed them to you for lunch."

Ida bit back the riposte that came to mind. Now was not the time for subtle, or even unsubtle, humor. "Geoffrey darling, I don't know any more than you do," she said. "But I've got my people working on it, and we should start getting some answers pretty soon."

"Pretty soon? How about right now? What if she's been kidnapped again?"

Geoff paced the floor of his office like a caged predator, and Ida kept moving to stay out of his path. Anger and frustration were combined with outright fear in his every word, every gesture. His voice was ragged with emotion, and he looked like a man on the brink of collapse.

"Will you stop that bloody pacing?" she finally said, having stepped aside for the dozenth time. "You're driving me bonkers! Are you absolutely positive Bess didn't leave you a message?"

"Of course I'm positive. Where would she leave it that I haven't looked? There's nothing in her room, nothing in the kitchen, nothing here. Bloody hell, Rocky, even you can see that."

"Wonderful as I am, Geoffrey darling, I'm not omnipotent. For instance, did you check your computer?"

"Of course I did. I'm not a total . . ." His voice drifted into vagueness as he sat down and began hammering at the keyboard, his lean fingers flying. Up came the current draft of "The Flower of Ballarat." He perused the pages quickly, then grunted with annoyance. "See? Nothing. Bloody nothing!"

Ida sighed, struggling to keep the impatience out of her own voice. "Are you certain she didn't have any other files going? It shouldn't be too hard to check. You wiped the computer clean just the other day."

Geoff gave no indication of having heard, but his fingers began to fly over the keys again, bringing up menus and submenus and lists of file names. "What the hell?" He clicked on something called "Kate's Confession," opened the file, and silently began to read.

Ida stepped forward and read over his shoulder.

"What's this all about?" Geoff pushed away his chair, almost taking off Ida's foot in the process. "The whole thing is out of context, and she's not making any sense. The scene is fine, a bit black, but who the hell is Paul Yeldarb? And why does she keep switching from Kate to Bess? There's even two or three Eliz . . ."

Abruptly, Geoff re-swiveled his chair into position and scrolled back to the hero's first line of dialogue.

Having already recognized the pattern, Ida crossed her arms and hugged her chest, instinctively shielding herself against Geoff's imminent reaction.

"Bloody hell," he said, reaching the end again. "This is written as if she . . . as if Bess had actually experienced . . . no!"

Ida pounced. "Would it matter if she had?"

"What kind of stupid question is that?"

"A pretty simple one to answer, I would have thought."

But his gaze was on the screen again, and Ida could see signs of strain in his clenched jaw and flaring nostrils.

"Yeldarb," he said. "That's Bradley spelled backward."

When he finally turned to face her, Geoff wore an expression of such utter sadness, she thought for a moment he was about to burst into tears.

"It's true, isn't it?" he said in a voice so ragged she could hardly make out the words. "Oh, Bess, you poor child. And what have I done but add to it?" His hand closed in a fist that slammed the desktop so hard the entire computer jumped.

"Instead of abusing your own sensibilities, or your desk, it might make a bit more sense if you tried to fix things." Ida kept her own voice carefully calm.

"Fix things? After the way I've treated her, she'd be perfectly justified if she wanted my balls for bookends."

"Yes, darling, most girls have that sort of justification at one time or another, and for some strange reason it's always because of a man they love. I do suppose it has crossed your mind that Bess might be in love with you. Or did you think she crawled into bed with you because you were in the right place at the right time?"

He raised one hand, and Ida backpedaled, fairly certain she'd gone too far, wondering if he'd actually hit her. But he lowered his hand as quickly as it had been raised, then simply sat there, staring at his palm as if it belonged to someone else.

"Settle, boy," she said, putting every ounce of authority she could manage into those two words. Geoff didn't move, just looked at her, and his eyes were burning ice. "No, darling, Bess didn't tell me anything, not even one teensy detail. However, despite the occasional lapse, I'm not stupid. May I say without fear of being turned to salt by your damn eyes, that your logic was stupid? I assume by now you've come to the conclusion that Bess never deceived you and didn't know about your association with her father. Because, if you don't bloody well believe that, I'm out of here!"

"I think I've always believed it."

"Rubbish, Geoffrey darling. Your child bride twisted your tightie whities. You wouldn't have believed someone who'd been given a dose of truth serum."

Whereupon Ida, mentally begging forgiveness from Bess if she ever found out, praying she never would, proceeded to tell Geoff exactly what she had told Bess she wouldn't tell. He sat there, silent throughout, but took every word like a separate lash from a whip. By the time Ida had finished, he was bent over, staring at the floor and visibly shaking.

When the phone rang, he snatched at it like a life-line. What followed was totally incoherent to Ida, who could hear only one side of the conversation. All Geoff seemed able to say was: "But that's not possible." And: "We sold them. We sold them all! There's no way they could all be here, and in my name." Finally: "Okay, thanks. Just let them sit a while until I figure out . . . to be perfectly honest, mate, Tascalypt is the least of my problems."

Upon hanging up, Geoff looked like someone in a trance. Even when Ida's cell phone rang, he didn't move, didn't hardly blink. Nor did he seem to try and follow her conversation, which was mercifully short.

"Right, darling, my people have solved the puzzle," she said, but had to reach out and pat his cheek to get a response. "Geoffrey, are you in there?"

"All those shares we threw on the market to ransom Bess. They're back. My broker doesn't understand it, says it was done through such a convoluted run of transactions, he can't even begin to trace the source. What the hell's going on?"

"Off the top of my head, I'd suspect your girl had something to do with it. But the only way to find that out is to ask her, and to ask her you're going to have to find her. Which means a little trip to Yankee-land, Geoffrey darling."

That pulled him out of his fugue. "She's gone back to America? But her clothes are all here, and her suitcases."

"Which only proves she might be the first woman alive to fly from here to New York without a change of underwear. Interesting woman you've chosen, darling. But that's what she's done, it seems, so what are you going to do?"

Rising from his chair, he stretched like a lean, predatory cat. "I'm going to go after her, aren't I? And I'm going to find her too, if it takes me three days or three months or three years. And when I find her, this business of the shares will be among the very last questions I'll be asking."

"You'll ask her if she knows how much bloody trouble she's caused you. You'll ask her why she's so featherbrained she didn't see from the beginning that you loved her. You'll ask her to forgive you for being such a half-wit. Hell, Geoffrey darling, get me your passport so I can make sure it's up to date. And while you're at it, get me your divorce decree too. I'd never forgive myself if I let you get all the way over there and you can't marry her, assuming she's bonkers enough to let you. Now, get packed. I'll start making your travel arrangements."

"Would you take Lady while I'm gone?"

"No bloody way! You've not seen my house. It's a tribute to the childhood I never had. Your spaniel would have a bloody field day with my peacock feathers." The last was added in a voice that suggested every feather was a trophy.

"How about phoning Rachel Greaves, Lady's breeder? Only thing is, Rachel would have to collect Lady at the Melbourne airport, or send someone—"

"Bloody oath, Geoffrey. Is this really the time to be worrying about that mad dog? Why not shoot the bloody thing and buy a Labrador, like you've always said?"

"You bet it's worth the time." He gave Ida his first real

grin of the day. "If anything happened to that mad dog, it wouldn't matter what I sorted out with Bess. She'd strangle me right there on the spot, and I've stuffed things up enough. I don't suppose you could somehow manage to get me out of here this afternoon?"

"Out of here, yes. Out of Melbourne, I'm not so sure. And what if I can't get hold of Rachel? What if I'm not able to reach her? You can't just walk off and leave your dog at the Melbourne—"

"If you can't find Rachel, go through my phone list. Try anybody in the TGTA. Sue Axton or Sid Drew would have her, in a pinch. Someone will have kennel space, but I'd rather Lady go to Rachel since I don't know how long this will take and Rachel knows spaniels."

"I suppose it would be silly of me to ask how long you expect it to take," Ida grumbled, speaking half to herself as she began writing a list. Then she paused and looked up to find Geoff standing there, grinning at her.

"Jees, Ida, you're a rum'n," he said, lapsing into pure Australian slang. "A week ago you'd have taken my head off if I tried to make you do any of this. I'm going to look forward to meeting Tom Rossiter properly, when I get back. He was a bit of a mess last time I saw him, but he must be coming good with a hiss and a roar if he can turn my woman of stone into such a bloody marshmallow while he's still in his sickbed."

"You keep that up and you can make your own flight arrangements," she said with a blush. "Now, go find your passport and divorce decree."

"They're right here." He fished out the passport from one desk drawer, his divorce decree from another. "What's this?"

"I'd say it was a necklace, Geoffrey darling. Of course, that's only a guess."

"I bought it for Bess at the Fair, left it under her dinner

plate the night I falsely accused her of . . ." He stared down at the slender chain and jade tiger. "She left it behind, as if it didn't mean anything at all to her."

Despite Geoff's stricken expression, Ida heaved an exasperated sigh. "That's always been your answer," she said, thrusting her opal ring in front of his eyes. "For the last time, I'm not your ex-wife and Bess isn't your child bride. Gifts are fun, I'd be the first to admit that, but material possessions don't mean anything when you really love someone. Rossiter doesn't have a pot to piss in, or a window to throw it out of . . ." She paused, her cheeks ruddy again, then continued. "Listen, and listen good, Geoffrey Barrett. If your girl truly wanted to make some sort of statement, she'd have left the necklace on your pillow. I think she threw it in the desk drawer because she was angry."

"She had every right to be angry. Still, she's getting the necklace back if I have to tie her to her chair and clasp it round her lovely throat!"

"Fine. But may I suggest a different gift?"

"What kind of gift?"

"The gift of words. You're a writer, Geoffrey. You've made women laugh, cry, even fall in love with you through your words. Surely you could sway one little Yank."

"One little spitfire of a Yank."

"Too true. Please get ready for your flight now, darling, and while I don't want to sound pessimistic, pack some underwear."

Geoff could only stand in shock and disbelief at the sight of the gnome-like figure who huddled in the big office chair behind the enormous desk.

Part of Geoff's mind told him this had to be some sort of cosmic joke!

Could this man actually be corporate giant Dover Warren Cornwall?

The bloke Geoff faced resembled some strange species of monkey in a rumpled, unkempt business suit. The eyes that peered from beneath a beetled brow were simian, unblinking, perhaps even uncomprehending, and certainly far from threatening.

"He can't help you, but I expect you've realized that." The voice came from Cornwall's personal assistant, Miss Dragonian, who had placed a small hand on Geoff's sleeve to attract his attention. "He doesn't know where Miss Elizabeth is. None of us here do, and it's causing problems because, as you can see, Mr. Cornwall is fading into a madness he, himself, created."

As Geoff left the office, he found himself thinking that Cornwall had already faded. All that was left was smoke and mirrors, and Geoff found it almost impossible to believe that this was the corporate raider who had used his own daughter as a company pawn. Dogging Miss Dragonian's footsteps, Geoff couldn't find contempt, much less hatred, for such a pathetic creature. What really bothered him was that he couldn't find any compassion, either.

"You're Miss Elizabeth's man," Miss Dragonian said, walking behind her desk, reaching for a thermos, and pouring Geoff a cup of coffee that smelled like coffee but looked more like mud.

It was neither question nor exactly statement, but it suited the context somehow. Geoff accepted the coffee, which he needed badly, and merely nodded, unsure what might be coming next.

Miss Dragonian gave him a small smile as she rummaged through some papers on top of her desk, scooped up a pen, and began to write. Reading upside-down, Geoff could make out an address, a telephone number, and something else he wasn't able to decipher.

"I don't know how much good these will do you," she said, handing over the page from her memo pad. "We've been trying without success to get through to Miss Elizabeth, but the telephone only provides an answering machine, she isn't answering her E-mails, and the person we sent to try and find her has reported that her apartment is empty and her car is gone."

"And that person is . . . ?"

"A highly respected, highly qualified detective agency man. Denver based, yet he seems to be having all sorts of problems operating in Colorado Springs."

"I can just imagine," Geoff said, gulping down his coffee and thinking: Mouse.

"Would you like another cup?" Miss Dragonian asked.

Geoff shook his head no. He desperately needed to return to his hotel, where he could make some phone calls, try the one long-shot he had in his own bag of tricks, and organize his flight back across the United States . . . to Colorado.

He was about to leave when the door to Cornwall's office clicked open just far enough for the old man to poke his head through, looking for all the world like a stubble-chinned Howard Hughes . . . at the very end of his life.

"I don't care what she says," Cornwall hissed in a raspy, breathless voice. "And I don't care what you say either, even if you are the father. He's my grandson, and if you try to keep him from me I'll fight you through every court in the land."

Cornwall retreated again, slithering out of sight like a lizard, the office door closing with a blunt thud of finality. Geoff stared at Miss Dragonian, who looked placidly back at him, clearly not at all concerned by her employer's bizarre behavior or his astonishing statement.

"He gets quite obsessive about that," she said. "In fact, he hasn't left his office since Miss Elizabeth told him she was pregnant. He has his own private bath, even a sleeping alcove, but he spends most of his time on the phone with his attorneys. Two have quit and the rest hang up on him." Removing her glasses, she rubbed her eyes. "When you find Miss Elizabeth, please give her my felicitations."

"Yes, ma'am, and we'll send you an invitation to our wedding," he said.

Hailing a taxi, Geoff's mind raced. It was, he supposed, vaguely possible that Bess could have become pregnant. But would she know already? Not a chance! She had some other game in play here.

"Bloody ridiculous," he said aloud, then turned his mind to figuring out how he could find this woman he loved when a local and highly-trained private detective couldn't manage it. The only advantage he, himself, might have was that he knew about Mouse, a circumstance that hardly leant itself to the creation of confidence.

Inside his hotel suite, he dialed Room Service and placed an order for a steak sandwich and a pot of caffeine. Then he found that the best-connected flight he could get took off tomorrow morning. Which, he thought, was just as well. He had flown virtually non-stop from Tasmania, hadn't slept in two days, and knew from experience he was running on fumes. His head ached, he felt stiff and cranky, and his mind was so fuzzy round the edges he had to go over everything a dozen times, just to make sure he hadn't missed something of vital importance.

Almost immediately, he discovered just how difficult finding Mouse might turn out to be, never mind going past that roadblock to find Bess. Geoff kept getting Mouse's voice mail. He left his name, the hotel number, his suite number, even offered to pay the bloody rodent one thousand times the cost of a return long-distance call.

Finally, he said, "Mouse, damn your soul, I swear I'm not the bad bastard you think I am. I love Bess. I want to marry Bess. Now please, in God's name, help me!"

Sending equivalent E-mails to the address he had copied from his computer at home proved just as futile, so he placed a wake-up call and booked a limousine for the airport. Then he collapsed on the bed and was asleep in moments.

Twined through his fingers was a fragile gold chain, and his large hand clutched a tiny Tasmanian tiger.

Geoff had never believed in talismans or magic, had always thought a person made his own luck, yet even in his sleep his thumb polished the jade.

CHAPTER NINETEEN

Having just returned from a writers' convention, where she'd been deluged with fellow mystery authors and fans, Denise Dietz wanted to take a long hot bath and finish reading Eileen Dreyer's latest medical thriller.

Instead, she listened to her friend Mouse, determined to hear him out before she argued. It took a fair bit of listening. In fact, the phone was beginning to hurt her ear before she found a chance to interrupt.

"Mouse, you're a sadist," she said. "You're treating this poor man like some sort of enemy, and he's not. He's in love with Bess and she's in love with him, even if she is in denial right at the moment . . . Well, of course I'm sure. I don't have to know her well to figure that much out. If she really didn't want him to find her, she'd have gone someplace where he wouldn't have a hope in hell of . . . No, Mouse, that's not fair. Geoffrey Barrett is a very nice man. I've been following his contributions to the Novelists Inc. authors' loop for years now and . . . So you call him Lucifer. Knowing you, it's the Cinderella cat, not the devil. Big deal. As a woman, I happen to find the name Lucifer very intriguing . . . What do you mean he hasn't made a move you haven't mapped out for him? Stop chortling and explain what . . . You gave every bookstore my address? How on earth did you do that? In any case, I'm sure Bess has contacted all the stores, told them she's back in town, and . . . If I was half awake, or even half alive, I would have figured out, on my own, that you can hack into bookstore computers, not to mention hotel computer hookups. Damn it, Mouse, is nobody's system safe? Look, sweetie, I just got back from a conference and I'm in no mood to . . . Well thank you very much and the same to you. Sometimes you can be such a rat! Stop laughing, or I'll hang up the pho . . . Yes, Mouse, I understand. You've called one bookstore owner personally and you're going to aim Geoffrey Barrett at me and I'm supposed to redirect him so he can find you. But why me? I hardly know Bess, and, at the risk of repeating myself, I just got back from . . . You rotten rat! You're playing that poor man like a fiddle and having the time of your life. Never mind about Bess, or me, or that poor lost Aussie who only wants to find the woman he loves. This is just a rat maze, isn't it? Honestly, Mouse, you should be writing mysteries. You have the most devious mind I've ever encountered, and the most evil, and . . . Yes, okay, I said I'd do it and I will, but don't expect me to like it. You've thrown me into this because I look enough like Bess to be her mother and you . . . Oh please, don't give me that sister crap. It's beneath you. Anyway, if you heard one word I've said, which I doubt, I just returned from a writers' convention. That means no sleep, and the circles beneath my eyes look like . . . No, Mouse, I prefer raccoon-eyes to Uncle Fester eyes."

Denise slammed down the phone and started thinking out her role for when Geoffrey Barrett arrived. She hoped he'd get here soon, because, after talking to Mouse, whom she owed a ton of favors, she desperately wanted to take her bath and get squeaky-clean.

Geoff climbed the seemingly endless steps to a second floor duplex. He had exhausted every possibility, chased down every lead, and was reduced to taking a punt on what was probably the least likely hope he could think of. Or the best. Certainly, at this point, the only course of action that seemed to offer any hope at all.

He had determined two things almost from the instant of his arrival in Colorado Springs. One was that the city had an astonishing over-abundance of not-too-tall redheads. The other was that Mouse was ineptly named. The elusive bugger was as cunning as a shit-house rat.

"You won't find him unless he wants you to." These words had been said to him so often, Geoff could recite the rest of the Mouse-legend in his sleep. The head of the city's best detective agency had practically laughed in Geoff's face.

"The FBI can't find him, the IRS can't find him, I sure as hell can't find him, and believe me, I've tried it a time or two," Geoff was told over a sympathetic but otherwise uninformative after-work drink.

Well, not totally uninformative. He'd been given a list of known computer gurus in Colorado Springs, and he'd done his best to work through each individual, hoping he'd get lucky. Hah! What a total waste of time that had been!

Then he'd tried bookstores, only to find that while Bess was certainly known, admired, and locally famous, no one had seen her for months . . . or at least no one would admit to it. Likewise, the travel agents. Despite his disappointment with the detective agency, he had put them to work. But Bess was now proving as elusive as Mouse.

"It isn't as if she's breaking the law," stated the firm's most successful private investigator. "Nothing says she has to live in her apartment, or drive her car, or use her credit cards, or even make calls from her own phone. Fact is, if she's tied up with that damned Mouse, she could be driving anybody's damn car and using anybody's damn phone, and they probably wouldn't even know it."

In the end, Geoff had gone back to the beginning, talking

to whomever would talk to him, using his own status as an author to try and get something useful out of the bookstore people, the library people, anybody.

And here he was, standing in front of a door with what sounded like a very large dog behind it threatening to come out and have him for brekkie, and he still wasn't sure what the hell he was doing here. A previously unhelpful woman at a bookstore had suddenly become at least somewhat informative, and it had gotten Geoff this far, which was the best he'd managed all week.

He raised his hand to knock, but the dog was evidently the occupant's doorbell. Before Geoff's knuckles could even graze the wood, the door opened and his uncertainty became total bewilderment.

The woman who stood there, holding back the Australian shepherd who clearly wanted to eat him, could have been Bess, had she aged twenty-five or so years. The same size, the same stance, the same mane of turbulent auburn hair, the second pair of truly turquoise eyes he'd ever seen in his life.

"I'm sorry to trouble you," he began, fumbling for words, his whole balance gone wonky. "But if you're . . . uhm . . . Denise . . . uhm . . ."

"I am. And you're the Aussie who's sworn to grace our fair city until he finds Bess Carson," she said with a grin. "I suppose you know you're the talk of our whole writing community. So much persistence, so much . . . well, persistence. You'd best come in, Geoffrey Barrett, and have some coffee. You sure look as though you need caffeine badly. Sydney, leave him alone," she said to the dog, and turned away to let Geoff follow her into the house.

"I wondered how long it would take you to get to me," she said, after putting two mugs, a coffee pot, and some chocolate doughnuts between them at the kitchen table. "Although

I can't see why. I don't know Bess all that well, and I certainly have no idea where she is."

"That makes two of us," he said, wishing her dog would stop sniffling at his crotch. "I'm beginning to wonder if I know her at all, and I'm sure as hell not making any progress at finding her. Running around like a blue-arsed fly is all I've accomplished so far, and to be honest I'm getting too frustrated for words."

"Here, have some chocolate." She extended the plate of doughnuts. "I've always found chocolate to be a great cure for the unhappiness caused by the failure of one's hopes, desires, dreams and expectations."

"Now you sound like a romance author, not a mystery author. Look, I'm working with what I've got, Denise, which happens at the moment to be nothing at all. Talk about spinning your wheels! Half my problem is that I'm a stranger in a strange land. I don't know the local rules, no bloke will give me the time of day once I mention why I'm here, and most of the time I don't even understand the language. Then, at long last, this bookstore owner suggested I talk to you. Buggered if I know what she's up to, since a few days ago she wouldn't tell me a damned thing. But, well, here I am."

"So it's getting near quitting time?"

Denise's voice was soft, but the question held inferences he couldn't ignore. Geoff met her gaze with a blistering glare. "I never learned to spell that word," he said. "So no, I'm not going to quit. I'm not ever going to quit, even it gets to where all I can do is sit down in front of the biggest bookstore in town and stay there until Bess appears. My next step is to take out full-page ads in all your bloody newspapers. By the way, if you don't mind me getting personal, you and Bess—"

"Look alike, bar a couple dozen years," she finished for him. "And no, I'm not her mother. Bess Carson and I aren't related, but we've exchanged E-mails and crossed paths at book-signings and conferences, where, naturally, everybody always does a double-take." A second grin lit up her face. "But I do know the local scene, and since you're a dinkie-die Tasmanian, I suppose I can't refuse to help you, lest my co-author on your fair island go cranky with me."

"Co-author? Bloody hell! You're . . . Calliope, on NincLink!"

"Too right, mate. I named myself for a protagonist in one of my books. And please, call me Deni; I prefer it, actually."

"I saw your collaboration post. That's when I first devised my scheme . . ." Geoff paused to fake a cough, thinking he'd sound like nothing less than a randy bugger if he admitted his collaboration with Bess had originally been a ruse.

Whereupon something flashed across those amazing Bess-like eyes. Just a flicker, hardly anything really, and yet Geoff somehow knew there was more than a writing collaboration going on between this splendid, mature redhead and his un-known colleague in Tasmania. Much more, and it was all too close to home for him not to catch the nuances.

"Ah," he said, borrowing Ida's favorite certification. "Not you, too?" And had to laugh with the irony of it all, the coinci-dence of it all, as Deni blushed. Then the two of them lost it completely, and seconds later were blind with their laughter, bent double with it. Sydney the Australian shepherd showed her disgust by leaving the room.

When they had recovered sufficiently to resume the dis-cussion, now with a sudden bond created by the coinci-dence of their circumstances, Denise raised the issue of using E-mails or the Internet to contact Bess.

"I've tried that almost daily, Deni. She won't answer my E-mails. I can't realistically expect her to access my website, and the messages I've left on hers aren't working. Honest,

I'm at my wits' end. There has to be something to do that's more positive than what I've tried so far."

Denise shook her tousled auburn curls. "I don't know where she's hiding out, Geoff. I'd tell you if I did, I swear. She hasn't posted on NincLink, where all this idiocy started, yours and mine, but she's posted on a few other author loops. So my suggestion is to find a computer expert who can trace the source."

"I've tried that, too." Geoff rose to his feet, aware that his face was now a mask of despair. "Thanks for the doughnuts and coff—"

"I'll bet you haven't tried my ex-husband. Ordinarily, I wouldn't send my worst enemy . . ." She shrugged.

"Is this a last straw?"

"Yes, but it's a viable straw, and I know for a fact that he's home. We've been arguing . . . by phone . . . over Sydney . . . my dog. He wants her. I'm fairly certain it's just a ploy to hurt me, but I stupidly forgot to list Sydney in the divorce decree and . . ." Denise's voice trailed off as she gave Geoff a second shrug.

For some strange reason, her story didn't ring true, Geoff thought. Maybe because she sounded as if she was making it up as she went along. Or maybe he was imagining things, emotionally drained by the laughter that, for his part, had teetered on the brink of hysteria. Or maybe he couldn't decipher the truth if it bit him in the bum. Bess and Ida would certainly agree with that.

He watched Denise write down an address, then add a crude map, and fervently hoped her ex-husband was a successful last straw. Because Geoffrey Barrett, prosperous businessman and author, was not only running out of straws, but needles in haystacks as well.

Crossing the threshold, he restrained himself from drop-kicking Denise's bloody dog over the fence as it forcibly hammered at his crotch with a cold, wet nose. Australian shepherd? It looked more like a feral, unshorn sheep.

"Where are you and your . . . co-author getting together, Deni?" he asked. "Tasmania? Here?"

"Tasmania. I leave next month. And believe me, Geoff, I wish you luck with Bess. Maybe we can all get together Down Under."

"Ripper plan," he said, giving her an impulsive hug.

Inside, Denise watched through the window as Barrett's car blasted like a rocket from her driveway. Then she turned to her phone.

"He's on his way," she said when the machine picked up at the other end. "And I hope to hell you know what you're doing, Mouse, because he really is a nice guy. I hated lying to him, and wouldn't have lied, except that we're playing by your ratty rules and I didn't think you'd tell him where Bess was unless I did. I told him that you were my ex-husband. And trust me, you prankish, perfidious, unprincipled piece of Rodentia! Your 'Lucifer' is *okay,* and he's also so in love with Bess, he'll strangle you if you mess around with him."

Geoff's last-straw euphoria had dissipated by the time he found the obscure address Deni had provided, and the person who answered the door did little to make him feel better. The face of a gnome, complete with wispy, almost-white hair, topped the body of a professional athlete, aging perhaps, but successfully fighting it. As Geoff was led through a veritable labyrinth of passages in what had once been a downtown warehouse, he could almost visualize the man ahead lumbering forward in full gridiron gear. It was no surprise to reach the nerve center of the guru's operation and find a Denver Broncos jacket hanging up near the door and a profusion of football trophies lining what wall space wasn't taken up with computer gear.

Just what I need, a bloody ex-jock, Geoff thought, and his heart sank.

"Deni phoned, so I think I know what you want," the guru said in a surprisingly soft voice, almost as if he was trying to disguise it. "One other thing I did think of, though. Have you considered hacking into her website? Hacking in is easy as pie. Getting out is only marginally more difficult. Might be worth a try. You want to locate this lady pretty bad, huh?"

"Try anything you think might work, please. I don't care how long it takes or how much it costs. There's only one thing that matters here, and that's finding Bess Carson and somehow arranging for me to talk to her. I'll do it on the courthouse steps in the middle of a blizzard, if that's what it takes, but I'm not leaving Colorado Springs until I find her."

"Suits me. Funny you should end up at Deni's house. I mean, it must have been a last resort . . ."

He let the comment run out on its own accord, but Geoff had the distinct feeling this aging athlete was playing with him, like a cat plays with a . . . mouse. Then, incongruously, Geoff remembered a long-ago list-serve comment Denise had once written, something about how her soon-to-be-ex-husband bore a striking resemblance to Icabod Crane. *Either there's been a lot of good tucker shoveled into this bloke since then, or . . .*

"Until you asked, I was wondering too," he said, and could actually feel his eyes harden along with his voice. "But now, I'm beginning to wonder if I wasn't directed toward Deni. I suppose you wouldn't know anything about that."

"Me? No way. One thing I stay out of as much as possible is other people's business." Turning toward his equipment, the guru chortled. "This is going to take a while, Barrett. Do you want to hang around? Or would you rather go back to the Broadmoor and wait until I get in touch with you?"

I didn't tell Denise . . . Deni . . . I was staying at the Broadmoor Hotel! Suspicions confirmed, Geoff had to think for a moment before he found the control to reply, and even when he did, it was an effort to keep his voice neutral.

"I could go get us some beer," he said, then threw caution to the wind. "Or do mice drink beer? On the other hand, I reckon a bit of Ratsac might be appropriate, except they tell me the FBI and the IRS and the Marines, for all I know, have already tried that. And why the hell did Deni tell me you were her ex?"

The broad muscular shoulders tensed before Mouse turned to him with a gargoyle's grin. "Bess said you weren't no dummy, Lucifer. I guess I should've listened better. By the way, Deni nearly bit my head off. You should hear what she called me. I aimed you at her and made her fib. Deni said it was a rat's maze, and she's right, but I had to make certain of you, myself. For Bess's sake. She's been hurt, and hurt bad, and I love her very much." He held out one huge paw and nearly crushed Geoff's more slender fingers as they shook hands.

Then Mouse leaned back in his chair, observing Geoff through eyes that belied his innocent appearance. "Okay," he said with another gargoyle grin. "So I'm a gamer and the best hacker in the western U.S. of A. And you're mad as hell and ready to take me apart. Fair enough. But it's over now, Lucifer, or at least my part is. If you unclench your fists and settle down a bit, I'm going to draw you a map. And then, if you promise to forget where you were as soon as you leave here, we can let the path of true love smooth itself out again. Deal?"

Geoff met Mouse's hard-eyed gaze, and found himself

liking this strange man, regardless of his quirky use of what must be a phenomenal intelligence. "No beer laced with Ratsac, Mouse? No satisfaction? You sure know how to spoil a bloke's fun."

"I think you'll have all the fun you can handle in about an hour." Then, surprisingly, the strangely ugly face softened to become appealingly human. "I wish I'd met you in person earlier, Geoff. I probably wouldn't have made you suffer. Not that I'm apologizing or anything."

"No more Lucifer?"

"I'll leave that up to Bess. Although Deni says Lucifer sounds intriguing."

Geoff shook the enormous paw again. "Thanks, mate, and you can be sure Bess'll thank you too."

"Yeah, well, just don't invite me to the wedding. I don't do weddings. But you have my permission to name your first child after me."

"Mouse?"

"What's wrong with Mouse?"

"Nothing. I like it. Mouse Barrett. Works for a boy or girl."

With yet another grin, the athlete-turned-electronic-guru zeroed in on his computers, leaving Geoff to find his own way out.

CHAPTER TWENTY

Bess stared at the accusatory screen. She almost wished her computer could acknowledge disgruntled facial expressions with: "You've got angst"—the same way her ISP announced: "You've got mail."

Having totally ignored her E-mail and focused on the book she'd begun before her Tasmania visit, she had rescued her heroine from the ravening Apaches. Or rather her hero . . . who looked and sounded and was too much like Geoffrey Barrett . . . had. Within shouting distance of finishing the historical romance, she couldn't, didn't, or didn't want to.

She had tried. Lord knows, she'd tried. But her climactic love scenes were provincial, boorish, not loving in any way she could discern. They'd been written, revised, scanned for spelling errors, and discarded. So had a dozen other more-or-less traditionally happy endings, most of which made her want to gag.

Happy endings! Hah! What a lot of old cobblers, as Geoff would say.

"No, no, no!" she cried, then buried her head in her hands. She would not think about Geoff. It was killing her.

And yet she couldn't help herself. He was here in her hero, in her life. She saw him everywhere. When she ate her "brekkie" cereal. When she took a shower. Especially when she strolled through the park and watched dogs of all breeds fetch air-borne Frisbees.

Her favorite Barbra Streisand CD was issuing forth "Who's Afraid of the Big Bad Wolf," so at first the rapping at the sliding patio door didn't register. Even when it did, Bess didn't look up, knowing her eyes would be blotchy, her face tear-stained.

Then she did look up, and fairly flew out of her swivel chair to stand just inside the door, hand on the latch, unable to make her fingers work.

Through the glass, Geoff's eyes caressed her, one dark brow raised in the slightly quizzical gesture she had always associated with his pirate persona.

Bess felt like a statue. She couldn't speak, didn't trust herself to move, and her heart thundered so loudly she couldn't hear his words, even though she was aware that his mouth formed words.

With an effort, she managed to shake her tousled curls, as if that would somehow restore the balance between her heart's clamor and her ears' sudden deafness, and, surprisingly, it did.

"Bloody oath, Bess, but you've led me a merry chase," he was saying. "Are you going to let me in, or do I stand out here until I get covered by the next blizzard? Look, I'm not the Big Bad Wolf. And even if I were, I'm completely out of huffs and puffs. I won't eat you, love. I simply want to talk to you."

"You are," she said, finding her lost voice. "Talking, I mean."

He shrugged. "Don't try my patience too much, Miss Carson. A week in this city, pleasant as it may be for ignorant Yankees, is already more than enough for a poor, innocent, Tasmanian country boy. So please, Bess, open the door."

As if they belonged to someone else, she watched her fingers move, then stood aside as he strolled indoors, calm as could be. Turning off the CD player, he wandered over to stand next to her computer, his gaze flickering across the screen.

"How did you find me?" she asked, joining him at the computer, wishing she could skitter a chair across plywood because, while her toes seemed substantial enough, her legs felt like spaghetti.

He glanced at the picture window. "This place has a wondrous view of the mountains, my little possum."

"Don't try my patience too much, Mr. Barrett," she retorted, amazed at how steady her voice sounded. "How did you find me?"

He reached down, picked up her computer mouse, and casually stroked the small manual device with his lean, mobile fingers.

Bess got the message. "I'll kill that little piece of vermin," she said. "He promised—"

"I hardly think 'little' is the right word." Geoff grinned. "Your mouse is a damned big one. I'm glad I didn't have to get physical with him in order to break his silence."

"What did you do, instead? Bribe him?" She was angry, now. Angry with herself for letting Geoff inside, angry with Mouse for betraying her, and angry with Geoff because he looked too much like the hero in her unfinished book.

"I appealed to his sense of romance." Geoff placed the mouse on a mouse pad, then turned to face Bess, whose arms were folded across the front of her Denver Broncos sweatshirt. "Now, all I have to figure out is how to appeal to yours."

"I don't have one."

"Like you don't have the most beautiful auburn hair in the world, even when it's three days off from a comb? Speaking of which, what the hell is the story on this Deni Dietz woman?"

"Denise Dietz? The mystery author? When did you meet Deni?"

"This morning, just before I saw Mouse."

"You saw Mouse? You actually saw Mouse?"

"Of course. That's how I know he's not little. You'd better sit down, Bess. You look as if you're about to fall over."

"No. No, I'm okay. How . . . how did you find Deni?"

"I thought I'd found her through a bookstore owner, but Mouse aimed me at her."

"Yes, that's exactly what he'd do, the little . . ." She almost smiled. "Rat."

"Deni says you're not related, but she could be your mother, going on looks alone."

"Nothing but pure coincidence, and as well as we get along it's been a nuisance for both of us. Every time we turn up anywhere together, we face questions like yours. So we try not to schedule book signings togeth . . ." Bess paused. She was rambling, and knew it, fighting the stress by letting her tongue run away with her. But she couldn't do anything else, didn't dare face the reality of having Geoff standing there, only inches away from her, within touching distance.

"Poor woman looks like she needs a decent night's sleep," Geoff said. "And you look like a good night's sleep wouldn't do you any harm, either. What's the matter? This hermit's life not agreeing with you? Or are you having problems with this epic of yours?" He glanced at the computer screen, then peered straight into her eyes. "Or are you feeling guilty about sticking the knife into your father's back and twisting it? Really, Bess."

"You saw my father? How did you get past Miss Dragonian?"

"My natural charm, and a bit of name-dropping."

"Your name or mine?"

"Yours, of course. After the Tascalypt fiasco . . . and by the way, we need to talk about that someday when we're horizontal."

"Horizontal? You're taking a lot for granted, Mr. Barrett!" Inexplicably, she felt her cheeks bake. "To tell the truth, I am feeling guilty about my father. I wanted to hurt him and got carried away."

"Now there's an understatement. Exactly when is our son due, Bess? I assume he was conceived the night we—"

"Our son? I didn't say we were expecting a . . . Father told you about that?"

"Yup. He's obsessing over it. And here I thought you were just a pretty face, an omnivorous, arboreal, Australian marsupial known as a possum. In truth, my love, you're a Tasmanian tiger."

"There's no baby, Geoff. My father has always pushed my buttons. That's his button, a grandchild, and I was paying him back."

"In spades! They're scouring Colorado Springs for you, Bess, and I'm not surprised. Your father is fading fast. Not dying," he added quickly, "just incompetent. I think you'll have some work ahead to sort out his empire."

"I already have a new chief executive officer in mind. I offered the job to Mouse, but he said he didn't 'do' executive decisions, which is a bald-faced lie. He makes them all the time. Still, I don't think I, or anyone else, could pry him out of his electronic mouse hole with a ten-foot piece of cheese. Besides, he'd have the FBI and IRS cutting off his tail with a carving knife. So I plan to offer the job to Deni's son, Jon, who's as smart as Mouse, only . . . legit. I truly have no interest in running Father's empire, just in seeing that it's run with some semblance of ethics."

"That's probably the right decision, love. I suspect you'll

have other things to occupy your mind. Are you sure you're all right?"

"I . . ." She paused, now totally uncertain what to say. Geoff had a look in his eyes she couldn't decipher, but she thought it might mean approval, and she felt better about her New York visit. "I'm fine, thank you. How's Lady? And Ida?"

"Lady's being properly cared for in my absence," Geoff said, his voice as gentle as his gaze. "And Ida . . . well, I think Rocky will have to change her name to Marshmallow. That bloke Rossiter seems to have found her soft spot, and she's so soppy you wouldn't believe it. Funny the effect you Yanks have on poor, innocent foreigners."

"You were never innocent in your whole life, Geoffrey Barrett, and I sincerely doubt you were ever poor."

"What say you go rustle us up a coffee? The last caffeine I had was with your little mate Deni, who makes it so strong I don't know why she doesn't just eat it and save the water."

Bess took his advice and fled to the kitchen, leaving him to man the makeshift office she'd rigged in her borrowed condo. For an instant, she considered escaping through the back door, only to glance toward the window and discover that Geoff had tidily blocked the driveway. Bloody wonderful, she thought, and tried to slow the action of the coffee maker by staring at it. Eventually, however, the coffee brewed, and she went through the motions of fixing it for both of them, putting sugar and milk into Geoff's cup as if she'd been doing it for years.

With that thought, Bess almost dropped the sugar bowl, then decided she didn't dare risk carrying the cups in to where her computer now lived.

"Coffee's ready," she said in a loud enough voice for him to hear, then slid her jean-clad rump into the confines of the kitchen's small breakfast nook. And waited. Until finally her curiosity took control and she slid out again to tiptoe cautiously over to the door-frame. From there, she could see him sitting at her computer.

What the bloody hell was he writing?

She crept up behind him, staying out of his line of vision, then peered over his shoulder, and watched his lean fingers fly across the keys, the words pouring forth in a steady, entrancing stream as he swiftly, decisively finished her book.

This time it didn't end with a vapid whimper. This time, under his direction, it ended with a love scene that fairly scorched the computer screen.

Her main characters returned to life, and returned with a passion! The intensity of the final love scene made her Apaches, with their petty tortures, look like nothing more than chinless wonders. Her hero took the heroine on a journey that lifted her to erotic heights and kept her there, trembling, begging for satisfaction that slowly eased her nearer and nearer the edge.

Until . . .

Darling Bess. I know you're reading this, and you've read enough to know I'm not kidding. So just stay there, don't move, and keep reading.

The words were crystal clear, typed in a large, bold font. Bess was so bemused, she only half realized her body had begun to shake. She didn't want to read anymore, but her gaze seemed glued to the computer screen.

All that stuff I wrote between your hero and heroine, finishing your book, is for you too, when you're ready. I expect you understand that, even if you'll deny it. But first, Bess, you have to know this . . .

And the fingers that had so thoroughly driven her to distraction in Tasmania now flickered across the keys with astonishing sensitivity and speed, pulling the focus to center screen and, now, capital letters as well.

I LOVE YOU BESS
I AM ALWAYS GOING TO LOVE YOU, BESS
THIS IS NOT GOING TO GO AWAY
AND YOU ARE NEVER GOING TO RUN AWAY EVER
AGAIN!
BECAUSE I AM GOING TO MARRY YOU AND YOU
ARE GOING TO HAVE MY CHILDREN . . . OUR
CHILDREN. IS THAT CLEAR?
I APOLOGIZE FOR THE AWFUL THINGS I SAID
ABOUT YOU.
I APOLOGIZE FOR ANYTHING I HAVE EVER SAID OR
DONE TO HURT YOU. BUT I WILL NOT APOLOGIZE
FOR LOVING YOU BECAUSE YOU ARE THE ONLY
WOMAN IN THE ENTIRE WORLD THAT I CAN LOVE,
OR WANT TO LOVE, OR WILL LOVE.
IS THAT CLEAR?
PLEASE PRESS "ENTER" TO CONTINUE

Bess stood, transfixed. To press the enter key would mean reaching out, putting herself in Geoff's hands, in Geoff's world. She hesitated, then realized that walking away was simply unthinkable. Slowly, trying not to physically touch him, she reached forward, laid one fingertip on the key, and pressed Enter.

Geoff didn't even turn around. His fingers flashed across the keyboard, bringing up a new message. Bess could only hover as she watched his words form on the screen.

ARE YOU SURE YOU WANT TO CONTINUE?
IF YOU CONTINUE YOUR ENTIRE LIFE WILL CHANGE FOREVER.
YOU WILL LIVE IN TASMANIA.
YOU WILL HAVE TO ACCEPT BEING LOVED.
PRESS "ENTER" TO CONTINUE OR "ESC" TO ESCAPE

Escape? Where was the escape key? She had a vague memory of it being on the top left-hand corner of the keyboard.

This time her hesitation was less, the result the same.

DOES THIS PLACE HAVE A BED?
PRESS "ENTER" FOR YES

As her fingertips hung suspended above the keyboard, the sound of horse hooves thundered in her head and she clearly remembered the last verse of Alfred Noyes' famous poem. Bess, the heroine of the poem, had two options. She could sacrifice herself by pulling the trigger on the gun aimed toward her and the sound of the shot would warn her highwayman away from certain death. Or she could refrain from pulling the trigger and let her highwayman ride to his death. For the poem's Bess, the choice had been both complicated and simple.

For Elizabeth Carson Bradley, the choice was no choice at all.

The tip of one finger touched it! The trigger at least was hers!

Bess breathed deeply, savoring the scent of Geoff as her head rang with the cadence of *The Highwayman*. It was like moving into a dream. Geoff was here beside her, and yet she could hear the *tlot-tlot; tlot-tlot* as clearly in her ears as the sound of her own breath thundering in her breast. Once again, the lines of the famous poem echoed inside her head.

Tlot-tlot, in the frosty silence! Tlot-tlot, in the echoing night!
Nearer he came and nearer. Her face was like a light.

Her eyes grew wide for a moment; she drew one last deep
breath . . .

And Bess's finger struck the "ENTER" key so hard the entire keyboard bounced.

ABOUT THE AUTHOR

Victoria Gordon is the pseudonym under which author and journalist Gordon Aalborg has written women's fiction for two decades, including *Sunset Woman* (Wildside Press; 2003) and twenty contemporary Harlequin/Mills & Boon romances.

Many, like *Finding Bess*, are set in Australia, which is also the setting for Gordon's feral cat survival epic *Cat Tracks*.

Finding Bess can only be described as a book of the heart. It was written while Gordon and his wife, mystery author Denise (Deni) Dietz, were courting via E-mail between Tasmania and Colorado. It is in no way autobiographical, but was surely influenced by their own long-distance romance.

Most of Gordon's novels have touched on an interest in various aspects of the arts, and outdoor activities such as gundog training and competition. He was the founding president of the Tasmanian Gundog Trial Association, and is generally credited with having brought that sport to Tasmania, where it now flourishes.

Gordon lives on Vancouver Island. In his spare time, he sculpts in wood. He is also the author of the stage play *Stumped,* which was inspired by his experiences as a streetscape artist, carving a huge cedar stump on the boulevard outside his home. Visit Gordon's website, which includes pictures of his carving exploits, on www.gordonaalborg.com.